By Alexander McCall Smith

THE NO. 1 LADIES' DETECTIVE AGENCY SERIES

The No. 1 Ladies' Detective Agency
Tears of the Giraffe
Morality for Beautiful Girls
The Kalahari Typing School for Men
The Full Cupboard of Life
In the Company of Cheerful Ladies
Blue Shoes and Happiness
The Good Husband of Zebra Drive
The Miracle at Speedy Motors
Tea Time for the Traditionally Built
The Double Comfort Safari Club
The Saturday Big Tent Wedding Party

The Limpopo Academy of
Private Detection
The Minor Adjustment Beauty Salon
The Handsome Man's De Luxe Café
The Woman Who Walked in Sunshine
Precious and Grace
The House of Unexpected Sisters
The Colours of all the Cattle
To the Land of Long Lost Friends
How to Raise an Elephant
The Joy and Light Bus Company
A Song of Comfortable Chairs

THE ISABEL DALHOUSIE NOVELS

The Sunday Philosophy Club
Friends, Lovers, Chocolate
The Right Attitude to Rain
The Careful Use of Compliments
The Comfort of Saturdays
The Lost Art of Gratitude
The Charming Quirks of Others

The Forgotten Affairs of Youth
The Uncommon Appeal of Clouds
The Novel Habits of Happiness
A Distant View of Everything
The Quiet Side of Passion
The Geometry of Holding Hands
The Sweet Remnants of Summer

THE 44 SCOTLAND STREET SERIES

44 Scotland Street
Espresso Tales
Love Over Scotland
The World According to Bertie
The Unbearable Lightness of Scones
The Importance of Being Seven
Bertie Plays the Blues
Sunshine on Scotland Street

Bertie's Guide to Life and Mothers
The Revolving Door of Life
The Bertie Project
A Time of Love and Tartan
The Peppermint Tea Chronicles
A Promise of Ankles
Love in the Time of Bertie
The Enigma of Garlic

THE CORDUROY MANSIONS SERIES

Corduroy Mansions
The Dog Who Came in from the Cold

A Conspiracy of Friends

THE VON IGELFELD ENTERTAINMENTS

The 2½ Pillars of Wisdom
Unusual Uses for Olive Oil

Your Inner Hedgehog

THE DETECTIVE VARG NOVELS

The Department of Sensitive Crimes
The Talented Mr Varg

The Man with the Silver Saab
The Discreet Charm of the Big Bad Wolf

La's Orchestra Saves the World
The Forever Girl

My Italian Bulldozer
The Private Life of Spies

A Song of
Comfortable Chairs

ALEXANDER McCALL SMITH

abacus
books

ABACUS

First published in Great Britain in 2022 by Little, Brown
This paperback edition published in Great Britain in 2023 by Abacus

1 3 5 7 9 10 8 6 4 2

Copyright © 2022 by Alexander McCall Smith

The moral right of the author has been asserted.

A CIP catalogue record for this book
is available from the British Library.

Paperback ISBN 978-0-349-14481-8

Typeset in Galliard by M Rules
Printed and bound in Great Britain by
Clays Ltd, Elcograf S.p.A.

Papers used by Abacus are from well-managed forests
and other responsible sources.

Abacus
An imprint of
Little, Brown Book Group
Carmelite House
50 Victoria Embankment
London EC4Y 0DZ

An Hachette UK Company
www.hachette.co.uk

www.littlebrown.co.uk

This book is for Deirdre Molina

Chapter One

Under Personal Management

Precious Ramotswe was the owner of the No. 1 Ladies' Detective Agency, if not the sole private investigation business in Botswana – one or two others claimed to offer such services – then certainly the longest established, most reputable, and definitely the only one run by ladies. This last attribute was important, she believed, and explained why Mma Ramotswe had declined to follow a suggestion made one evening by her husband, Mr J. L. B. Matekoni that the word 'Ladies' might be dropped from the agency's name.

'These days,' he remarked, 'we do not think of this thing being just for men and this thing being just for women. People do not think that way any longer, Mma.'

Mma Ramotswe rarely disagreed with her husband – nor he with her – but on this occasion she felt she had to defend the status quo. 'But we have always been called the No. 1 Ladies' Detective

Agency,' she pointed out. 'That was painted on our sign, right at the beginning, and it is still there.'

'I know that, Mma Ramotswe,' he said. 'I see that sign every day. And, let me tell you, I am very proud of it. I think: this business was started by my wife. And then I feel very proud indeed, Mma.'

She thanked him. 'You are very kind, Mr J. L. B. Matekoni. There are some husbands who do not pay much attention to what their wives are doing. You have never been like that.' She paused. 'But why change a name we're all used to? Why are people always trying to find new names for things that have perfectly good names already?'

He shook his head. 'I am not saying that we should change names all the time, Mma. All I am saying is that these days we are encouraged to share things. People do not like to see things *reserved* just for one sort of person. That is why it might be better to say that this is not just a detective agency for ladies, but one that will help anybody, even men. After all, that is what you do: you help everyone who needs help – not just ladies.'

She was patient. 'But, Rra, the name does not say that our services are only for ladies. We have never said that. What the name tells us is that it is ladies who run the agency. That is something quite different.'

Mr J. L. B. Matekoni considered this. 'It is true that the agency is run by ladies. That is very true, Mma.'

'Well, then, Rra, why should the name be changed – if what it says is true?'

Again he took some time to respond. Then he replied, 'Think about my own business, Mma Ramotswe.'

'Tlokweng Road Speedy Motors?'

'Yes. Tlokweng Road Speedy Motors – my garage. Now, may I ask you, Mma: who runs that business?'

She smiled. 'You do, Mr J. L. B. Matekoni. Everybody knows that Tlokweng Road Speedy Motors is your business. It is one of those things that is well known.'

He raised a finger to emphasise his point. 'That means that it is a business that is run by men – or by one man, I suppose. There is Fanwell, but he is just an assistant. And Charlie, who is part-time. All men, Mma.'

She waited.

'But we do not say "Tlokweng Road Speedy Men's Motors". We do not say that, do we, Mma?'

Mma Ramotswe could not resist the invitation. 'No, Rra, because that name would mean that it was a garage for speedy men. That is not what you would want to say, I think.'

Her point took him by surprise, and he corrected himself. 'Or "Tlokweng Road Speedy Motors for Men". That is what I was thinking of, Mma. So why do you feel you have to say that a business is run by ladies? That is what I cannot understand.'

Mma Ramotswe saw what he was driving at, but she remained unconvinced. For so long men had assumed that everything would be run by them – that was the problem, she felt. And now that women were claiming their rightful place in business, as elsewhere, it seemed reasonable enough for them to stress that a particular enterprise was one under their exclusive management. It might sound like the staking of a claim, but that was justified, she felt, after all those long years of being held back by men.

She could have explained all this to Mr J. L. B. Matekoni, but she felt they had dwelled long enough on the issue, and it was time anyway for her to cook their dinner. The children, Puso and Motholeli, were both away, spending the night at the houses of schoolfriends. They were on the sleepovers that they loved so much and that made them so tired and irritable the next day.

3

Tomorrow would be a Friday, though, and that was quite a good day on which to be tired and irritable. That was because the school day ended early on a Friday and they could come home and be tired and irritable in their rooms.

She and Mr J. L. B. Matekoni had been sitting out on the veranda of their house on Zebra Drive. Now she left him there, nursing the last few sips of his cold beer, while she made her way into the kitchen. There was a packet of rice on the kitchen table, waiting to be measured out into a cooking pot. There was also a large pile of broad beans that she had harvested that very evening from her vegetable garden and that would need to be podded for their meal. Mma Ramotswe was proud of the vegetables she grew – each crop a victory, she thought, in the face of conditions that made growth challenging. Firstly, there was the soil that was inclined to be too sandy and that had to be dressed with the dried donkey manure that she bought in large sacks from her friend, Mma Potokwani. The Orphan Farm raised donkeys that were then sold on to villagers to use for their carts, and Mma Potokwani, not one to waste anything, sold the manure from the makeshift stables to help pay for the cost of their feed. Mma Ramotswe was happy to buy this fertiliser, as she was strongly of the view that there was a direct connection between the use of donkey manure and the growth of healthy vegetables. And the proof of that was now on the table before her. Her beans, large, pale green and very slightly furry, in the way in which broad beans are furry, would be boiled, salted, and then fried for a short time in butter. There were few things more delicious than fried beans, Mma Ramotswe thought, although pumpkin, also generously enriched with butter and sprinkled with ground black pepper, would be a close contender. They had no pumpkin that evening, though, and so it would be the beans and a small helping of boiled

4

maize meal that would accompany the stew that she would shortly begin to make. The main ingredient of that, of course, would be Botswana beef, which everybody knew was the tastiest of all meat. That was because of the country on which the cattle grazed – those wide plains, dotted with acacia trees, that went on forever, on which the sweet grass grew and over which the cattle moved, under the watchful eyes of their herd boys. That was what made Botswana beef so special, as her father, the late Obed Ramotswe, had explained to her so many years ago, when he had first started talking to her about cattle. Not a day went past on which she did not think about her late daddy, and the things that he used to say to her, and now she thought of him once more as she sat at the kitchen table and began to pod the beans. She had loved him so much, and he had loved her, and she dreamed that one day she might see him again, when she, too, was late, whenever that would be.

Of course, there were other things to think about – things to do with the No. 1 Ladies' Detective Agency and with her assistant – or rather, her colleague – Mma Grace Makutsi, that distinguished graduate (with ninety-seven per cent) of the Botswana Secretarial College. Mma Ramotswe was always careful to leave the worries of the working world where they belonged – in the office – and not to bring them back home. It was important, she felt, to keep your working life separate from your home life; she knew far too many people who allowed the cares of the job to intrude upon their home life, and these were the people who tended to become depressed or suffer from something that she had recently read about in a magazine – something referred to as *burn-out*. She had been intrigued by the description of this condition, which the magazine told her affected a very large proportion of those who were successful in their jobs. 'Success can come at a cost,' the article warned. 'Those who are ambitious and spend all their time thinking about their work may get to the top of the tree, but what do they find there? They find that they are too exhausted to enjoy the fruits of their labours. They are burned out.'

Mma Ramotswe had given this some thought. She knew many hard-working people, and she felt that what the magazine said about them was probably true. Some of those people seemed to be struggling under the burden of their success. They were probably burned out, she thought. They certainly did not seem to be enjoying their success – if you were burned out, then presumably you could not enjoy it because you felt too ... well, burned out to do so.

Learning about the dangers of burn-out had stiffened her resolve to keep work firmly in its place, but that did not mean that she could not think, from time to time at least, of what was going on in the office. And now, as she prepared the evening meal, she found herself thinking of Mma Makutsi and of something that had happened in the office the previous Friday. It was a little thing, but she knew only too well that little things had a habit of becoming major things. A single strand of wool protruding from the sleeve of a favourite sweater could, if ignored, lead to the unravelling of the whole garment; a tiny crack in a pane of glass could become a lengthy fault line; an unchecked act of incivility on the part of a child could become a full-scale rebellion. It was true that there were cases when turning a blind eye was the best thing to do, but then there were many other situations where the opposite was the case. Mma Makutsi was not only a valued colleague, she was a friend – perhaps the closest friend she had (after Mma Potokwani, of course). But there were times when Mma Makutsi's ambitions worried Mma Ramotswe. It was all very well to have achieved ninety-seven per cent in the final examinations of the Botswana Secretarial College, but that did not necessarily entitle you to endless promotions – even to the point of taking control of a business that somebody else had started. Mma Ramotswe was not in the slightest bit selfish, and was prepared to share her agency with Mma Makutsi, but she did not think she should be eclipsed by her colleague. The notepaper they had recently had printed bore both names immediately under the address: *Under the personal management*, it said, *of Mma Precious Ramotswe and Mma Grace Makutsi, Dip. Sec. (BSC).*

There had been some discussion of that wording. The first draft that Mma Ramotswe had intended to send to the printers had read, simply, *Directors: Mma Precious Ramotswe and Mma Grace Makutsi*. She had shown that to Mma Makutsi, who had spent some time gazing at the paper, before she raised her objections.

'I am not sure about this, Mma,' Mma Makutsi said eventually. 'If we call ourselves directors, then people may think we are a limited company. And we are not a company, Mma – we are a firm. We are unincorporated, you see.'

She looked across the office to where Mma Ramotswe was sitting at her desk.

'There is a difference, you see, Mma Ramotswe,' she continued, her tone becoming slightly condescending, as of one delivering a simplified lecture on a complex technical point. 'We were taught all about companies at the Botswana Secretarial College. Not having been there, you may not know about them.'

Mma Ramotswe raised an eyebrow. 'I know what a company is, Mma.'

Mma Makutsi looked as if she might not quite believe that. 'Well then, Mma, we should not use the word *directors*. That is only for people who run limited companies. We are not directing a business – we are managing it. How about *Under the personal management of* . . . and then we put our names. Something like

7

Under the personal management of Mma Makutsi and Mma Ramotswe? How about that?'

Mma Ramotswe noticed whose name came first. Gently, she voiced an objection. 'But that sounds as if you founded the firm, Mma. I think I did that.'

'No,' said Mma Makutsi. 'It is alphabetical. M comes before R, Mma.'

'That is true, Mma, but I think I would still like my name to go first. I was here first, I think – then you came and joined the firm.' She paused. 'That is how things are usually done, Mma. Look at Adam and Eve. Adam was there first, I think, Mma, and then Eve was made out of one of his ribs. You do not say Eve and Adam, do you? It is always Adam and Eve.'

'I do not believe that rib business,' said Mma Makutsi. 'I think that is just a story.'

'You are probably right, Mma, but the point is that we still talk about Adam and Eve.' She paused. 'So if you give me back the paper I shall take out the bit about directors and write instead *Under the personal management of Mma Precious Ramotswe and Mma Grace Makutsi.*'

Rather reluctantly, Mma Makutsi got up from her desk and handed over the piece of paper. 'I can take it to the printers, if you like, Mma,' she said. 'Their place is near Phuti's store and I shall be going that way this afternoon.'

The draft was delivered as promised, and a few days later the printer delivered a cardboard box containing the printed stationery. Mma Ramotswe took a sheet of notepaper out and examined it with pride. But then she saw the letters after Mma Makutsi's name.

'There is something extra here, Mma,' she said.

Mma Makutsi looked at the new stationery with an affected

nonchalance. 'Oh, yes, Mma,' she said. 'I made a little change before I delivered it to the printer.'

'You have put in your secretarial diploma,' said Mma Ramotswe. 'And you are claiming to have a BSc too. I do not think you are a Bachelor of Science, Mma.'

Mma Makutsi laughed. 'That is not a BSc. Those letters stand for Botswana Secretarial College.'

'But I have not put anything after my name,' said Mma Ramotswe.

Mma Makutsi stared at the floor. 'I am sorry that you do not have anything to put after it,' she said. 'That is a great pity, Mma.' But then she had an idea. 'You could have mentioned your driving licence, Mma. You could have put DL after your name. Maybe you could do that next time we have notepaper printed.'

The memory of that conversation brought it home to Mma Ramotswe that there was always a possibility that Mma Makutsi might stage a coup. That, Mma Ramotswe feared, was a danger that now seemed to be presenting itself, and that was the reason why she found herself thinking of office affairs when she should have been concentrating on the podding of beans in the kitchen of her house on Zebra Drive.

The following day, Mma Ramotswe slept in rather longer than usual. The absence of the children meant that the house was unnaturally quiet, and she barely noticed Mr J. L. B. Matekoni slipping out of bed. Nor did she hear him making his breakfast in the kitchen, or calling out, at the front door, 'That's me off to work now, Mma. Don't forget to go to the office!' It was a well-worn joke between them: he would remind her to go to the office and she would respond by telling him that he should not forget to come home after work. On such small sayings and customs are marriages built – comfortable familiarity; and that,

Mma Ramotswe always felt, made a better basis for a marriage than any amount of novelty.

She experienced a moment of panic when she eventually emerged from drowsiness and looked at the clock on her bedside table. It was already eight-thirty, a recklessly late hour for her, but then she remembered that the children were at their friends' houses and did not have to be got ready for school. The agency was going through a quiet spell – several major inquiries had recently been satisfactorily concluded – and she had no appointments that day. Mma Makutsi would open up the office and together they would tackle some of the administrative tasks that had been piling up and needed to be attended to. She knew that Mma Makutsi would be keen to do some filing and she herself would work on the bills for recently completed investigations. There would be time for several tea breaks, of course, and in this way they could expect to spend a pleasant and not unduly stressful day in the office. It was also possible that a new client might walk in off the street – one never knew when that would happen, and that was often the way in which some of their most interesting clients contacted them. Of course there were factors at work in the background, foremost of which was the word of mouth on which every business ultimately would succeed or fail.

She did not hurry. A leisurely breakfast of a fried egg, toast spread with honey, and a large cup of redbush tea was followed by a walk around her vegetable garden and a quick tidying-up of the living room. After that she was ready to prepare a sandwich for her lunch, have a final cup of tea, and then set off in her tiny white van for the short drive to the office. The traffic was light, as the morning rush was over, and she did not push her van beyond a stately fifteen miles an hour, a speed at which it seemed to be most comfortable and at which the fewest rattles and other worrying noises emerged from the engine compartment. Mr J. L. B. Matekoni would have replaced the van at the drop of a hat, but Mma Ramotswe was as loyal to machinery as she was to people, and steadfastly refused to countenance the purchase of a new vehicle. One day the white van would finally expire, but that day had not yet come, and until then it did what was asked of it patiently and with dignity.

Parking the van in its accustomed place under an acacia tree, Mma Ramotswe walked past the entrance to the garage. Mr J. L. B. Matekoni was busy performing open-heart surgery on a battered Land Rover, and did not see her, but Fanwell, his face streaked with grease, raised a spanner in salutation. Mma Ramotswe continued to the side of the garage, where a white-painted door constituted the entrance to the agency office.

Habit, more than anything else, made her knock. You did not have to knock on your own door, but she did, so deep was her engrained courtesy.

From within a voice invited her to enter.

'But Mma Ramotswe, it is just you!' exclaimed Mma Makutsi. 'I thought it might be somebody important.'

Mma Makutsi realised how unfortunate that sounded, and quickly apologised. 'I mean, you are very important, Mma – it's just that I thought it might be a client.'

Mma Ramotswe laughed. 'I know what you mean, Mma. Don't worry. Sometimes things come out the wrong way.'

She made her way towards her desk, but before she reached it, she noticed that something was different. It caught her eye from the side – a small name-plate, of engraved brass, mounted upon a wooden base, reading *Mma Grace Makutsi*. It was not a large sign, but at the same time it was not exactly small, and it was positioned on the side of Mma Makutsi's desk so that it could be seen by anybody entering the room.

'My goodness!' exclaimed Mma Ramotswe. 'What is that, Mma?'

At first Mma Makutsi affected not to know what Mma Ramotswe was talking about. 'What is what, Mma?' she asked.

'That,' replied Mma Ramotswe, pointing at the name-plate.

Mma Makutsi allowed her gaze to drift to the sign. 'Oh, that. That's a name-plate, Mma. You see them on desks in offices. They tell the public who it is who's sitting behind the desk. They are very modern things.'

Mma Ramotswe lowered herself into her chair. The sign was still visible, at an angle. 'It's very impressive, Mma Makutsi,' she said.

Mma Makutsi inclined her head. 'Thank you, Mma. I think it will be helpful, too.'

Mma Ramotswe thought about this. 'Yes, you would not want people not to know who you are.'

'Precisely,' said Mma Makutsi.

'And it will be helpful for me too,' Mma Ramotswe went on. 'I might be sitting here at my desk and when I look across the room I might think: who is that lady sitting at the other desk? And then I shall see the sign, and all doubt will be removed. I shall say to myself, "That lady over there is Mma Grace Makutsi." At least, according to the sign it's Grace Makutsi.'

The irony was lost on Mma Makutsi, who simply nodded her agreement.

Then Mma Ramotswe said, 'Is there a sign for me, Mma?'

Mma Makutsi frowned. 'I paid for the sign myself, Mma. I did not expect the office to pay for it.'

Mma Ramotswe thanked her. 'That was most considerate, Mma, but I wondered whether you had one made for me at the same time.'

There was a silence that seemed to last for some time. 'I'm

sorry,' Mma Makutsi said at last. 'I did not think of that, Mma. I am very sorry.'

'That is all right,' said Mma Ramotswe. 'I think that people coming here for an appointment know who I am. I do not think they need to be told.'

If there was reproach in Mma Ramotswe's voice, it was mild; so mild, in fact, that it seemed to go unnoticed. 'I can order one if you would like me to,' said Mma Makutsi. 'Phuti knows the man who makes them. He made mine at a special rate. It was not expensive.'

Mma Ramotswe bit her lip. Her reply was measured. 'I don't think that will be necessary,' she said, then after the shortest of pauses added, 'Thank you, anyway.' She tried not to sound hurt, but Mma Makutsi's thoughtlessness had surprised her. She would never have done something like that – she would never have ordered a sign for herself and forgotten all about Grace, but that was another matter: Mma Makutsi had her little ways and it was always possible that her apparent selfishness had been entirely unintended.

'Are you sure, Mma?' Mma Makutsi pressed. 'It would be helpful, I think, for us both to have these signs on our desks.'

Mma Ramotswe shook her head. 'Don't worry, Mma, there are many more important things to think about.'

They set about their work, Mma Makutsi having already started filing the pile of papers on her desk and Mma Ramotswe having invoices to compile. It was while they were both engaged in these tasks that a knock came on the door and Mma Makutsi leaped up – somewhat guiltily, thought Mma Ramotswe – to admit the unexpected caller; except that he was not unexpected, as Mma Ramotswe was soon to discover.

Chapter Two

The Relative Size of Desks

A man stood in the doorway.

'Is this the place?' he asked.

Mma Makutsi adjusted her glasses. '*Dumela, Rra,*' she said, pointedly. Both she and Mma Ramotswe were firmly of the belief that you always – *always* – started a conversation with a stranger, as with anybody else for that matter, with a polite greeting. You did not have to go through the whole gamut of enquiries as to whether they had slept well, whether their family had slept well, and so on, but you never simply launched into whatever it was that you were planning to say without at least a few preliminary words of salutation. And even then, after you had greeted the other person, it was polite to approach the business in hand by a slightly circuitous route rather than start talking directly about it. So, if one had some business relating to cattle, it would be polite to say something about cattle in general, about the grazing, about the prospects of rain, and only then begin to talk about any particular cattle in question. That was the way things had always been done in Botswana, and, as far as Mma Ramotswe was concerned, the way that things had always been done in Botswana was the way they should always be done. What was the point of having a country, she thought, if you were all going to do things differently from one another? There were two parts to a country, she believed: the land, the people, the cattle – the things that you saw when you looked about you – they all made up the outside part; and then there was the inside part, the memories, the ways of speaking and acting, the feelings of attachment and love – these made up the inner part, the soul of the land. And countries did have a soul – she was convinced of that – just as we ourselves had a soul, however you might describe it. It was dangerous, Mma Ramotswe felt, to say that there was no such thing as a soul, to suggest that we were not much more than *things*, because if you did that, what was there to stop you treating people badly, to stop you casting them aside, or ignoring their feelings, or hardening your heart to their suffering? If you believed that other people had souls, then you treated them respectfully; you treated them, in other words, as a brother or a sister. And that lay at the heart of what Mma Ramotswe believed: that you should be able to go up to anyone, anyone at all, and address him or her as your brother or your sister – *and mean it*.

And now this man stood in the doorway and did not say *dumela* and made no enquiry about their health. But when Mma Makutsi said, '*Dumela, Rra,*' pointedly, he could hardly remain unaware of his rudeness, and so he lowered his eyes, shifted his weight from one foot to the other, and began again, this time uttering the appropriate greeting. Mma Makutsi glanced over at

Mma Ramotswe, with a look that said, *That's him told*. It was a look that Mma Ramotswe knew well; Mma Makutsi often put people in their place, gently but firmly, although sometimes not so gently, when they transgressed in some way. There had been several instances of this recently, most notably when she and Mma Ramotswe, travelling together to visit Mma Potokwani, had been pulled up at a police roadblock and asked through the passenger window, rather rudely, where they were going. 'That is my business, Rra,' Mma Makutsi had snapped at the young policeman. 'This lady ...' and here she had gestured towards Mma Ramotswe, 'This lady, as you can see, could be your aunty, and you would not ask your aunty where she was going like that, would you? You would not. You would say, "Excuse me, aunty, do you mind telling me where you are going?"'

The policeman had been taken aback, and had stammered an excuse.

'Do not let it happen again,' said Mma Makutsi. 'And also, do not waste valuable police time in asking respectable ladies where they are going. There are plenty of bad men driving round on the roads. You should be asking them that question – not us.'

The exchange over, and with the tiny white van once again on its way, Mma Makutsi turned to Mma Ramotswe and gave her the *That's him told* look. Mma Ramotswe smiled; she had to admire Mma Makutsi's self-assurance, which was just what over-zealous or impolite policemen – and other officials – needed to encounter from time to time. There was no excuse for rudeness: the old Botswana morality was unambiguous on that matter. You treated other people with courtesy, no matter who they were. An important, powerful person should always listen to a small, unin-fluential person. A poor man was as worthy of respect as a rich man. Women should not be bullied by strong men, and weak men should not be brushed aside by strong women. Everybody had the right to stand up straight and speak their mind. And if you were in some way on the outside, born on the margins, you should still count for as much as somebody born in a much more privileged bed. A country that recognised these things would always be a good place, and Botswana, as everybody knew, was a good place.

Now their visitor took a step forward, and Mma Ramotswe noticed that he was carrying a toolbox. 'You must be looking for Mr J. L. B. Matekoni,' she said. 'The garage is next door. You'll find him there, Rra.'

The man shook his head. 'No, Mma, I'm looking for the No. 1 Ladies' Detective Agency.' Putting down the toolbox, he extracted a piece of paper from his pocket. 'I'm looking for the managing director – for Mma ... Mma ... ' He re-examined the piece of paper. 'For Mma Grace Makutsi, BSc.'

Mma Ramotswe gasped. She could not help herself. Who could refrain from gasping in such circumstances?

Mma Makutsi intervened. She seemed unfazed – and certainly unrepentant. 'That is me, Rra. You're looking for me, I think.'

Mma Ramotswe stared at Mma Makutsi, but the other woman seemed indifferent to her gaze of wonder and reproach. BSc, thought Mma Ramotswe. *BSc!* But that was the least of it: *managing director!* Should she speak to this man; should she correct him? Should she point out that you should not believe everything you read after a person's name? She decided that she would not. She would not embarrass Mma Makutsi in front of a stranger, and so any reproof – and there would have to be one – would come later, and would be gentle. The BSc could be ignored, but Mma Makutsi should not go round misleading others as to her being the managing director of the agency.

The man had now noticed the name displayed on Mma

Makutsi's desk. 'Ah yes, I see the name now, Mma.' He turned to Mma Ramotswe. 'And you work here too, Mma?'

Mma Ramotswe inclined her head. She said nothing; it was so obviously for Mma Makutsi to rectify any misapprehension.

And Mma Makutsi did. 'That is Mma Ramotswe,' she said. 'We work together.'

The man smiled at Mma Ramotswe. 'I have never met any lady detectives before, Mma. In fact, I have never met any detectives at all.' He paused. 'My name is Mr Serumola. You were in touch with us. My firm is called General Woodwork and Shopfitters.'

Mma Ramotswe replied, 'That will be Mma Makutsi who was in touch.'

'Yes,' said Mma Makutsi. 'That was me. This is the desk in question, Rra. This one at which I am sitting.'

Mma Ramotswe watched in astonishment as Mr Serumola opened his toolbox and took out a measuring tape. Making his way to Mma Makutsi's desk, he proceeded to measure it, noting down the dimensions in a small black notebook. Then he stood back and stroked his chin thoughtfully.

'I think it will be easy enough,' he said at last. 'I can add a small leaf at either end, on a hinge, you see, so that it can be lowered if you do not need the capacity. Flexibility is the answer these days, ladies.'

Mma Ramotswe looked to Mma Makutsi for an explanation, but Mma Makutsi was busy with Mr Serumola.

'Will the wood look the same?' she asked. I do not want part of my desk to be one colour and the rest another. I do not want a two-tone effect, Rra, if it can be avoided.'

'It can be avoided very easily,' said Mr Serumola. 'Wood can be stained, Mma. It is not hard. I should be able to match the colour without any difficulty.'

'That will be very satisfactory,' said Mma Makutsi. Turning to address Mma Ramotswe, she continued, perfectly coolly, 'You may be wondering what all this is about, Mma.'

Mma Ramotswe confessed that that was precisely what she was wondering.

'I decided that my desk was too small,' Mma Makutsi explained. 'These days there are so many papers, as you know, Mma. And then there are the other things that you need to put on a desk – the pens, the rulers, the things for punching holes in paper . . . '

'Punches,' contributed Mr Serumola. 'I think they call those punches.'

Mma Makutsi nodded. 'That is the correct name, Rra. And all these things take up desk-space.' She paused. 'And there is the telephone too. The telephone needs space and if you are drinking tea, you must also find a place for your teacup. That is an issue too.'

'There are so many things to think about,' said Mr Serumola. 'But you are very wise, Mma Makutsi, to be thinking ahead like this. There are many people who do not anticipate what their needs will be. Those people are short-term in their thinking.'

'You are quite right, Rra,' said Mma Makutsi. 'You should plan ahead.'

'I'll give you an example,' Mr Serumola went on. 'The other day I saw in the paper that the government said there were not enough nurses. They said that this was because not enough had been trained. They were hoping to get some from Zambia, they said.'

Mma Ramotswe and Mma Makutsi waited.

'But do you know what I thought?' he continued. 'I asked myself one question, just one simple question. That was: why did the hospitals not train more nurses in the first place? It is not complicated mathematics, you know. You look at the figures. You ask how many people there are, and then you find out how many nurses do you need for every five hundred people, say.'

'That would not be many,' said Mma Makutsi. 'Maybe not even one.'

'I do not know about that, Mma,' said Mr Serumola. 'The point is that you can take the whole population and divide by that figure I do not know, and that will give you the number of nurses you need. Then you advertise for young women to train—'

'Or men,' Mma Makutsi interjected. 'It's men too, Rra. There are nurses who are men these days.'

Mr Serumola looked puzzled. 'We are talking about nurses, Mma.'

'I know that,' snapped Mma Makutsi. 'There are male nurses, Rra.'

Mr Serumola was doubtful. 'Male nurses?' he said. 'What do these male nurses do?'

Mma Makutsi laughed. 'Where have you been these last few years, Mr Serumola?'

He frowned. 'I have been here in Gaborone, Mma. Except for six months, when I was up at Selebi-Phikwe, working with a contractor on the mines up there. They need carpenters, you see.' Then he added, 'Why do you ask, Mma?'

Mma Makutsi was patient. 'What I meant, Rra, was that you seem to have missed some very important changes. There are male nurses now. They have been around for many years. And they do all the things that other nurses do – there is no difference in the jobs they do.'

Mma Ramotswe had been following the exchange with inter-est. Now she interjected, 'Sometimes they have special jobs to do, Mma Makutsi. If you have a very traditionally built patient, for instance, and the nurses have to lift the patient out of the bed, then they may ask a male nurse to do that, because they are stronger and can lift heavier weights.'

Mma Makutsi pursed her lips. 'Not all men are stronger than women,' she said.

'Some are,' said Mr Serumola.

'That may be true,' agreed Mma Makutsi. 'But it depends, I think, on whether you are talking about a small man or a big man. There are some very small men, and they may not be very strong.'

'They can be,' interrupted Mma Ramotswe. 'There is a very small man who lives near the bus station. I have seen him there sometimes. His legs are very short, but they are very muscular. They look like tree trunks.'

Mma Makutsi laughed. 'That would be dangerous if there were any termites around, I think. You know how termites like to march up the side of tree trunks. And then suddenly the tree falls over because the termites have eaten the trunk.'

Mr Serumola seemed to appreciate that. 'That small man could fall over too,' he remarked. 'I hope he is being very careful.'

Mma Makutsi tapped a finger against her desk. 'You were talking about forward planning, Rra. And I agree with you. That is why I am happy that I shall have a large desk.'

Mr Serumola replaced his tape measure in his toolbox. 'I will cut and sand the wood,' he said. 'Then I shall come back next week to fit the extensions. I will stain them once they are in place.'

Mma Makutsi thanked him and rose to escort him out of the office. When she returned, she glanced at Mma Ramotswe. 'I hope you do not mind my making these arrangements for a bigger desk,' she said. 'I was going to talk to you about it.'

Mma Ramotswe shook her head. 'It is your desk, Mma. And it is important in this life to feel happy with your desk.'

'Exactly,' said Mma Makutsi. 'That is what I feel too, Mma.'

Mma Makutsi returned to her filing while Mma Ramotswe sat lost in thought, gazing up at the ceiling. Mma Makutsi wanted to have a bigger desk than the one that she, Mma Ramotswe, had. That was very obvious. She wanted an ostentatious name-plate; she wanted a desk with an extension on either side. Two questions arose from this. The first was this: why should Mma Makutsi suddenly be visited by this burst of ambition, so obviously, even carelessly, displayed? And the second flowed from that: where would it all end?

These were the questions that she put to Mr J. L. B. Matekoni when the two of them sat on the veranda that evening during that special half-hour or so when the sun is clearly committed to sinking but has yet to do so. It was a favourite time of the day for Mma Ramotswe: the day, with its attendant cares, was largely over, and the sky, so unrelenting in its heat and immensity at midday and in the early afternoon, seemed somehow kinder, more forgiving. Birds were still to be seen – and heard – chattering their final messages and announcements, but would soon disappear into the shelter of their acacia branches. There was woodsmoke on the air, a whiff from a fire lit by a nightwatchman in his shack, and dust, too, waiting to be settled by the cold air of night. It was a time for sitting still and thinking, or, if you were fortunate enough, for going over, with a spouse or a friend, the affairs of the day. At this time, and under this sky, such affairs could almost always be reduced to their proper proportions, and could be put away for the night ahead.

That was how it was on Zebra Drive, which of course was in Gaborone. Outside the bright circle of the town, only a few miles beyond its outer boundaries, it was not all that different, although there was more of everything when you were in a village or at a cattle post: more sky, more land, more trees, more sounds of birds and insects and creatures for which one had no certain name. Mma Ramotswe would sometimes close her eyes when she was sitting out on her veranda, and imagine that she was back in Mochudi, where it had all begun. There had been no electric light in those days, or at least there had been none in their house, where she had sat as a small girl and watched her aunt and her mother's cousin stirring the pot or, against the soft hiss of a paraffin lamp, sewing some garment by hand. And outside, in a chair under the tree, her father might be sitting with a friend or two for company – a friend, perhaps, with whom he had worked in the mines all those years before, and with whom he could go over stories of the people, good and bad, whom they had known in the deep shafts of the gold reefs.

But now she sat beside Mr J. L. B. Matekoni, who had had an exhausting day repairing the suspension on a hearse. 'Does it matter, Rra?' Mma Ramotswe had said. 'The late people won't mind if the ride is bumpy.' He had looked at her reproachfully, but then they had both laughed and he'd reported that Fanwell had made the exact same point. He had told him off for lack of respect, but had spoiled his own reproof by smiling.

Mma Ramotswe was drinking a cup of redbush tea, which she now refreshed from the pot on the table before her. She did not want to burden Mr J. L. B. Matekoni after a tiring day, but she felt the need to speak to him about Mma Makutsi and her puzzling manoeuvres. So she told him about the arrival of Mr Serumola and of the revealing of Mma Makutsi's plan to enlarge her desk.

'I understand why she might find it convenient to have a bigger surface,' Mma Ramotswe conceded. 'But we all have limited desk space. All you have to do is pile things up on top of a filing cabinet, or stack papers on a shelf until you can deal with them. You'd think that somebody who is a graduate of the Botswana Secretarial College—'

'With ninety-seven per cent,' interjected Mr J. L. B. Matekoni.

'. . . with ninety-seven per cent, would know that you can shelve papers and then deal with them later. You'd think that a first-class secretarial graduate would know that and would not go to all the trouble of having a desk extension. But no, that is what she has arranged to have.'

Mr J. L. B. Matekoni received this information thoughtfully. 'Of course,' he said, 'it's not about space. It never is.'

'No?' asked Mma Ramotswe. 'What is it about, then?'

'Importance, Mma. It is all about importance. She wants to have a bigger desk than you so that people will think she is more important. I have seen that sort of thing before. One of the people in the Botswana Motor Trades Association has a brother who works in a government office. He told him that there are very firm rules for the size of desk that government officials have. If you are a senior official, then your desk must be such-and-such a size. If you are promoted, they give you a bigger desk. And office space too – the same rules apply there. You can tell where somebody is on the ladder by the size of their office. It is all laid down and people are very sensitive about it.'

Mma Ramotswe asked him if he thought it was the same thing with Mma Makutsi.

'It will definitely be the same thing, Mma,' he replied. 'That is what she is doing.'

Mma Ramotswe shook her head. 'It makes me feel sad, Mr J. L. B. Matekoni,' she said. 'Mma Makutsi and I are very old friends. We have worked together for many years now. I do not understand why she should be so keen to promote herself like this.'

She watched him ponder this. Mr J. L. B. Matekoni, too, was fond of Mma Makutsi, and he did not like the thought that she was unhappy. And that could be the only reason for such behaviour, he thought. People who were secure and happy did not feel the need to boost themselves in this way and to seek the advantage of a few extra square inches of desk space.

'I think you have to see the whole thing as part of a long story,' he said. 'Every problem is like that, you know, Mma Ramotswe. You think you know the reason why something is the way it is and then you start to look at what went before, and what went before *that*, and you end up with a far longer story than you first imagined.'

He paused. This was an unusually long speech for Mr J. L. B. Matekoni, and Mma Ramotswe was rapt.

'Go on, Rra,' she encouraged him. 'I am listening to what you are saying.'

Mr J. L. B. Matekoni drew a deep breath. 'You have to remember, Mma,' he began. 'Mma Makutsi comes from Bobonong. That is where she is from.'

'Yes, Rra, Bobonong. It is way up there.' She pointed vaguely northwards.

'And her people were not very well off,' Mr J. L. B. Matekoni continued.

'That is true,' said Mma Ramotswe. 'She did very well to get herself down to Gaborone and into the Botswana Secretarial College. That is a big jump, I think – from nothing to attending a course in Gaborone. That is quite an achievement.'

'Involving a lot of sacrifice,' said Mr J. L. B. Matekoni.

Mma Ramotswe nodded. She did not disagree; Mma Makutsi had achieved a great deal, but did that, of itself, explain why she should be so touchy about status? After all, she had made a very good marriage – Phuti Radiphuti was not just anybody; he was the proprietor of the Double Comfort Furniture Store and a member of a family that owned a considerable herd of cattle. If you married into a family like that, then surely there was not much about which you needed to worry. The size of your desk should be irrelevant if you had what Phuti and Grace had.

'I think she is insecure,' said Mr J. L. B. Matekoni. 'I think that she is worried that she might lose everything. That sometimes happens, you know. People who are very comfortably off sit and worry about losing all their money.'

'But that's ridiculous,' protested Mma Ramotswe. 'Phuti has that business. He does very well. She is not going to find herself penniless. That will never happen.'

Mr J. L. B. Matekoni was not so sure. Now he lowered his voice, although there was nobody to overhear: only two Cape doves, on their branch in the cool of the evening, content in the company each of the other; only the cicadas in their cease-less chorus.

'I have heard something, Mma Ramotswe,' he said.

She waited.

'Yes, I have heard something. I am told that there is fresh com-petition for a very important part of Phuti's business.'

This was news to Mma Ramotswe. She had heard that the Double Comfort Furniture Store had a good grip on its markets and that none of the other furniture stores came anywhere near it in the volume of their sales. Had Mr J. L. B. Matekoni learned something that contradicted that?

It seemed that he had.

'Do you know what the biggest part of Phuti's business is?' he asked.

Mma Ramotswe guessed. 'I know that they sell a lot of dining-room tables.'

Mr J. L. B. Matekoni shook his head. 'No, Mma. That is no longer true. They used to sell many of those tables, but now people are eating in the kitchen. Or they are eating off their laps. So, there are not many people who sit down in a dining room and eat from a dining-room table.' He paused. 'Some people are not even using plates any longer. They eat out of cardboard boxes.'

Mma Ramotswe had seen that. When she was last at the supermarket, she had spotted some young people sitting on a bench outside, eating pizza from a cardboard box. When they had finished, they had simply tossed the box away. The sight had troubled her, and had she not been in a hurry to get her shopping done before the supermarket closed, she would have gone over and remonstrated with them. It was not responsible behaviour to add to the burden of litter in that way. That was not what Botswana stood for, but perhaps these young people had not been told what their country represented – what ideals had been set out by Seretse Khama when the country emerged from its colonial past, when the butterfly that was the new state had broken out of the chrysalis of the Bechuanaland Protectorate and had spread its delicate wings. Botswana had made it; it had become the finest country in Africa because of sacrifice and hard work and determination to make the recipe work. Did they know that, these young people who threw litter about with such thoughtlessness? She sighed. She should not be too disapproving, because one could end up shaking one's head all day over the things that one saw. You would end up with a bad crick in the neck that way, or your head might even fall off. Perhaps that had already happened somewhere – some poor person had been so shocked by everything that his head had fallen off and rolled away. And of course, nobody liked people who spent their time complaining about the behaviour of the young. They were probably perfectly decent young people who just were not think-ing – and how many of us really *thought* about things when we were their age?

'So,' she said to Mr J. L. B. Matekoni, 'it is not tables. Then is it chairs, Rra?'

He seemed disappointed that she had arrived so quickly at the right conclusion. 'Yes, Mma. You are absolutely right. It is chairs that are the main item. Phuti told me that the sale of chairs accounts for sixty-seven per cent of their turnover. That is a lot, I think.'

Mma Ramotswe agreed. She did not claim to know a lot about business, but she did know that it was important to diversify. If you relied too heavily on one product, or one client, then there was always a danger that that product might become unfash-ionable or the client would disappear. Mma Makutsi had said something about that once, when she was talking about what she had learned at the Botswana Secretarial College, but Mma Ramotswe's attention tended to wander when Mma Makutsi was talking about such matters and she rarely remembered the details.

She looked at Mr J. L. B. Matekoni. 'Somebody else is selling chairs to Phuti's customers?'

Mr J. L. B. Matekoni looked grave. 'There is a new company,' he explained. 'They call themselves Twenty-First-Century Chairs. They have opened up now in Gaborone.'

'I do not like that name,' said Mma Ramotswe. 'We know that it is the twenty-first century, Rra. We don't need these chair people to tell us that.'

He smiled. 'They think it is very modern. They believe that people will think their chairs will have more features than other chairs. Everything has to have features these days, Mma Ramotswe. Have you noticed that?'

She had. 'Whatever you buy has a long list of what it does. Nothing is simple any longer. Nothing.'

It was a subject on which Mr J. L. B. Matekoni had strong views – at least, when applied to cars. There had been a time when cars took you from one place to another and that was that. Now they had to have automatic this and automatic that. They had to have headlights that swivelled when you turned a corner and alarms that sounded if you were about to reverse into something. There had been a day when you could reverse into things if you wanted to, and the car would say nothing about it. Now it gave you a dressing-down if you did what the car thought was the wrong thing. And as for the diagnostic systems that told you which bit of the engine to replace, that just discouraged people from fixing anything; you just threw things away and replaced them with new – and expensive, needless to say – parts. If this went on, there would no longer be any role for mechanics and everybody would be able to fix their own car by simply replacing bits of it as they went along. Well, that was not the sort of world that he wanted to live in, and sooner or later everybody would learn that lesson. They would wake up one day and discover that we had used up all the spare parts we could make and we would have to go back to basics and start fixing things once again. That day, he thought, could hardly come soon enough.

He told Mma Ramotswe what he had heard about these new chairs. 'They are completely adjustable,' he said. 'There is a lever that you pull and the angle of the back changes. And then another lever controls the height of the chair. And of course they are very modern in their lines. They call them minimalist, I think. That is the new word for chairs like that. Minimalist. They do not have thick cushions – in fact, there are no cushions at all.'

Mma Ramotswe shook her head. 'No cushions? But everybody

wants cushions on their chairs. How can you sit for long periods of time if you do not have cushions?'

'True,' said Mr J. L. B. Matekoni. 'But these new chairs do not look at all comfortable – unlike the chairs that Phuti sells.'

'Then why are people buying them?' asked Mma Ramotswe.

Mr J. L. B. Matekoni sighed. 'People like to think they are being up to date,' he said. 'And they are undercutting Phuti's prices, I've heard.'

It did not look good to Mma Ramotswe. But what she heard next made the whole situation look even worse.

'They have had quite an advertising push,' said Mr J. L. B. Matekoni. 'And they're planning a big new campaign.' He paused, waiting to deliver his bombshell. 'And do you know who will be the face of these new advertisements?'

Mma Ramotswe hesitated. She had her suspicions, but it was almost too painful to give voice to them. Then she ventured, 'Violet—'

'Yes,' interjected Mr J. L. B. Matekoni. 'Violet Sephotho.'

Mma Ramotswe gazed up at the veranda ceiling, as if she expected help to come from that quarter. A small gecko, white to the point of translucence, attached, upside down, to the ceiling board by its tiny sticker feet, looked down at her.

'Oh,' she said. It was all she could think of to say, and after a few moments she said it again. 'Oh.'

What was there to say about Violet Sephotho, the well-known lady about town, the would-be nemesis of Mma Makutsi, the ruthless pursuer of every opportunity to make money – and trouble – that came her way? That was enough, but there would be so much more if one set out to enumerate the full list of Violet's wicked schemes. Mma Makutsi knew all about those, because Violet had been at the Botswana Secretarial College at the same time as she had, but had managed to graduate at the end of the course with the barest pass available. And even then, she had been lucky to get the low mark she did because it was widely rumoured, although never proved, that she had only passed one of the examinations because she had become close to one of the male lecturers – 'Close enough to pass any examination,' as Mma Makutsi had put it. 'Close enough to see the examination paper the day before it was issued to the candidates. That close, if you see what I mean, Mma Ramotswe.'

Violet Sephotho had done nothing but foment trouble, and here she was at it again – this time associating herself with a firm that seemed set on gobbling up the hard-won market of a well-established furniture company, and doing so by dazzling people with so-called minimalist chairs with numerous, perfectly unnecessary functions. It was no coincidence that her latest venture should involve a direct attack on the interests of the Radiphuti business – there had existed ill-feeling between Violet and Mma Makutsi from the very first day they had met, all those years ago, at the Botswana Secretarial College. New students embarking on their course were invited to have tea with the principal and selected members of the college staff in the hall used for examinations and other large meetings. For Grace Makutsi, fresh from Bobonong, it was a significant occasion. Here she was, after all those sacrifices, mixing with people who had seen so much more of the world than she had; young women whose parents actually owned a car, in some cases, rather than a donkey cart of the sort that, in those days, the Makutsi family had used for transport. She had two proper dresses – the one she was wearing, and the other one in the laundry; she had two pairs of shoes, and one lace handkerchief, of which she was inordinately proud. She did not have much else. But she had embarked on the journey that would open doors for her – as she had been told education would always do – and she had been filled with pride at having got this far. And then Violet Sephotho, looking Mma Makutsi up and down, as they stood in a small cluster, waiting for the principal to come and have a word with them, had said, in that tone that she came to recognise as Violet's put-down voice, 'So you're Grace Makutsi, are you? You come from Bobonong, they tell me.' She did not explain who *they* were, and Mma Makutsi had wondered who would be talking about her this early in the course, and what would they be saying?

Mma Makutsi answered politely. 'I am,' she said.

'I have never been up there,' said Violet Sephotho. 'It's very far away from everything, I think.'

Mma Makutsi bit her lip. 'Or everything is very far from Bobonong,' she said – or should have said, because it only occurred to her to say that well after the event. So she was silent, while Violet Sephotho continued to look at her in a slightly disdainful way.

Later, at their very first lecture, Mma Makutsi had noticed that Violet sat in the back row, painting her nails while the lecturer talked about the syllabus they would be following – a fascinating combination of shorthand, typing skills, accountancy and, most interesting of all, the principles of filing. In due course there would be courses on staff management, business structures, and advanced telephone skills. Violet looked bored throughout, and Mma Makutsi realised that here was somebody who had had too much given to them too early, and now could not be bothered with anything.

And after that inauspicious beginning it had become worse. When Mma Makutsi married Phuti Radiphuti, Violet's anger and envy were unconcealed. She could not accept that Mma

Makutsi, a young woman from Bobonong, of all places, should end up with one of the most eligible bachelors in Gaborone – at least in financial terms. Phuti was no catch in terms of looks, of course, but Violet would have been quite happy to overlook such shortcomings in the light of his evident liquidity, and she had even tried to lure him away from Mma Makutsi with blatant flirting. That had not worked, of course: Phuti was a good and loyal husband, and he was happy in their marriage. That was a challenge to Violet, of course, and when the opportunity arose to involve herself with a business that could chip away at his and Mma Makutsi's prosperity, then how could she possibly resist? She did not even try.

Chapter Three

A Big Crisis in the Early Morning

The following morning, Phuti Radiphuti drove Mma Makutsi to work as he usually did. Mma Makutsi now had a driving licence, but preferred not to drive because of the difficulty she experienced in driving on the left side of the road rather than in the middle, which to her seemed safer. If you favoured one side of the road, she felt, you were far more likely to stray off onto the verge, and from there it was but a short drift into the surrounding bush, should one's attention wander for a few moments, as was quite possible – especially on a hot day, when drowsiness might come upon one unannounced. She had heard of one driver who, when driving up to Francistown, on that straight road that cuts through the bush like an arrow, had dozed off and had woken up in a small village some miles off the road, having made his way there, across various fields, without waking up from the sleep that had overtaken him. Such tales, of course, tended to be apocryphal, and were often embellished on each telling, but could be salutary nonetheless, and some attention should be paid to them. No, the less you were at the wheel, the less risk there was of anything untoward happening to you. And in Mma Makutsi's case, there was no real need to drive when she had the good fortune to be married to a husband who was prepared to drive her to work in the morning and to get the driver from his furniture store to drive her home at the end of the day. And if she needed to get anywhere from the office, there was always Fanwell or Charlie, both of whom were allowed to drive Mma Ramotswe's white van – if they applied for permission – provided, of course, that one of them was available. In general, Mma Makutsi felt safer if Fanwell was at the wheel, as he tended to observe the speed limit, while Charlie would put his foot right down on the accelerator, causing the van's ancient engine to whine in protest as the last drop of torque was wrested from it.

'I have some things to buy in the supermarket,' she said to Phuti, as they set off down the drive that led to the gate at the bottom of their plot. 'You might like to come in with me and help choose some things you'd like to eat.'

Phuti was in no hurry; the Double Comfort Furniture Store had conscientious and entirely reliable staff. His under-manager, a slight, rather worried-looking man from Molepolole, was always at the store well before Phuti arrived in the morning and could be completely trusted to open up at eight o'clock on the dot.

'I can help you shop,' Phuti said. 'I would like to choose some chocolate biscuits. And perhaps some cake. You know that cake that has four differently coloured squares running through the centre.'

'They call that Battenberg cake,' said Mma Makutsi.

'I call it delicious,' said Phuti.

'It is very good if you like sweet things,' agreed Mma Makutsi. 'Mma Ramotswe is like you. If she sees that cake, she likes to eat it all up – every last piece.'

'We can buy some of that cake,' said Phuti. 'And some other things too. I need nail clippers, Mma. I used to have some, but I don't know where they are now. They have disappeared.'

'We can see if they have them,' said Mma Makutsi. 'Stores do not always have everything you need.' She paused. 'Are you sure you need nail clippers, Rra?'

He was sure. 'My toenails are making holes in my socks,' said Phuti. 'It is not good for the ends of my socks.'

They discussed socks and other items of clothing for much of the journey to the supermarket at the Riverview Shopping Mall. Phuti needed more socks, he said, and he could also do with new underpants, as there were holes appearing in several pairs that were still in commission. They were only six months old, he complained, and he felt that underpants should last longer than that. 'Sometimes I think they make these holes deliberately. They have weak points in all underpants, so that holes will appear and then people will go out and buy more. I have read about that sort of thing, Mma. It is called phased redundancy.'

'I do not approve of that sort of thing,' said Mma Makutsi. 'Underpants should last for at least eighteen months, I think. Maybe two years. There is not an unlimited supply of underpants in this world.'

Phuti agreed. 'And they should be local,' he said. 'It is no good our buying all our underpants from China. Those underpants have a long way to come. That cannot be a good thing.'

'I think you are right,' said Mma Makutsi. 'But I don't think that anybody will do anything about it. People are lazy when it comes to things like that. They say, "Oh, there are many under-pants in China – we can just order some of them." So all the men in Botswana are now wearing Chinese underpants. Not that anybody talks about it, of course – at least, not publicly.'

Phuti was silent, and Mma Makutsi shot a glance in his direction. Her observation, it seemed, had made him think, although she was not sure what he was thinking. He was, in fact, not sure that the majority of underpants were made in China; some were made in the Philippines, he thought, and they used to make underpants down in Cape Town in the old days. But factories, once so busy making thousands of pairs of underpants a day, now stood silent, and he pictured them for a moment, in their abandonment.

'Do you think we could make more underpants in this country?' he asked eventually, as their car negotiated the traffic circle near the hospital.

'Of course we could,' said Mma Makutsi. 'All you need is some industrial sewing machines and some underpants material. And a pattern, of course. I think you can get machines that cut the material.'

Phuti was interested. 'Do you feed the pattern into a computer? And then does the computer then control machines that cut the material? Is that how it works?'

Mma Makutsi was not entirely sure, but her knowledge of clothing manufacture, although slender, was enough to allow her to answer with some confidence. 'Yes, that is how these things work these days, Rra.'

Phuti stroked his chin. 'But it might still be possible to employ actual people, Mma – real people, that is, not robots – to lay the patterns out on the cloth and then cut it with scissors. Would that still be possible, do you think?'

Mma Makutsi thought that it would. Machines had not entirely replaced human beings, she said, although there were many machines that were planning to do just that. That was potentially worrying. If you made a machine like, for instance, Mma Ramotswe – embodying all her fine qualities – then that would be uncontroversial. Such a machine would undoubtedly be of great benefit to any community. The same might be said of a machine that somehow replicated Mma Potokwani, a machine that could automatically wash, scrub, dress and feed orphans on a production-line basis; such a machine would be objected to by few. Of course the housemothers, those hard-working and uncomplaining ladies who cooked the children's meals, who mended their clothes, who swept the neat, small houses that were home to the charges of Mma Potokwani's Orphan Farm, might have something to say about being replaced by machines. Could machines love children? Could machines love *anybody*? And would they ever invent a machine that could hold a child's hand and stroke a child's brow after a nightmare or in a time of illness? She thought not.

Worse still was the prospect of a malignant machine. It was all very well to imagine machines resembling Mma Ramotswe or Mma Potokwani, but what if some perverse engineer were to design an artificial Violet Sephotho? A machine with its buttons and switches painted in the same bright red nail varnish with which Violet adorned her rather long fingernails? Mma Makutsi shuddered at the thought.

'There is a problem, though,' Mma Makutsi warned. 'If you have people cutting the cloth by hand, and then sewing it themselves, even on big sewing machines, the cost of each garment will be very high. It might be twice the cost of the same thing made by a machine.'

Phuti gazed at the road ahead. 'That is not good,' he said.

She agreed. 'People have to watch where their money goes. There is no such thing as a money tree.'

Phuti laughed. 'If you listen to what some people say, Grace, you'd think there was. Oh, yes.'

They both found themselves thinking of examples. Phuti recalled that there had been a local politician who had said, on the radio, so that everybody might hear, that the government should give everybody a free car. This, he suggested, would lead to increased productivity and would mean that the government actually made more money in the long run through taxation. Phuti had not forgotten that interview, and still smiled at the memory, although his smile faded as he recalled the effect on the politician's popularity. That had risen almost beyond measure, which had in turn resulted in his rapid promotion to the deputy leadership of his party. For her part, Mma Makutsi thought of Charlie's recent request that his part-time salary, as an assistant at the agency, be doubled in view of the birth of his baby. Mma Makutsi had been astonished at his boldness, but Mma Ramotswe had taken it calmly and had compounded Mma Makutsi's surprise by offering Charlie a rise that, although not what he had asked for, was nonetheless typically generous. Mma Makutsi knew that the extra money would come out of Mma Ramotswe's own funds, and had considered directly reproaching Charlie for that, but had decided to say nothing. She had, however, made a pointed remark about how, in general, money had to be earned, rather than conjured up from imaginary sources, but Charlie had simply stared at her and made no comment. If there were believers in money trees, then she thought that Charlie was almost certainly numbered among them.

Nothing further was said about the technical side of clothing manufacture, and they were now drawing into the car park at the supermarket.

'Nail clippers,' Phuti muttered as he switched off the car engine. 'We must not forget nail clippers.'

'Nail clippers,' said Mma Makutsi. 'Yes, nail clippers. I shall put them at the top of my list, Rra.'

'So I shall not need to remind you once we get inside?' asked Phuti.

'There will be no need for that,' said Mma Makutsi as she got out of the car. She closed her eyes briefly. The way to remember things was to see them. Mma Ramotswe had told her that a long time ago, during the first month of her employment at the No. 1 Ladies' Detective Agency. Mma Ramotswe had confided that that was the system she had always used, and that it almost always worked. Now Mma Makutsi saw, in her mind's eye, lined up before her, a pair of nail clippers, a large tin of pilchards in tomato sauce, a packet of strong bread flour, a bottle of sunflower oil (for all cooking purposes), a packet of chocolate biscuits, a Battenberg cake and ... She frowned, and opened her eyes. The final thing she saw was a person. There was a woman standing at the end of all these objects, a woman who was looking at her and smiling. She closed her eyes again in an attempt to call up the image once more, but all that came was the nail clippers, with the inscription, worked into the metal: *Made in China*. She tried again, but with no success. Who had it been?

Phuti was waiting for her, and together they began to cross the car park towards the supermarket entrance. Phuti said something to Mma Makutsi that she did not really hear.

He was bemused. From time to time, his wife seemed to withdraw into a realm of her own. She had explained that this tended to happen when she was thinking about office affairs, about some case on which she and Mma Ramotswe were engaged, and he wondered whether that was the case now. 'Are you somewhere else, Mma?' he asked. 'In the office, maybe?'

She shook her head. 'I was thinking of the things we need,' she said. She would not tell him about the woman who had popped up at the end of the list. That was just too complicated, and Phuti was always telling her not to allow her imagination to run away with her.

They entered the supermarket. Like so many supermarkets the world over, it was a place of bright lights and that indefinable smell universal to food shops – a combination of food overlaid with soapy odours unknown to even the most acute of noses. It was also a place of chilled air, which was refreshing in the hot season, even now at this early stage of the day. Phuti fetched a shopping trolley and they began their progress through the shop's aisles. One by one, the items on Mma Makutsi's mental shopping list were located and placed in the trolley.

The nail clippers were hardest to find, but they eventually located them alongside the nail varnishes and related beauty products. Phuti was amused.

'Some of these things appeal to vanity,' he said. 'I do not want to clip my toenails out of vanity, Grace.'

'Oh, I know that,' said Mma Makutsi. 'But I think these days men should pay more attention to these questions, Phuti. Gone are the days when men had to pretend not to care about these things.'

Phuti selected a pair of clippers. 'I think these will do for my nails,' he observed. And then, with a smile, he continued, 'I shall feel much better once my nails look a bit nicer. I think I need a big nail make-over, Mma!'

He had spoken in jest, but there are occasions on which words not intended to be taken seriously are nonetheless uttered at the worst possible time – and this was one of them. The height of the supermarket shelves in that part of the shop was lower than elsewhere and it was possible for shoppers in the neighbouring aisle to see, over the top of the shelves, the heads of those on the other side. And it was at that precise moment that a head appeared from the other side – a head attached to a body that had been bending down to retrieve an item on a lower shelf, but that was now raised, craned over the top, to see who it was who was involved in this discussion of nails. And that head belonged to none other than Violet Sephotho, arch-nemesis of Mma Makutsi, troublemaker, husband-stealer, and what was worst of all, at least in this particular context, one who would love to exaggerate to others an instance of apparent male vanity.

Mma Makutsi was still shaking when she entered the office of the No. 1 Ladies' Detective Agency that morning. Mma Ramotswe was already at her desk, and the kettle on top of the filing cabinet had just boiled, sending a small cloud of steam into the still office air. That steam was symbolic, it suddenly seemed to her, of the turmoil of emotions that had erupted following the unfortunate incident in the supermarket. That encounter had eerie echoes of an earlier occasion, not all that many months ago, when Mma Ramotswe and Mma Potokwani had been falsely accused by Violet Sephotho of stealing chocolate biscuits that Violet herself had blatantly taken out of their box and consumed before replacing it on the supermarket's shelves. Had Violet dreamed of revenge for having been found *in flagrante delicto*, she could not possibly have imagined anything better than overhearing Phuti expressing concern about the state of his toenails. 'And they say that we women are too concerned about our appearance,' Violet would say. 'But you should have heard him going on about his nails!' What delight she would have in passing on that juicy little snippet to her friends; what pleasure, indeed, had she felt in seeing the look of consternation on Mma Makutsi's face when she realised that she had been overheard. That alone, Violet must have thought, was reward enough for being in the right place at the right time, even were she not to spread the story to others, which of course she had a firm and fixed intention of doing.

Had it been anybody else who had overheard them, Mma Makutsi would not have worried too much. She knew, though, that Violet Sephotho would love to paint Phuti in an unfavourable light – as being someone who was excessively vain. That was something Mma Makutsi simply could not accept, because Phuti was just not like that at all. And so she tried to deal with the situation as best she could, saying, in as careless a tone as she could muster, 'You're just joking, of course, Phuti.' Then, as her voice became stronger, she added, 'You're not really concerned with these things at all. That's a joke, you see.' Finally, after a short pause, in a voice raised to an even higher pitch, she went on, 'A joke, of course. Hah! A joke about nail clippers because modern men ...' And at that point words drained away from her, like water from a reservoir in which a large sinkhole has suddenly opened.

She was not sure whether Violet was still there. Her head had been visible because she had craned her neck to see what was going on. Now there was no sign of anybody, and there was certainly no sound of a trolley being pushed up the adjoining aisle. Mma Makutsi looked at Phuti again. He seemed to have been struck dumb. His mouth was open, and she could hear him breathing – it sounded more like gasping, she thought – but not a word escaped him.

Mma Makutsi acted. There was only one thing to do, and that

was to run round the end of the aisle and see if she could find Violet. She would explain to her that what she had heard was a bit of banter, and that Phuti was not in the slightest bit vain. And so, urging Phuti to follow her with their shopping trolley, she started to make off in search of the other woman.

There was no sign of Violet in the adjoining aisle, and so Mma Makutsi, followed by Phuti Radiphuti behind a squeaking and protesting shopping trolley, set off to the tills where she thought Violet might be unloading her goods.

She found Violet handing over her items to a bored-looking male cashier.

'Violet,' spluttered Mma Makutsi.

Violet looked round. Mma Makutsi saw that she was smiling at her in a fixed and insincere way. It was a smile she knew only too well, an expression that combined disdain and condescension in roughly equal measure.

'So, it's Mma Makutsi,' said Violet. And then, looking past Mma Makutsi at Phuti, standing with the shopping trolley, Violet added, 'And Phuti too, if I'm not mistaken. Mr Furniture himself.'

Violet's gaze went to Phuti's nails. It was a deliberate stare – quite deliberate.

Grace swallowed hard. 'Phuti was joking back there,' she said. 'I was looking at cosmetics, you see, and ...'

Violet glanced into their shopping trolley. 'None in there, I see. Tinned pilchards, chocolate biscuits, flour, cooking oil ... I do not see any cosmetics, Mma Makutsi.'

'I did not get any,' said Mma Makutsi quickly. 'But Phuti doesn't usually spend his time thinking about his nails.'

Violet shrugged. 'Oh, I think men can do that these days, Mma Makutsi. There are plenty of men who spend a lot of time preening themselves, even right here in Botswana. They call them new men.'

Mma Makutsi laughed carelessly. 'Oh, new men ... I do not think there are all that many new men in Botswana.'

Phuti had followed this exchange in embarrassed silence. He was a mild man by nature – in that respect not all that unlike Mr J. L. B. Matekoni, who was famously diffident. But now he felt that he had to contribute; after all, men were being discussed here, and men were entitled, surely, to have the occasional say when they were being discussed by women. So now, clearing his throat politely, he said, 'I don't think I am a new man, Violet.'

Violet ignored this. It was as if the supermarket's public address system had transmitted some routine remark about a special offer in the cold meats section – the sort of announcement that you hear but do not really hear. 'Men can spend as much time as they like on their nails,' she said. 'I don't care if a man is vain. Do what you like – that's what I always say.'

Mma Makutsi opened her mouth to protest. It was intolerable, this being lectured by Violet Sephotho of all people, with her bare pass mark in the final examinations of the Botswana Secretarial College – what was it? Somewhere in the lower fifty per cents? Well, that said it all, did it not? Perhaps she should simply remind her of the disparity between their academic achievements, although she imagined that Violet knew full well where the two of them stood in that regard.

But Mma Makutsi did not have the chance to give voice to any of this, as Violet continued, 'Anyway, let's not waste time talking about things like this.' And, having said that, she now addressed Phuti: 'You and I are in the same business now, Phuti. You know that, of course – you'll have seen our chairs.'

Phuti stood quite still. For a moment it looked as if he might respond, as his mouth opened, but then it closed again. Mma Makutsi frowned.

'What business?' she said. 'What chairs?'

Violet transferred her gaze back to Mma Makutsi. She looked scornful. 'Doesn't your husband keep you informed, Mma?'

'I do not know what you're talking about,' Mma Makutsi said. 'What is this business, Phuti?'

He did not reply, but stared morosely at his wife. The cashier looked at his watch and yawned.

'Oh,' said Violet, 'I see that there's not much pillow talk in your place.'

Phuti shifted from foot to foot. 'Chairs . . .' he began, but went no further.

Violet now began to pay for her purchases, speaking over her shoulder as she did so. 'No doubt you'll see the ads, Mma. There is a big push about to start. Everyone is going to go for our chairs – no question about it.' She paused. 'Still, as you and I were taught in our college days, Grace – competition is a good thing in business.'

That was her parting shot, and her purchases in her bag, she gave the cashier a flirtatious smile and left. Mma Makutsi looked down at the floor while Phuti cleared his throat to give an explanation.

'I've been meaning to talk to you, Grace,' he began.

The cashier tapped his fingers against the card machine. 'Please, Rra, attend to this business outside. We are very busy.'

They were not. There were no customers standing behind them and the shop was unusually quiet. But they completed their business in silence and walked out, still in silence, to the car.

Mma Ramotswe could tell immediately that something was gravely wrong.

'*Dumela* . . .' she began as Mma Makutsi came into the office.

She got no further than that first word of greeting before she rose to her feet, instinctively, as she saw her friend and colleague appear to teeter before her.

'Mma, what is wrong?' she said as she rushed forward to steady the figure before her. 'You must sit down, Mma. You must sit down right away.'

She helped Mma Makutsi to her chair, inadvertently knocking over the *Mma Grace Makutsi* name-plate, which fell, with a clatter, to the floor.

'My name-plate,' muttered Mma Makutsi, stooping to pick it up, but being prevented by Mma Ramotswe.

'That can wait,' said Mma Ramotswe. 'You must sit down, Mma, and tell me what is wrong.' She paused. 'Have you had an accident? Is everybody all right?'

Mma Makutsi was in her chair now, but Mma Ramotswe stayed beside her, an arm around her shoulder. She shook her head as she answered the question. 'There has been no accident, Mma Ramotswe. And yes, everybody is all right – but not all right. No, everything is not all right – everything is *very* not all right.'

Mma Ramotswe crossed the room to bring the spare chair up to Mma Makutsi's desk. Then she sat down, reaching out for her friend's hand as she asked her to explain.

It emerged slowly, each sentence being punctuated with a pause in which Mma Makutsi sniffed or dabbed at her nose with a handkerchief.

'Phuti and I have had a row,' she said. 'We never fight. Never. Now I have shouted at him – this very morning, Mma, and sent him off to the office like that. It is very bad.'

Mma Ramotswe waited. She tried to imagine what might have happened. Their marriage, she believed, was fundamentally sound – in fact, she had always been impressed with its closeness and stability. Phuti had never shown any sign of having a wandering eye, and Mma Makutsi would be the last person, Mma Ramotswe thought, to have an affair. Yet you could never tell what was going on in a marriage when you surveyed it from the outside, as she had learned in the practice of her profession. As a private detective, you discovered things about people and their domestic arrangements that you would never have guessed from the outside and that only became apparent when you probed behind the façade that people presented to the world.

Of course, couples had their tiffs, and there would be few marriages in which no cross words had ever been spoken. In this case, she reminded herself, there was an additional factor: Mma Makutsi could be touchy, and there were occasions on which she had made a mountain out of a molehill. It was perfectly possible that she and Phuti might have had a minor disagreement and she had promoted this into a full-scale row. If she had done that, then the fact that the original issue was a trifling one would mean that the whole thing would soon blow over and be forgotten about. And so Mma Ramotswe decided not to be too concerned, but to calm Mma Makutsi down with a few reassuring words and a cup of tea. Tea had remarkable calming properties when administered mid-crisis, and that, perhaps, was what was needed now.

'I think we should have tea, Mma,' said Mma Ramotswe. 'When you look at things with a cup of tea in front of you, they often seem very different.'

Mma Makutsi was having none of this. 'But this is very serious, Mma. This is not something that a cup of tea will fix.'

Mma Ramotswe decided to postpone the tea. 'Tell me, Mma – what happened?'

Mma Makutsi told her of the visit to the supermarket and

of Phuti's loud remark about needing a nail make-over. Mma Ramotswe smiled. 'Everybody knows that Violet Sephotho is a gossip and a troublemaker,' she said. 'People will not care about what she says.'

Mma Makutsi shook her head. 'But it was not just that, Mma. It was not just that she overheard. It's what she said to us later.'

Mma Ramotswe waited. Now she remembered what Mr J. L. B. Matekoni had told her about the emergence of competition in the chair business – and of Violet's involvement in the advertising campaign. This put a totally different complexion on the whole matter.

'About the business?' prompted Mma Ramotswe. 'About the chairs?'

Mma Makutsi looked surprised. 'You know, Mma?'

Mma Ramotswe told her that she had heard the previous evening. As she spoke, she saw Mma Makutsi's surprise turn to dismay.

'He did not tell me any of this,' Mma Makutsi said. 'It seems that everybody knows about this problem except me. Probably even Fanwell and Charlie know.'

'Oh, I don't think so, Mma,' said Mma Ramotswe.

'But they will,' said Grace bitterly. 'And everybody will be talking about it and saying, "Don't let Mma Makutsi hear about it." That is what will be happening, Mma Ramotswe.' She paused, and gave Mma Ramotswe a look of reproach. 'Why would he keep a big problem like this from me, Mma?'

Mma Ramotswe looked up at the ceiling. Sisterhood was all very well, but when it drew you into disagreements between husband and wife you had to be careful.

'I think that Phuti loves you very much, Mma,' she said. 'I have always thought that.'

Mma Makutsi thought about this for a moment. 'That is not the point, Mma.'

'But it is,' replied Mma Ramotswe. 'Phuti loves you very much and does not want you to worry.'

Mma Makutsi took off her glasses and polished them. It was a mannerism that Mma Ramotswe knew well, and she knew that it meant that Mma Makutsi was preparing to re-evaluate a position.

Mma Ramotswe pressed home with her advantage. 'And you have been worried, I think, Mma. You have been worried about ... about security? About money?'

Mma Makutsi hesitated. Then she said, 'Yes, I have, Mma. I knew that something was wrong. I knew that he was worried about the business, but I couldn't talk to him about it. I thought that it would go away – that maybe it was something temporary. But now ... '

'So, you have both been worrying away and you have not been able to speak to one another. You became cross with him for not telling you about this crisis, and all the time he was only trying to shield you.'

'It would have been better to talk,' muttered Mma Makutsi.

Mma Ramotswe agreed. It was always – *always* – better to talk.

Mma Makutsi went on to tell Mma Ramotswe about the fraught conversation she had had with Phuti in the car after they had left the supermarket car park. 'He said that it is very serious,' she explained. 'And I shouted at him. I shouted, Mma, because he should have told me. And anyway, he said that the Double Comfort Furniture Store could go bankrupt in a couple of months. He said that is all the time that it has left.'

Mma Ramotswe spread her hands in a gesture of sympathy. 'That is very sad news, Mma.'

'And we will lose everything, Mma,' Mma Makutsi went on. 'Even our house.'

Mma Ramotswe did not hesitate. 'You can come and stay with me,' she said quickly. 'Mr J. L. B. Matekoni will want that too. We have plenty of room.'

That was not true, and they both knew it. The children would have to sleep in the kitchen if the Radiphuti family came to stay.

'You are very kind, Mma Ramotswe,' said Mma Makutsi.

'We are friends,' said Mma Ramotswe. 'You can always stay with your friends.' She paused. 'But it will not come to that. I'm sure that there is something we can do.'

Mma Makutsi sighed. 'What, Mma? What can we do?'

'I shall think of something,' said Mma Ramotswe.

But the truth of the matter was that she had no idea. It was hard enough keeping the No. 1 Ladies' Detective Agency and Tlokweng Road Speedy Motors afloat. Adding the Double Comfort Furniture Store to the burden would be the proverbial straw that caused the camel to stumble and fall, even if its back remained unbroken.

Mma Makutsi had now stopped shaking, but Mma Ramotswe felt that she was still in need of calming – never before had she seen Mma Makutsi quite so upset.

'Let me make a suggestion, Mma Makutsi,' she said. 'Take a deep breath. Then, once you have done that, close your eyes and think of some good things.'

Mma Makutsi stared at her. 'What good things, Mma?'

Mma Ramotswe shrugged. 'The good things in your life, Mma. I think there must be some.'

'Yes, there are,' said Mma Makutsi. 'There are many good things.'

'Well, then, think of some of them. That will put things in perspective. Is your husband one of them?'

There was only the slightest hesitation before Mma Makutsi said, 'Yes, he is. He is a very kind man.'

'And your baby?'

'He is a very good baby.'

Mma Ramotswe persisted. 'And you have good friends?'

'Yes,' said Mma Makutsi. 'I have good friends. You are one, Mma. You are a very good friend to me.'

Mma Ramotswe lowered her eyes. She did not seek compliments. 'And many others too, I think, Mma Makutsi – including Mma Potokwani.'

'Yes, her. She is a good friend ... even if sometimes we have not seen eye to eye.'

'You cannot always do that,' said Mma Ramotswe. 'But that does not mean that somebody is not a good friend.'

Mma Ramotswe waited. Then she went on, 'Your eyes are still open, Mma. Close them now and think about these good things.'

Mma Makutsi closed her eyes. She took another deep breath, which increased her sense of calm, and it was at this point that she heard a small voice, a tiny voice from the floor down below, a voice from which she had not heard for some time. *What about us, Boss? Don't forget your shoes.*

Mma Makutsi opened her eyes wide. She looked at Mma Ramotswe. Would she have heard the shoes? 'Did you hear something?' she asked.

Mma Ramotswe hesitated. 'Not really, Mma. Although there was something – although it was very faint.'

'Very faint, Mma?'

'Yes,' said Mma Ramotswe. 'You know how sometimes you think you hear a voice? You're not sure, but you think you have. It was a bit like that, I think. A voice from a long way off. But it's usually just your imagination.'

'Yes,' said Mma Makutsi. 'Just your imagination.'

She looked down at her shoes. They were one of the good

things in her life, these beautiful shoes in green leather with blue lining and small bows. Phuti had been with her when she bought them; he had encouraged her, saying that she deserved shoes like that and should not think about the price. How many husbands would say something like that? Very few, she thought; most would say, 'There is no need for green leather and blue lining, nor for bows.' That is how men thought about shoes; so few of them *understood*. And yet Phuti did; he understood what shoes meant.

Chapter Four

The Temptation of Pies

By noon, Mma Makutsi seemed to have recovered from the gloom that had beset the earlier part of the day. Mma Ramotswe was relieved and decided to mark the uplift in spirits with a suggestion that the two of them should go out to see Mma Potokwani for lunch. No lunch invitation had been received, but Mma Potokwani always welcomed visitors, especially if they brought with them, as Mma Ramotswe was planning to do, a take-out lunch of pie and chips, perhaps with added baked beans in tomato sauce. It was not a healthy lunch by any stretch of the imagination, but Mma Ramotswe had always believed that the psychological boost given by delicious but unhealthy food went at least some way to compensating for the negative effect of all the carbohydrates and fats and other undesirable ingredients that made such food so tasty. Cheerful people, she had read, lived longer than miserable people. People who laughed were less likely to suffer from all sorts of complaints (except, perhaps, a stitch in the side) than those who refrained from laughter. And there was a great deal of other evidence to the effect that allowing yourself the occasional, or even not-so-occasional treat made you feel better and ultimately healthier. Traditionally built people, such as she was, were under attack, of course, and there were many who seemed dead set on making their lives as unhappy as possible. In these circumstances, the traditionally built needed to stand up for themselves and indulge themselves from time to time. And you really could not expect your dresses to fit you forever – as you went through life and became more prosperous, you should expect to take a slightly bigger size of clothing. That was better, surely, than wasting away and taking a smaller and smaller size. That sort of thing often ended only one way.

'I was thinking, Mma,' Mma Ramotswe said, 'that we might go out to see Mma Potokwani. We could perhaps take some lunch with us – you know how she appreciates that.'

Mma Makutsi did not require much persuasion. 'That would be a kind thing to do,' she said. 'A pie, perhaps . . . '

'My thoughts exactly,' said Mma Ramotswe. 'And chips, I think.'

Mma Makutsi opened a drawer in her desk and tidied away the papers she had been working on – a tricky report to a difficult client, one who was convinced that his wife was having an affair with his brother-in-law. The husband was unwilling to take the risk that his wife should discover herself to be under surveillance, and so he had suggested that attention be focused on the brother-in-law instead. He was a man called called Tabo Seno, and he was the manager of a restaurant. Mma Makutsi had followed the brother-in-law over a period of three days, borrowing the tiny white van, along with Charlie as driver, for the purpose. On the second day of the observation she had discovered that he was, as suspected, having an extra-marital affair – but with another woman altogether. That had given rise to what she had immediately identified as an ethical quandary, and she had duly raised the issue with Mma Ramotswe who had a good sense of how such difficult situations should be resolved.

'That man is a very slippery one,' Mma Makutsi said. 'Charlie and I sat in the van for hours, waiting for him to come out of his restaurant. Eventually he did, and we lost him almost straight away.'

Mma Ramotswe asked how that had happened. 'Was it the traffic, Mma? If you're following somebody and cars slip in between you, it's only too easy to lose your person.'

Mma Makutsi looked sheepish. 'I know what you mean, Mma. It is very frustrating, particularly since your van cannot go very fast. Walking pace is not always enough, you see.'

Mma Ramotswe did not rise to the bait. Her tiny white van could do no wrong in her eyes, and if Mma Makutsi, or Charlie, or anybody else for that matter thought it too slow, well so be it.

'But to tell the truth,' Mma Makutsi continued, 'the reason why we lost him is that we were slow getting started. It was a very hot day, Mma, and when he came out of the office, I must admit that we were drowsy. We were very drowsy.' She paused. 'In fact, we were asleep.'

Mma Ramotswe raised an eyebrow. Had Clovis Andersen not said something about that in *The Principles of Private Detection*? Had he not written, *There are many things you will miss if you are asleep. Sleep is the enemy of vigilance, and vigilance is the enemy of sleep. Remember that.*

Well, she remembered it now. And although there could be no argument about the first of these propositions, she was not sure about the significance of the second. Sleep was indeed incompatible with a state of vigilance – that might go without saying, but why was vigilance the enemy of sleep? Did it mean that being vigilant meant that you could not sleep? That, surely, was too extreme: a vigilant person needed sleep, just like everybody else, and it was hard to imagine a person being vigilant if he or she was too tired to keep a proper look-out.

That was the trouble with sayings that sounded good, but that might not make complete sense when you started to look at them more closely. And yet some of them made absolute sense when you mulled them over. Her father, for instance, the late Obed Ramotswe, had said to her when she was a young girl, 'You take care of the cattle and the cattle will take care of you.' She had laughed at this at the time, because she could not think of how cattle could take care of human beings. Would there be a cow whose job it would be to watch over people as they wandered through the bush, just as cattle wander? Or did it mean that cattle would give warning to those who were looking after them if they sensed the presence of danger – a lion, perhaps, or a snake? Animals could tell when such things were about, even if people could not. And there had been more than a few cases over the years of young boys, looking after cattle at remote cattle posts on the edge of the Kalahari, who had been taken by hyenas, or even by lions. 'Look at what the cattle are doing,' Obed Ramotswe had said. 'If they are restless, they are restless for a reason.' Years later, the real meaning of what her father had said came to her, and she realised how right he was. He – her daddy, as she called him – was not just talking about cattle, he was talking about everything: about friends, about family, about the world. If we looked after the things in our lives then our care would be repaid. It was as simple as that, and, when the understanding of it came upon her, she wished that she had been able to say to him, 'Yes, yes, Daddy, you are so right.' Because the things our parents say to us often are sometimes proved true, even if we ignore them, or think that they are quaint examples of a folk wisdom for which we are too sophisticated. It was too late, though, because Obed Ramotswe was late then, and had been late for years, and she would never have the chance to tell him that now she knew exactly what he had meant.

Now, as Mma Makutsi slipped the report into the drawer, she felt a certain out-of-sight, out-of-mind relief. It was true that problems dealt with in this way did not altogether disappear, but they might nevertheless loom less large on a temporary basis. And this problem of what to do about Mr Tabo Seno was one that she was particularly keen not to have to think about for a few hours. The difficulty was one that she and Mma Ramotswe had encountered on a number of occasions before this: what to do about information that you uncovered that had nothing to do with the client. This information might be important to somebody else, though, and a question might then arise as to whether it should be passed on to that person.

She had raised the issue with Mma Ramotswe, who had reminded her that one had to be very careful about getting involved in other people's matrimonial affairs. 'Not all husbands are perfect,' she had said. 'And neither are all wives. It is not always helpful to tell a woman that her husband is keeping secrets from her – or, of course, that she is keeping secrets from him.'

'Unless we are asked directly about that?' Mma Makutsi said. 'Then we must tell.'

'Of course,' said Mma Ramotswe. 'Most of the time, that is true. But then ...'

Mma Makutsi waited. 'You may discover something that is long past,' said Mma Ramotswe. 'Remember that case—'

Mma Makutsi interrupted her. She had not forgotten. 'That woman from Lobatse,' she said. 'That woman who wore that very tight dress? That one, Mma?'

Mma Ramotswe smiled. 'It was a very tight dress, Mma. You are right. I was surprised that she could move in that dress – it hugged her legs so tightly. All the way down.'

'It made her look as if she had been wrapped up in cellophane,' mused Mma Makutsi. 'It was a very uncomfortable-looking dress.'

Mma Ramotswe looked thoughtful. 'Normally, I would be very wary of a woman wearing a dress like that,' she said. 'If I was investigating a case of suspected adultery and a woman was wearing that sort of dress, I would immediately think: this woman is guilty.' She paused. 'I would think that, Mma, although I know that you should never jump to conclusions.'

Mma Makutsi nodded her agreement. What Mma Ramotswe said about jumping to conclusions was undoubtedly true – and had the endorsement of no less a person than Clovis Andersen behind it – but even as she accepted the truth of the proposition, she reflected on the fact that whenever she had jumped to a conclusion in the past she had been right: the facts had, in due course, borne her out. And that had been so in that case, where their investigation had revealed that the woman in the tight dress had indeed conducted not one, but three affairs, all with younger men and, oddly enough, all with footballers. But what had complicated the case was that these affairs had all taken place between six and eight years earlier, and since then there had been no evidence at all of any straying on her part. Rather to the contrary, she had become involved with a group of women who engaged in running a centre for abused women. The tight dress had meant nothing, it seemed: she was now a loyal wife and a useful citizen with a solid record of charitable work. What had made the husband suspicious was the circulation of an old story about his wife and a young footballer – a story that was, as it happened, true, but nevertheless had no bearing on what his wife had become. Should something that was so clearly in the past be brought up to tarnish the present? That had been the issue they had faced, and they had decided in favour of silence. 'We all change,' Mma Ramotswe observed. 'And you cannot always judge people for what they were, if they are now something quite different.'

'But what about Tabo Seno?' Mma Makutsi asked. 'This is different, Mma Ramotswe. This is not the past. What I have discovered there is happening right now. He is having an affair, but not with our client's wife.'

'Then I am afraid it is not our business,' said Mma Ramotswe.

'Even if we see some poor woman being deceived by some man? Is that not our business?' Mma Makutsi protested.

Mma Ramotswe sighed. There was so much wrong with the world. There were so many cases of people behaving badly in one way or another, of people doing things they should not do, and the more we scrutinised what was going on around us, the more we discovered just this sort of thing. Under every stone, she sometimes thought, there is bound to be a scorpion.

Did we have to do something about every instance of bad behaviour we encountered? She found it difficult to answer that question. She was satisfied that there was a duty to report crime to the authorities – that was part of being a good citizen – but where the issue was a private one, one between husband and wife or employer and employee, it was not so clear that we had to act. And when it came to marriage, you simply never knew. There were some marriages where it might be best for a husband or wife not to know about something because the marriage was far from failing. And there might be children, too, whose interests had to

60

be considered. An erring husband might be a good father, and might also be a caring and considerate partner for the wife he was otherwise deceiving. You could never tell, and that was one of the main reasons why you should not interfere.

And so Mma Ramotswe had said to Mma Makutsi that she should tell their client that his brother-in-law was not having an affair with his wife. She should just say 'No evidence' and leave it at that because if she told him about who the woman was, he might be expected to reveal that to his sister, whose marriage might be incapable of surviving the infidelity.

Mma Makutsi had accepted this advice, but felt uncomfortable about it and was having difficulty in writing the report. 'It is not easy not to say things that you want to say but that you feel you cannot say,' she observed.

And Mma Ramotswe thought for a moment before remarking that sometimes it was not easy to say things that you knew you had to say but that you would prefer not to have to say.

And on that note, they closed the office and drove off in the van to the take-away restaurant where the delicious, but unhealthy, pies and chips were already being heated for the first of the lunchtime customers. The smell of this preparation was tantalising, and reached them as they parked the van directly outside the restaurant.

'The smell of lunch,' said Mma Ramotswe. 'It is always a very good smell, that one.'

'And breakfast,' Mma Makutsi observed. 'That is a good smell to start the day with. If there is bacon and maybe sausages too, Mma, and fried bread.'

For a few moments they were both lost in olfactory recollection. Then Mma Ramotswe broke the silence. 'Dinner, too, Mma. I like the smell of dinner.'

'Who doesn't, Mma Ramotswe? All of these are very good smells. I do not think there are many who will argue with you about that.'

Mma Makutsi had been hungry when they started the trip; this conversation, and the subsequent purchase of the pie and chips, all boxed up and ready to go, only made her hunger pangs more acute. Neither she nor Mma Ramotswe was known for having exemplary self-control when it came to food, and now, as they drove out to the Orphan Farm at Tlokweng, the temptation to sample their lunch proved too great.

'I shall just check on the lunch,' said Mma Makutsi, prising open the lid of the take-away carton.

'I am sure it is in order,' said Mma Ramotswe, struggling not to laugh. 'They are very careful about things at that shop. There will be nothing missing.'

'You can never be too sure,' said Mma Makutsi, gazing at the crust of the large pie nestling alongside the golden-brown potato chips.

Mma Ramotswe took her eyes off the road long enough to sneak a look at the contents of the carton. A wisp of steam rose from the pie; a tiny curve of white, quick to disappear.

'It is certainly very nice and hot,' said Mma Makutsi.

Mma Ramotswe took her foot off the accelerator.

'Is there something wrong with the engine?' asked Mma Makutsi. She did not entirely trust the tiny white van, having been stranded on two occasions in the past when its engine had inexplicably ground to a halt.

'No,' said Mma Ramotswe, bringing the van to a halt by the side of the road. 'There is nothing wrong ... It's just that I thought we might try one of the chips, and it is safer to stop than to eat while you are driving.'

'That is very true,' said Mma Makutsi. 'There are many people who have had accidents because they have been eating while driving. That happened to one of Phuti's clients. He crashed his car and was found unconscious in the driving seat. There was half a roast chicken on his lap, along with a salt cellar and a bottle of tomato ketchup.'

Mma Ramotswe did not approve. 'He must have been trying to add those things while he drove,' she said. 'I hope he is not late.'

'He is not late,' said Mma Makutsi. 'But his car was written off. I think he has learned a lesson.'

Mma Ramotswe turned off the engine. It was a quiet section of road. On either side, the scrub bush, brown in its earth and in its vegetation, stretched out towards a thicker growth of acacia trees and, in places, eucalypts. Cattle tracks, those paths that wandered with a seeming aimlessness across the Botswana countryside, negotiated their way into the trees before turning back upon themselves or disappearing into the eroded scars of natural ditches and dongas. It was land that gave shelter to snakes and the prey that sustained snakes; it was land that made the plains on which termites had constructed, here and there, towering mounds of packed mud, six feet high and more, in which their cities and civilisations rose and fell.

'We can try one of the chips,' said Mma Ramotswe. 'We can eat in the car and then go on to Mma Potokwani's place.'

'Should we be doing this, Mma?' asked Mma Makutsi. 'We are only twenty minutes away from the Orphan Farm.'

Mma Ramotswe struggled. Mma Makutsi was right to express these doubts – they could easily hold back but, on the other hand, they could as easily succumb to the temptation to sample the fare. 'We are all weak, Mma,' she said eventually. 'Please help yourself.'

The take-away had provided four small single-bladed forks with which the meal might be tackled, and Mma Makutsi now used one of these to spear two chips. These she laid down on one of the paper napkins that had come with the order. Then she did something that Mma Ramotswe was later to describe in detail to Mr J. L. B. Matekoni when she spoke to him that evening. It was something that she thought said more about Mma Makutsi's qualities as a friend than any of her words ever could.

Mma Makutsi surveyed the two chips she had extracted from the carton. Mma Ramotswe saw that they were not what she would call chips of equal merit. One was thin and slightly distended – as if it had been pulled at each end, or as if it had been carved from a twisted or deformed potato. The other was an example of what any chip might aspire to be: regular and evenly fried, with the result that it was a golden brown of the most delicious hue. The misshapen chip, moreover, looked soggy, while the other was firm and dry, and of just the right consistency.

Mma Makutsi hesitated, and then, using the original wooden fork, she took for herself the thin and distended chip, leaving the other one for her friend.

Mma Ramotswe saw this, and her heart leaped. This was her friend who had made this choice. This was her friend who had chosen the defective chip for herself, leaving the delectable one for her. A lesser person would not have done that. Indeed, *most* people would not have done that – because most people have a slight tendency, sometimes unthinking, to selfishness. But Mma Makutsi did it, and Mma Ramotswe, noticing the choice that had been made, was grateful.

Mma Ramotswe popped the chip into her mouth. It was as tasty as it looked.

'That was very good,' she said to Mma Makutsi. 'Perhaps another one, Mma?'

Mma Makutsi's eyes widened. 'Are you sure, Mma?'

'Well, I think it is very difficult for anybody just to have one chip,' said Mma Ramotswe. 'It would be like eating one salted peanut. Have you ever heard of anybody who could restrict themselves to eating just one salted peanut, Mma?'

Mma Makutsi had to admit that she had never heard of such a thing. So Mma Ramotswe speared another two chips, passing one over to Mma Makutsi.

'Delicious,' said Mma Ramotswe, and absent-mindedly, perhaps, helped herself to a third, and a fourth after that – as did Mma Makutsi.

Before long, all the chips had been consumed, leaving only the pie in crusty isolation.

'We appear to have eaten all the chips, Mma,' said Mma Ramotswe. 'And now the pie has nothing to go with it.'

'That is a big shame,' said Mma Makutsi. 'I did not mean to eat them all, Mma, and I suspect that you did not either.'

Mma Ramotswe shook her head. 'Sometimes things happen,' she said. 'They happen even if we really don't want them to happen.'

'That is very true,' said Mma Makutsi, staring at the pie. The crust was perfect, she thought: brown, but not too brown, and made of that lovely, light pastry that seemed just right for a steak pie. It was a pie into which one might sink one's teeth and allow, even encourage, the gravy to trickle down one's chin. It was a reassuring pie; a pie that must have been made by one who simply wanted other people to be happy. It was that sort of pie.

Mma Ramotswe cleared her throat. 'I do not feel proud of myself, Mma,' she announced. 'It was not necessary to eat all the chips.'

'It was not,' agreed Mma Makutsi.

'And now we can hardly take Mma Potokwani a pie with no chips. She will ask – as she is fully entitled to do – where are the chips?'

Mma Makutsi looked down at her hands, complicit, as they were, in the act of appropriation. Looking up, she made her suggestion. 'I think it would be best not to take the pie, Mma,' she said. 'That would mean that we would not have to explain what happened.'

Mma Ramotswe considered this. 'So, we'll take the pie back?'

Mma Makutsi hesitated. 'Unless . . . '

Mma Ramotswe sensed what was coming next, but thought she would ask anyway. 'Unless what, Mma?'

'Unless we ate the pie ourselves,' said Mma Makutsi. 'It would be a pity to let it get cold. And it is not a good idea to re-heat food, I think. There is always the danger of bacteria, Mma. There are many bacteria around these days, Mma.'

Mma Ramotswe smiled. 'It is our pie, I suppose. And we didn't tell Mma Potokwani that we were bringing her a pie. So that means, I think, that we would not be doing anything wrong.'

Mma Makutsi was pleased to be given clear permission. 'I will break it in two, Mma,' she said, reaching to extract the pie from the box. 'Then we can eat it before we continue our journey.'

The pie was in due course shared.

'Delicious,' said Mma Ramotswe, as she licked the last few crumbs from her fingers. 'We shall get one for Mma Potokwani next time.'

'Yes,' agreed Mma Makutsi. 'And there is another thing, Mma. You know how Mma Potokwani is always saying that she needs to lose weight?'

'I have heard her say that,' said Mma Ramotswe.

'Well, what we have just done,' went on Mma Makutsi, 'is to

have helped her in that. We have done something helpful for Mma Potokwani in eating that pie. Had you thought of that?'

Mma Ramotswe had not, but she thought of it as they completed their journey along the rough dirt road to the gates of the Orphan Farm. It was an interesting idea, but she found it hard to agree with Mma Makutsi. They had done the wrong thing, she now decided, and they had been led into doing the wrong thing by appetite. There was nothing to be proud of in that, whatever Mma Makutsi might say, and Mma Ramotswe felt that when she reached the Orphan Farm she should perhaps confess what had happened to Mma Potokwani. She was not sure that Mma Makutsi would approve of that, but Mma Makutsi's conscience was one thing, and hers was another.

Chapter Five

A Friend from Bobonong

Mma Potokwani, redoutable matron, tireless defender of orphans, matriarch, maker of the finest fruit cake in Botswana (and possibly all southern Africa, although she would be far too modest to assert *that* claim), was looking out of the window of her office when Mma Ramotswe drove up in a cloud of dust – timely rain would settle that – and parked where she always left her tiny white van, under an obliging acacia tree. Above them was the wide sky of Botswana, a sky of the palest, attenuated blue, drained of any other colour by the sun; all around them was the air, which was filled with the screech of cicadas in their incessant, protesting love call, and with the sound, too, emanating from somewhere not too far away, of children at play. The sound made by children in a playground, Mma Ramotswe had once remarked to Mma Makutsi, was very similar to the sound of cicadas, in that it, too, was high-pitched and continuous, and not composed of any words that an adult ear might intercept and decipher. Mma Makutsi had agreed. 'It is like singing,' she said. 'Except that it is not like singing.' And Mma Ramotswe had replied, 'That is true, Mma, except that it is not true.'

Mma Potokwani had somebody with her in her office – a woman in her mid-thirties, wearing a simple blue skirt and a white blouse. She was an attractive woman, but the style was modest and neat, and an observer might have said, 'This is a woman who is dressed for a job interview.' And that, in fact, was why she was there, watching as Mma Potokwani rose to her feet and glanced out of the window to see who had arrived.

'I have some visitors,' the matron said. 'But I think we have talked enough anyway. Do you have any questions you would like to ask me?'

The woman, whose name was Patience, said that she felt they had covered all the matters that she had raised, but she just wanted to check that if she got the job of book-keeper and office manager, she would be able to live in Gaborone and travel to work each day by minibus. Mma Potokwani assured her that as far as the Orphan Farm was concerned, the only requirement was that she should be in the office by eight-thirty each morning and would leave at five o'clock. 'Furthermore,' Mma Potokwani continued, 'I think I can offer you the job right now. I think you are just the person for us.'

Patience clapped her hands together. 'Oh, Mma, that is good news. I am very happy – very, very happy.'

'I'm glad,' said Mma Potokwani. 'We are very much a family in this place. We all pull together.'

'I shall definitely do that,' said Patience. 'You tell me which direction to pull in, and I shall pull. There will be no trouble with that.'

Mma Potokwani smiled. 'I think there are some ladies who

have come to see me,' she said. 'There is a lady called Mma Ramotswe. Perhaps you have heard of her.'

Patience shook her head. 'I have heard of nobody, Mma. I am from Bobonong, you see. I do not know many people down here.'

Mma Potokwani looked interested. 'Bobonong, Mma? You say that you are from Bobonong?'

'Yes. I was born in Bobonong, Mma. And I went to school there and had a job and everything. Then I met a man, who works for the Department of Water Affairs here in Gaborone. He was up in Bobonong for six months, on an assignment, and he asked me to come back to Gaborone with him. Me and my son, you see. I have a son: I had him when I was very young. The father is ...' She made a gesture to suggest disappearance into thin air. 'The father is nowhere. My son is fourteen.'

Mma Potokwani did not probe further. It was a familiar story – a young woman, sometimes still a teenager, had a child by a young man who then deserted her. There were thousands of young women in that position, Mma Potokwani reminded herself, and many of them had no help from the father of their child. It was left to the women and their mothers to bring up the children: grandmothers in Africa had broad shoulders.

Patience continued with her story. 'We are living now in Gaborone with this new man. My son is at school there,' she explained. 'He transferred from a school in Bobonong. The school in Gaborone is not so good, I'm afraid. We had some very good teachers up in Bobonong.'

'I see,' said Mma Potokwani. Bobonong? Of course – that was where Grace Makutsi came from. So now she said to Patience, 'One of the ladies who is outside right at this moment – she is from Bobonong. Perhaps you even know her.'

'It is possible,' said Patience. 'But there are more people

in Bobonong than you might think. We do not always know one another.'

'Of course not.'

The visitors were outside now, as Mma Potokwani heard the floorboards of the entrance to her small office building protest under Mma Ramotswe's weight.

'The lady from Bobonong is called Grace Makutsi,' said Mma Potokwani. 'She is a lady who has glasses and—'

She got no further. 'Grace Makutsi?' exclaimed Patience. And then said, 'Grace Makutsi, who went to the Botswana Secretarial College ...'

'I believe that is the same lady,' said Mma Potokwani. 'But you shall see her in a moment as they are outside and I must invite them in.

'Grace Makutsi!' muttered Patience in wonderment, as Mma Potokwani went to the door. 'Grace Makutsi!'

Mma Potokwani was out of the room for no more than a minute or two before she returned with Mma Ramotswe and Mma Makutsi. 'These are my visitors,' she announced to Patience. 'This is the Mma Ramotswe I mentioned and the other lady, Mma Makutsi. Here they are, Mma.'

Mma Ramotswe smiled at Patience. Then, turning to Mma Potokwani, she said, 'I hope we aren't interrupting anything important.'

'We have just finished our meeting,' said Mma Potokwani. 'And it has been very satisfactory. Patience will be joining us on the staff here. She has—'

She did not get any further. On seeing Patience sitting in the chair opposite Mma Potokwani's desk, Mma Makutsi let out an exclamation of surprise, followed by a quick lifting of her hands to cover her mouth.

'I think you two know one another,' said Mma Potokwani. 'Old friends?'

Mma Makutsi recovered her voice. 'Oh my! Oh my! This is unbelievable, Mma Potokwani. I must be imagining things. I must.'

Mma Potokwani laughed. 'The world is a small place, isn't it, Mma Makutsi?'

Mma Ramotswe joined in. 'And there are old friends in every corner of it, it seems.'

Patience had now risen to her feet and taken Mma Makutsi's hands in hers. 'Grace, it is you. I can see it is you. And this is me, you see. I am here.'

Mma Makutsi began a quiet ululation – the traditional way of expressing extreme pleasure. 'Oh, this is an important day,' she said. 'I have found my old friend.'

Mma Potokwani beamed with pleasure. 'I am very happy. I had no idea, only a few minutes ago, that you two would know one another. And then Patience here mentioned that she came from Bobonong, and I immediately thought: Bobonong. And then I thought: who do I know who comes from Bobonong? And then a tiny white van draws up and out gets a lady from Bobonong. That is a very big coincidence, I think.'

'*If* it is a coincidence,' said Mma Ramotswe. 'Sometimes, when these things happen, it even looks as if there has been some planning – somewhere.' She paused, and, looking slightly disappointed, added, 'Although I think such things are probably just coincidence. I do not think that there is any other explanation for them.'

Mma Potokwani looked doubtful. 'You cannot be sure, Mma Ramotswe. One thing I have learned is that you cannot be sure of anything these days.'

Mma Makutsi did not want to be distracted by discussions of how things happened. They occurred because of the things we did, and that was all that mattered. Her life had turned out the way it did because she had worked hard to get herself to the Botswana Secretarial College; had she simply let life flow over her, she would have got nowhere and would still be in Bobonong – working in a store, perhaps, or eking out a living on the land. And she had met Phuti Radiphuti because she had taken herself to those dance classes and had persisted with the unpromising and unprepossessing man whom she had met there, who had at that time a bad speech impediment and who could barely dance a step; and she had turned all that round so that Phuti had come into his own, had blossomed, and had eventually proposed to her. After that, everything changed. Penury and its discomforts became a thing of the past. She was able to buy new clothes, and new shoes. None of that, she thought, had come about through the operation of coincidence; none of that was pure chance.

So now she steered the conversation away from conjecture and asked Patience what she was doing here, so far from Bobonong, looking for a job with Mma Potokwani.

'It is a complicated story,' answered Patience. 'Perhaps I can tell you later.'

Mma Potokwani looked at her watch. 'According to my watch, ladies, it is lunchtime now. If you have no other plans, I think we could all go and have lunch with one of the housemothers. There will be plenty for everybody.' She turned to Patience. 'And over lunch, Patience, you can answer Mma Makutsi's questions.'

Mma Ramotswe and Mma Makutsi exchanged glances. It would be rude to turn down an invitation to lunch and so they nodded their assent and tried to look enthusiastic. But the pie had been a large one, and the chips had been numerous. If they were to be honest, then they might confess to having no appetite, but neither felt she could do that, especially as Patience greeted Mma Potokwani's suggestion with evident pleasure. 'I am very hungry, Mma,' she said. 'I did not have breakfast this morning because I was so nervous about my interview. Now, I am hungry enough to have breakfast and lunch rolled into one.'

Mma Potokwani smiled. 'And Mma Ramotswe and Mma Makutsi both have healthy appetites. So we shall all have a very good lunch, I think.'

They went outside and began to walk the short distance to one of the small bungalows in which each housemother lived with a group of ten or twelve children, creating for the children a small family. In the doorway of one of these they saw a familiar figure standing – one of the housemothers well known to both Mma Ramotswe and Mma Makutsi.

'That is Mma Bopa,' said Mma Potokwani to Patience. 'She knows Mma Ramotswe and Mma Makutsi well. And she is one of the best cooks we have.'

'I am keen to meet her,' said Patience.

'She will give us a very good lunch,' said Mma Potokwani. 'Very filling.'

They drove down the dusty track that led from the Orphan Farm to the main road into Gaborone. During the first few minutes of the journey, neither Mma Ramotswe nor Mma Makutsi spoke. Then Mma Makutsi turned in her seat and said, 'Oh, Mma Ramotswe, I am feeling very uncomfortable.'

The van swerved as Mma Ramotswe looked at her friend. Then it slowed down. 'Would you like me to stop, Mma?'

Mma Makutsi shook her head. 'No, I am not going to be sick. I do not feel all that well, but I don't think it is that bad.'

Mma Ramotswe sighed. 'I am feeling a bit uncomfortable too,' she said, touching her stomach gingerly. 'It is a judgement on us, Mma. That is what it is.'

Mma Makutsi considered this. 'Because we have been greedy?' she asked.

'I'm not sure if I would use that word,' said Mma Ramotswe. She hesitated. She might not use the word greedy to describe what they had done, but others would, she suspected – and they would be right.

'At least you did the right thing,' said Mma Makutsi. 'I would not have had the courage, Mma. But you did it.'

'It was not courage,' said Mma Ramotswe. 'It was guilt, I think.'

It had happened towards the end of the lunch. Mma Bopa had prepared lamb chops, sausages and slices of pumpkin, and Mma Potokwani had urged the housemother to give large helpings to her guests. Mma Ramotswe had watched with growing alarm as Mma Bopa had heaped food on her plate, and she saw the same alarm in the face of Mma Makutsi as the same thing was done to her plate. They had no alternative but to eat the food given them, as it could have caused offence not only to Mma Potokwani, but also to Mma Bopa had they refused. And so they had struggled to dispose of their generous helpings and then, in spite of their protestations, had been faced with liberal seconds.

The serving of pudding, an apple crumble topped with a thick layer of demerara sugar and cream, had proved the metaphorical final straw, and Mma Ramotswe had suddenly blurted out what had happened in the van.

'To tell the truth, Mma,' she said to an astonished Mma Potokwani. 'To tell the truth, we had bought pie and chips to share with you, and we ... ' She faltered, but she was always truthful, and now she had to continue. 'We couldn't help ourselves,

Mma Potokwani. We stopped on the way and ate it all up. It started with a single chip – yes, just one – and then it led to more chips and, finally, to the whole pie.'

Mma Ramotswe saw that Mma Potokwani was staring at her in astonishment. But then she began to smile. 'You ate it all?' she asked.

'Yes,' said Mma Ramotswe. There was both misery and regret in her voice. 'We should not have done it.'

'But it was yours,' said Mma Potokwani. 'You had not given it to me. You were fully entitled to eat it, Mma Ramotswe.' She paused. 'But you must be feeling very full now.'

Mma Ramotswe nodded. 'People who eat too much – people like Mma Makutsi and me – feel very full, I think. They deserve to feel very full.'

Mma Potokwani laughed. 'You will not feel full forever, Mma. By this evening you will be hungry once more. You need not worry.'

And now, in the van, Mma Makutsi said, 'Let's not talk about food, Mma. There are other things to discuss.'

'Such as your friend, Patience?' asked Mma Ramotswe.

Mma Makutsi nodded. They were passing a small store, one of those rural shops that crop up along the byways of Africa, and that sell all the necessities of life – soap and paraffin and maize meal and salt, and things that look useful even if one cannot tell exactly what they do. Outside the shop, leaning against a pillar of the veranda, stood a man in sunglasses, holding a cigarette. As they drove past, he drew on the cigarette and then exhaled a cloud of smoke to be waved aside with his free hand.

'Silly man,' said Mma Makutsi. 'He can have nothing better to do than stand outside that store and blow smoke in the air.'

Mma Ramotswe was more tolerant. 'We do not know what is happening in his life,' she said. 'He may be unhappy, Mma.'

'He would be happier if he did something constructive,' Mma Makutsi retorted. 'There are too many people moaning about things these days, Mma. Moan, moan, moan. And they like to blame everybody else – never themselves.'

Mma Ramotswe had not heard Mma Makutsi blaming herself recently – or ever, if it came down to it. But she said nothing about that; she wanted to know about Patience. 'Your friend,' she said. 'I think she is very pleased to be getting a job with Mma Potokwani.'

Mma Makutsi said that she, too, had formed that impression. 'Mind you, Mma, she'll have to work hard. Mma Potokwani never sits about very much – unlike that man back there outside the store.'

Mma Ramotswe ignored the sting in the tail of that remark. 'And is she a hard worker, this Patience?'

Mma Makutsi was unequivocal. 'Yes, she is a very hard-working woman. She has had to be.'

Mma Ramotswe waited. It would be a familiar story, she thought. Women worked and worked. They brought up the children; they kept the house; they made the meals; and then they went to work on top of all that. That was the lot of women in so many places but especially, it seemed, here in Africa, where so many people had to struggle to make ends meet. And yet they did it; and yet they made the most of their lives, and kept smiling through difficulties that might floor the strongest. Whatever she heard from Mma Makutsi about Patience's past, nothing would surprise Mma Ramotswe.

'I remember her when we were very small,' Mma Makutsi began. 'We were five, maybe. Five or six. I cannot remember very much before that – can you, Mma?'

'No, Mma.' Except for happiness, she thought. She could remember being happy. And her father – she could remember him carrying her in his arms when she must have been even younger – three or four. She was sure she could remember that. She could remember being loved.

'She did not live very far from us, up in Bobonong,' Mma Makutsi continued. 'They had a very small house – one of those traditional ones, with packed mud walls. They had an old cart outside, one that had lost its wheels a long time before, and a grain bin. There was a grandmother and an aunt and some children who were Patience's cousins, I think. There had been two brothers, people said, but they were late.'

'Then I remember her at school. She was always hungry – I remember that – and the teachers used to give her food. They did that with some of the children who came from poor families. They had bread and syrup in a cupboard and they would give them thick slices of bread with syrup dripped over them. The other children were envious but were told that there was none for them.

'Patience was often bullied. I knew the girls who were doing that – there were one or two like that at school. They were Violet Sephotho types, Mma Ramotswe. There is always a Violet Sephotho type. Always. And then, in later life, you go out into the world and you meet the real Violet Sephotho ...'

Mma Ramotswe smiled. 'That is unfortunately true, Mma.'

'I was friendly with Patience,' Mma Makutsi continued. 'She was very good at sewing, and she taught me some of the fancy stitches she had learned. She even earned a bit of money by sewing things for the clinic that the French priests ran. She fixed sheets for them. She also mended the priests' clothing. They were kind to her, I think. When she became a Catholic, they told her that

78

she would almost certainly get into Heaven when she died because she had been baptised. And she had a picture of the Pope in her schoolbook. I remember how she showed it to me and said that she prayed for the Pope every night before she went to bed. She also had pictures of some saints who would protect her, she said, if she said the right prayers.

'I remember one of these pictures, Mma Ramotswe, because Patience showed it to me more than once. It was of a Ugandan saint. He was called St Charles Lwanga – I remember that name – and terrible things were done to him. Many of the saints had terrible things done to them, Mma Ramotswe – do you know that?'

'Yes, Mma Makutsi, I have heard that. There is much dreadful unkindness in this world – even today, Mma.'

Mma Ramotswe looked up from the road ahead, just briefly, as she was driving, and there was a small herd of goats nibbling at the grass by the roadside; she would not want to knock one of these down, agile though they were at avoiding passing traffic. She looked up at the sky for a moment, and thought about the things that it had seen, the suffering and the wrongs; the wars; the small acts of cruelty too. Yet this was Botswana, and they were protected from most of those things because they had a constitution and laws that people obeyed, as Seretse Khama had hoped they would; and they had a flag, their precious flag, to remind them who they were and what was expected of them. *We are so fortunate*, she said to herself; *we are so fortunate.*

Mma Makutsi looked grave. 'Then, when she was sixteen,' she continued, 'Patience was attacked by a man. It happened at night, when she was walking along a path at the edge of the village. He was waiting behind some trees and she did not see him in the darkness until it was too late to run away. She could not see his face and was unable to tell the police very much about him. She could tell, though, that he was not a local man. She said that she did not think he spoke Setswana.

'The awful thing, Mma, was that he was only a short distance away from a house, and there were people in that house. They were playing music, though – loud music from a radio station – and they did not hear her screaming. So, afterwards, the man ran away and she was left by the path until a woman walked past her and saw her. This woman was a nurse, and she helped her. Then she took her to her home and spoke to Patience's mother.

'They took her to the French priests at their clinic. They said that it was a terrible thing that had happened and they called the police. The police came, but said that they did not have much to work on, and that these things were happening all the time, and young women should not be walking about at night by themselves. I don't think they would say things like that these days, Mma Ramotswe, but this was before people started to complain.

'Patience found that she was pregnant because of this attack. She was very upset, as she was only sixteen, and she did not want to have a baby. The French priests said that she had no choice and they sent her to a place they had where women could go to have their babies if their village did not want them. They looked after her well there, she said. There was always plenty to eat and they had a room where the young women could do jigsaw puzzles and read the Bible. It was not very exciting, Patience said, and she was pleased when she had had her baby and was allowed to go home.'

'Well, I am glad that she was all right,' said Mma Ramotswe. 'And the baby was all right, too?'

'He was healthy,' said Mma Makutsi. 'She had her mother to help her look after him, and there was her grandmother too. They looked after the baby while she went off to work in the

80

government office up there. She was a cleaner at first, but she took a correspondence course in book-keeping. The government people gave her a better job after a while and she had a bit more money, but she found a man who was not very good, Mma. Some people say that he was the same man who had attacked her. Many people said that, in fact, because he was always taking her money and sometimes it would be obvious that he had beaten her about her face. She should have left him, Mma Ramotswe, but she did not. Even after I left Bobonong, I used to hear from people I had known back there, and they told me about how the French priests had tried to speak to this man and get him to change his ways. They even said that he had hit one of the French priests, which is something you should never do, Mma. You should never hit anyone, but particularly not a French priest.'

Mma Ramotswe shook her head. 'This story is not unusual. Women stay with bad men – sometimes for a long, long time. I do not know why they find it so hard to leave them.' But even as she said this, she thought about how she had stayed with Note Mokoti, her first, and unkind, husband all those years ago, because she had been young, and because it had been so hard, for whatever strange reason, to leave him. It had broken her father's heart – she found that out later – to see her with that man, but when at last she broke free, Obed Ramotswe had not said anything about how she should have done it much earlier, he had simply put his arms about her and wept, in the quiet way in which men sometimes weep, but which means so much, perhaps because it is so quiet.

'And then, Mma?' asked Mma Ramotswe.

'She told me after lunch,' said Mma Makutsi, 'when you and Mma Potokwani were looking at that quilt that Mma Bopa had been making, she told me then that she had met this other man only three months ago, this man who works for Water Affairs, and she had come down to Gaborone with him. She said that he is the complete opposite of that other man, and that she is very pleased that at long last she has found somebody who can make her happy.'

Mma Ramotswe was relieved to hear this. She was not one to deny the harsh side of the world – of course that side existed – but she was always pleased when she heard of things taking a turn for the better. She liked it when she heard the scales of justice had been righted; that bullies had been humbled; that the downtrodden had been relieved of at least some of their suffering. She liked such stories because it helped people to believe in justice, which we had to believe in if we were not simply to give up in the face of adversity. She believed that, and it would take more than the occasional setback to make her believe otherwise.

Then Mma Makutsi added, 'She is worried about something, Mma Ramotswe. She is pleased with her new boyfriend, but she is still worried. She said it is something very serious.'

'Did she tell you what it was?' asked Mma Ramotswe.

'No,' replied Mma Makutsi. 'She said that she would come to see me sometime next week. She said we can talk then.'

They were now getting close to town and Mma Ramotswe glanced at her watch. It was close to three o'clock, lunch having been a slow affair.

'Is it worth opening the office just for a couple of hours?' asked Mma Ramotswe.

'If we had not had such a large lunch,' said Mma Makutsi, 'I would have said yes. But when you have had a very big lunch—'

'Or two lunches,' interjected Mma Ramotswe with a shy grin.

Mma Makutsi hesitated. Having had two lunches was a serious matter, and one might not admit to it too readily. But then she saw the amusing side of their situation, and she, too, began to grin. 'Yes, or two lunches – when you have had two lunches, it is probably best to go home and sleep everything off.'

'That is true,' said Mma Ramotswe. 'That is undoubtedly true.'

She took a turning onto the road that would lead to Mma Makutsi's house. She would drop her off there and then go on to Zebra Drive, where she would make herself a cup of redbush tea before sitting on the veranda as the day cooled down, thinking of the day's events, and in particular of her meeting with Patience. Patience was a stranger she had not met before, and yet now, for better or worse, she felt somehow involved in her life. She would no doubt find out from Mma Makutsi what it was that was troubling Patience and then, perhaps, she might even be able to help. That was why she had started the No. 1 Ladies' Detective Agency in the first place – to help people with the problems in their lives. That is what she and Mma Makutsi did, and it was possible that they would be able to do that for this woman from Bobonong who had had, it seemed to her, rather more than her fair share of troubles. If they could help her, they would do so – or at least try to help, because one could never be sure what success, or otherwise, awaited our efforts in this life. That, she thought, was one of the things that was definitely well known.

Chapter Six

Gum Disease Is Serious

It was the following day that Mma Ramotswe had her first encounter with Twenty-First-Century Chairs. She was not prepared for this, as it took place when her mind was on other things entirely – a trip to the dentist that she had arranged for Charlie, the young mechanic and trainee detective – mostly the former, according to Mma Makutsi – who, a few days previously, during the mid-morning tea break, had complained of sore gums. The conversation had turned to dental matters when Mma Makutsi had remarked that Phuti Radiphuti had recently found a set of false teeth in a restaurant in which he had been having lunch with his accountant.

'He went to wash his hands before the meal,' she said. 'He always does that. Every time. I have never seen Phuti sit down for a meal without washing his hands. Not once.'

As she spoke, she glanced at Charlie, who was leaning against one of her filing cabinets, nursing his mug of tea. Fanwell had just come in from the garage, and was pouring tea for himself as the subject of washing hands came up. Looking down at his hands, he reached into his pocket for a piece of the blue absorbent paper that Mr J. L. B. Matekoni provided for the wiping away of engine oil and grease.

'Not everybody washes their hands before they eat,' Mma Makutsi went on, throwing a pointed glance in Charlie's direction. 'There are some people who don't seem to bother. Not that I am thinking of anybody in particular; I am talking in general terms here.'

Charlie looked up at the ceiling.

Mma Ramotswe was aware of Mma Makutsi's tendency to needle Charlie, and sought to deflect the criticism that she now saw looming. Charlie and Fanwell were young men, you had to remember, and young men often failed to do the things they should do. That was just the way they were, and always had been: you should not be too hard on young men – or on anybody, really. 'We shouldn't wash too much,' she observed casually.

Mma Makutsi looked across the room. The sun streaming in through the window caught her large glasses, sending back a sliver of light, a glint of warning. 'Washing your hands is very important, Mma Ramotswe – as I am sure you know.'

'Oh, I would never argue with that,' Mma Ramotswe replied. 'There are times when you must certainly wash your hands.'

The light flashed again. 'Well then . . . '

'All I was saying is that our skin makes certain oils, Mma Makutsi. They are natural oils. And these oils allow friendly bacteria to live on us and protect us from . . . '

'Warthogs,' suggested Charlie, winking at Fanwell.

Mma Makutsi transferred her gaze to Charlie. 'What is this about warthogs? Who said anything about warthogs?'

'I'm just pointing out that warthogs do not like bacteria, Mma Makutsi. That is all I'm saying.'

Mma Makutsi gave a dismissive snort. 'You are talking complete nonsense, Charlie.' She turned to face Mma Ramotswe on the other side of the room. 'What was this about bacteria, Mma?'

'All I was saying is that there are friendly bacteria and unfriendly bacteria. Unfriendly bacteria make us ill. The friendly bacteria stop that from happening, and that is why you shouldn't wash all of them away.'

Fanwell now entered the conversation. 'That is very true,' he said. 'When I was at school, I learned all that. They said that we have friendly bacteria in our stomachs that help us to digest. That is why they have those bacteria drinks in the supermarket. They are like sour milk but they are one hundred per cent bacteria.'

'Hah!' said Charlie. 'Can you go into a bar and ask for a glass of bacteria? Is that the latest thing, Fanwell?'

Fanwell shook his head. 'No, you cannot do that.'

'People could drink bacteria rather than tea,' said Charlie, smiling broadly. 'Mma Ramotswe and Mma Makutsi could sit here in their office and drink bacteria all day, rather than tea.'

This brought a swift rebuke from Mma Makutsi. 'We do not drink tea all day, Charlie. We have regular tea breaks, because that helps us to work. You need liquids in this hot weather. That is why we drink a lot of tea.' She paused. 'And that is nothing to do with washing. It is still a good thing to wash your hands.'

'False teeth,' prompted Mma Ramotswe. 'You were telling us about Phuti finding some false teeth.'

Mma Makutsi took a sip of her tea. 'Yes, it was very odd. He had gone to that restaurant down near the tax office, you know the one, Mma – the one that is owned by that man with the beard.'

'That is very unhygienic,' said Fanwell. 'I do not think that you should have a beard if you are handling food. Your beard will get in the food.'

Charlie disagreed. 'I don't see how that would happen. There is no risk from beards, Fanwell. Too many people are saying this thing is risky, that thing is risky. There are always women telling men that they are very risky and shouldn't be doing things.'

Mma Makutsi was quick to respond. 'Women, Charlie? You say women are telling men not to do things?'

Charlie shrugged. 'Mostly it is women, Mma. Not always, of course, but mostly.'

'Nonsense,' expostulated Mma Makutsi. 'You are talking nonsense, as usual, Charlie.'

'Oh yes?' Charlie retorted. 'Those advertisements in the paper – the ones with that government nurse. The one with that big smile and all those teeth. She should be a stewardess on Air Botswana, I think. Hah! Big smile and *Please take your seat!* But all she does now is say: "Remember to eat vegetables. Blah, blah! Remember to go to the clinic to get your toenails checked. Remember to get your vaccination for this thing or that thing. Remember to feed your baby—"'

'They do not say that,' interrupted Mma Makutsi. 'I have never heard anybody telling you to feed your baby. That is complete nonsense, Charlie.'

The young man defended himself. 'I am making that bit up, Mma. Maybe that is made up. But the rest is true. It is always women who want to stop men enjoying themselves.'

Fanwell looked thoughtful. 'I have been thinking about the chef with the beard. I think that the danger would come when he leaned forward to sniff the food. That is when his beard might end up in somebody's mashed potato, or in the sauce – something like that. And then all the bacteria would jump from his beard onto the plate. That would be the danger.'

'And what if they're friendly bacteria?' challenged Charlie. 'Why should the bacteria in his beard not be friendly, Fanwell?'

'I do not think that is where friendly bacteria live,' Fanwell answered him, looking slightly embarrassed.

Mma Ramotswe had been following this conversation with amusement. But now she brought it back to false teeth. 'So Phuti found these teeth in the bathroom?' she asked. 'Just sitting there, Mma? On the basin?'

Mma Makutsi nodded. 'He said that they were on the side of the basin. There was nobody around.' She paused, as if to give effect to her words. 'Nobody, Mma Ramotswe.'

Mma Ramotswe frowned. It was an extraordinary picture. 'A whole set?' she asked.

'Yes, Mma – a whole set. Sitting there.'

Charlie shook his head in amazement. 'I can't understand why anybody would remove his teeth in a restaurant. Why would you do a thing like that?'

Fanwell laughed. 'He might have been washing them after a meal,' he suggested. 'If he didn't have his toothbrush with him, he might think, I'll just give my teeth a quick wash before I go back to work. Then perhaps he thought of something else and forgot about his teeth altogether.'

Mma Makutsi waved a dismissive hand. 'That is highly unlikely. He would know immediately that his teeth were not in place. People who have false teeth always know whether their teeth are in their mouth or not. They can tell.'

Mma Ramotswe asked whether Phuti had reported the teeth

to the proprietors of the restaurant. Mma Makutsi replied that
he had – and done so timeously – but that they were unable to
say whose teeth they might be. 'The waiter who had been serving
that lunchtime was asked, and he said that everybody had had
teeth. He said he would have noticed if there had been somebody
without teeth.'

'So what happened?' asked Charlie.

'The owner of the restaurant put them on a table in the
entrance,' Mma Makutsi replied. 'Then he put a notice next to
them saying, "Are these your teeth?"'

'And nobody claimed them?' asked Fanwell.

'I don't know,' said Mma Makutsi.

Mma Ramotswe thought this a rather disturbing story, made
all the more unsettling by its lack of resolution. She did not like
the thought of some unfortunate person losing his or her false
teeth. It would have been an expensive loss, as false teeth were
far from cheap. And if they had belonged to an elderly person –
perhaps to somebody whose memory might not be what it once
was – then such a person might be unable to remember where
he had been and where his teeth might have ended up. It was all
rather sad.

Then Charlie had remarked, 'My teeth are all right – they are
very sharp, very powerful, but my gums are not so good.'

Mma Ramotswe looked at him with concern. 'What is wrong
with your gums, Charlie?'

Charlie did not seem unduly concerned. 'They bleed. When I
brush my teeth, there is blood. Not all the time – just every other
day, maybe.'

Mma Makutsi wrinkled her nose in disgust, but Mma
Ramotswe was solicitous. 'That is very serious, Charlie. Have you
not heard of gum disease?'

Charlie shrugged.

'Gum disease is serious,' Mma Ramotswe insisted. 'Many people do not know how serious it is. They think that nothing can go wrong with their gums, but it can. Gum disease can set in and then suddenly one day you wake up and discover that all your teeth have fallen out.'

Fanwell pointed an admonitory finger at Charlie. 'You had better watch out, Charlie. That will be you one day. No teeth. All your teeth on the floor, being carried away by ants. Ow!'

'My teeth are not falling out, Fanwell,' said Charlie, reaching into his mouth to demonstrate the firmness of his dentition. Unfortunately, the tooth that he seized proved to be loose, and, as he wiggled it, it moved in its socket. Charlie froze.

'You see!' crowed Fanwell. 'That tooth is ready to fall out. Maybe tomorrow, maybe the day after. But that tooth is going, Charlie. Goodbye tooth!'

Mma Ramotswe beckoned Charlie to her side. 'Open your mouth, Charlie,' she said.

He did as he was bid. The loose tooth had alarmed him.

Mma Ramotswe peered into the young man's mouth. Gingerly, she slid a finger past his lips to push, very gently, against the bottom line of teeth. She hesitated. She thought there had been some movement, but she could not be sure.

'Did you feel anything, Mma?' Charlie asked once she had withdrawn her finger.

'I think they might be a little loose, Charlie,' she said.

After that, it had not been difficult to persuade him to accompany her to a dentist, and she arranged the appointment herself. 'I shall take you there,' she said. 'You must not worry. The dentist is very good. He will look at your gums and tell you what to do.'

'It might be too late,' said Fanwell, adding, helpfully, 'If it is, then the dentist will have some false teeth for you and you will be fine, Charlie. There will be no problem.'

Now, they stood together outside the dental clinic in the small shopping centre near the golf course while Mma Ramotswe reassured Charlie that this visit to the dentist would involve no pain and would be over before he knew it. And it was while she was doing this that she noticed the shop that had sprung up in the building immediately next to the dentist's surgery. Mma Ramotswe was sure that on the last occasion she had been in this particular shopping centre, the shop premises had been empty – now they boasted a large, rather garish sign above the doorway: Twenty-First-Century Chairs. And beneath that, in smaller lettering, but still hard to miss, were the words: 'The Future Arrives and Takes Its Seat.'

'Charlie,' said Mma Ramotswe, 'the dentist is expecting you. You go in there and I will take a look at this chair place.'

'You said you would come with me,' protested Charlie. 'You said that, Mma.'

'It is not necessary to hold your hand all the time,' Mma Ramotswe soothed him. 'I shall come and fetch you very soon.'

'So, Mma,' said the young man who appeared from the back of the shop. 'So you are interested in a chair.'

Mma Ramotswe had been bending down to examine what looked like an office chair. It was covered in black leather and had several levers protruding from beneath the seat. As the salesman approached her, she straightened up to address him.

'I see that this is an adjustable chair,' she said. 'I assume that these levers make it go up and down.'

'Up and down and backwards and forwards,' intoned the young man. 'This is called an omni-directional chair, Mma. This chair will adjust to your needs. It is an intelligent chair.'

Mma Ramotswe stared at him. An intelligent chair! How could a chair possibly be intelligent? Could it tell you what the capital of Lesotho was or what distance the earth was from the moon? Did this chair know all the answers?

'I am not looking for a chair that knows more than I do,' she said.

The young man laughed. 'Hah! That is very funny, Mma. I am laughing at that, as you see. It is very funny.'

He became serious. 'No, Mma, that is called an intelligent chair because it is adjustable. Most chairs are suited to just one sort of person, but there are, in fact, many different shapes of person. Even in this country, even in Botswana, we have many different types of . . . of rear.' He averted his gaze briefly. There were some topics, though, that could not be avoided. 'You see,' he went on, 'there are people who are larger in that department, and then there are people who are not so large in that region. A chair must be capable of accommodating both types.'

He allowed himself a quick glance at Mma Ramotswe's figure. 'I think you are a larger lady, Mma. I am not being rude; I am just stating a fact. You are a larger lady and might need a bit more room across the way. That is why there is this lever here. You see, if I press it like that, the arms of the chair move to the side. That is to give more room to those who need it. That is called chair intelligence.'

Mma Ramotswe pointed to the chair. 'May I try it, Rra?' she asked.

'That is why it is here,' said the young man. 'You are very welcome to try it, Mma.'

She sat down, and was immediately uncomfortable, as the seat of the chair had virtually no padding. 'It is very hard,' she said.

'That is as it should be,' said the young man, a note of

92

defensiveness coming into his voice. 'The days of soft chairs are over, Mma. That is not what employers want.'

'Employers, Rra? What is this to do with employers?'

The young man explained. 'This is a chair for office use, Mma. Employers do not want their employees to go off to sleep while they are meant to be working. They want them to be sharp and focused on the job in hand. That is why these chairs are not padded.'

Mma Ramotswe looked doubtful. 'But they would not want their employees to be complaining about discomfort. That would not be good for the workforce, I think.'

The young man did not argue. He was pointing to another chair. 'This is one of our special family home chairs,' he said. 'This is the chair that is getting into all the living rooms of Botswana. This chair is getting everywhere.'

Mma Ramotswe saw a large garishly patterned armchair, the legs of which, fashioned in the shape of a talon clutching a ball, appeared to be made of ornately carved wood.

'That chair,' said the salesman proudly, 'is outselling all our other chairs – even the office ones. There is a waiting list for that chair.'

Mma Ramotswe moved closer to the chair, bending down to examine its legs. She reached forward, and her touch confirmed her suspicions. The wood was moulded plastic, and not carved at all.

'One hundred per cent plastic,' said the young man, again with pride in his voice. 'Isn't that amazing, Mma? Pure plastic that is made to look like wood. There is a special process for that. But unfortunately I am not at liberty to reveal it.'

Mma Ramotswe straightened up. 'It is a pity that it is not wood,' she said. 'The people who made that chair obviously think that wood is better. That is the reason why they make it look like wood, I think.'

'Yes!' exclaimed the young man. 'That is very good, Mma. That is a very good point. Yes, wood can look fine, but what happens to wood? That is the big question that everybody needs to answer.'

She waited for him to continue. She had noticed that his collar was frayed and that his shirt was missing a button. He does not have anybody to look after him, she thought, and for a moment she forgot the boasting sales talk and the plastic chair-legs and the uncomfortable office chair, and thought, instead, of this young man going home at night to a shared room somewhere in a high-density suburb, and not having a girlfriend or a mother to make him feel better about things, and having to worry about whether his sales commission that week would meet the target set for him by some distant manager who might not even know his name.

The explanation began, delivered in a monotone that suggested the words had been learned and committed to memory: 'Plastic, Mma, is a very hard-wearing substance. There are many things made of plastic now. You can make anything. And plastic, you see, does not rot, as wood does. Plastic can get wet and you don't have to dry it. If you let wood get wet and leave it that way, then it can crack and develop mould. Mould is very bad, Mma: if you get mould in your lungs, then you can die, sure-sure. That is happening every day.

'And there is another big advantage to plastic over wood, Mma ... If you would give me your name, then I could address you personally, which is what I would like to do.'

She gave him her name, and he listened carefully. Then his eyes widened. 'You are that lady who has that detective agency? Are you that lady, Mma?'

Mma Ramotswe smiled. Word had got around, but she found

that she was still occasionally surprised to find out how widely the agency was known. 'Yes,' she replied, 'I am that lady. There are two of us—'

'I know,' he interjected. 'There is you and then there is another lady who is not quite so fat. I have heard of her too.'

Mma Ramotswe let the remark pass. There had been a time when such a thing would have been a compliment, but attitudes had changed now. She did not mind it, though, if people passed tactless remarks – she was happy being who she was. There were thin people and then there were people who were not so thin. There were tall people, and then there were some very short people, although sometimes they did not stand out so much as the tall ones, and you could easily miss them. But they were there, just as all the other sorts of people were there. The real art in going through life with dignity and with a modicum of happiness was to accept what you were, and, at the same time, to accept others – *and to love them all equally*. That was hard, and for some people it was impossible, but you had to try. We were all brothers and sisters, after all, and should embrace one another as such. That seemed so obvious, and yet there were people who refused to accept it, and made others unhappy because of their refusal.

'I used to want to be a detective myself, Mma Ramotswe,' the young man said, lowering his voice, as if he were imparting confidential information; there was nobody to hear, though. 'I think I might have been good at it.'

Mma Ramotswe smiled encouragingly. 'I am sure you would be. But you must tell me your name, Rra.'

'I am called Freddie,' he replied. 'I have a Setswana name, of course, but I don't use that very much because it is one of those names that people used to give their children although they sound odd. My name meant *short nose*, which is a very stupid name, Mma. My nose is not very short, and it is not very long.'

Mma Ramotswe found her eyes drawn inexorably to Freddie's nose. There was nothing exceptional about it, she decided.

'Your nose is a very good-looking nose,' she said. 'There are many men who would give a lot to have a nose like that, Freddie – I can tell you that.'

Freddie grinned with pleasure. 'Are you sure about that, Mma Ramotswe?'

'I am very sure,' she replied. 'In fact, I am certain.'

Freddie looked thoughtful. 'I think that I would have made a good detective because I am always looking at the things *behind* things, Mma. Do you see what I mean?'

'Looking for reasons?' asked Mma Ramotswe.

'You could put it that way. What I am doing is looking for what things really mean. So, if somebody says something, I think: is he saying that, or is he really saying the exact opposite?'

Mma Ramotswe frowned. 'That sounds very interesting, Rra. Could you give me an example?'

'Well, if somebody says to me, "I'm going to Francistown tomorrow to see my mother," I think: why is this person going to Francistown? Is it because he wants to visit his mother, or is it because he wants to do something quite different – visit his girlfriend, perhaps? And then I think: if he is really visiting his girlfriend, then why does he want to hide the fact? That is a very big question, Mma Ramotswe, but it is exactly the right question to ask if you want to get to the truth.'

Mma Ramotswe encouraged him to continue. She was interested in this example because it was rather close to a situation she had encountered in one of her investigations. The young man was right in at least one respect: people often concealed the real reasons for their actions. Clovis Andersen had something to say about that, although she could not quite remember what it was.

'This person going to Francistown,' she prompted. 'What would be the real reason?'

'To see his girlfriend,' replied Freddie.

'But why would he not say that?'

Freddie raised a finger to emphasise his reply. 'Because his girl-friend is really the girlfriend of somebody else, and neither he nor she wants anybody to find out. You see? You see how that works?'

Mma Ramotswe nodded. 'Of course, it always possible that there is no girlfriend in Francistown.'

Freddie looked taken aback. 'No girlfriend, Mma?'

'But what if he is going to Francistown for another purpose altogether?'

Freddie looked blank.

'What if he is going to Francistown to rob a store? What if he has some bad friends up there and one has been in touch to ask him whether he would like to help them do some stealing. He might say: lots of things to steal up here – something like that. And so your friend—'

'He was not my friend,' interjected Freddie.

'So this person, then, thinks of a reason he can give that he might later use as an alibi. He spreads word round that he is going to see his mother, but he is really going to rob a store. Very clever.'

Freddie stared at Mma Ramotswe for a while as if to work out whether she was making fun of him. He decided that she was not. 'All very interesting,' he said. 'But I really need to tell you about another advantage of these chairs. Termites do not eat plastic, Mma. They are completely uninterested in it. So you will never find the legs of these chairs eaten by termites. That is guaranteed.'

'That's very good,' said Mma Ramotswe.

She turned her gaze back to the armchair. 'Where do these chairs come from?' she asked.

Freddie waved a hand in the air. 'They are imported, Mma. You could not make a chair like this in Botswana. The plastic legs need to be made in a big factory, and we do not have one of those in Botswana.'

Mma Ramotswe asked where they were imported from.

'From over there,' said Freddie, again waving his hand.

'From South Africa?'

'Yes, I think they come from South Africa. There are many places there where they make chairs like this. We bring them into our warehouse out at Tlokweng. That is where we keep them.'

Mma Ramotswe absorbed this information. 'They might be made in China, Rra? Could they come from China, do you think?'

Freddie considered this. 'There are many things that come from China,' he said. 'They are always making things, the Chinese.'

'That is true,' said Mma Ramotswe. 'Perhaps the chairs are made in China and then they ship them to South Africa, and then from South Africa they send them here.'

'That is probably what happens,' said Freddie. 'That is international trade, you see, Mma Ramotswe.'

'And we send them our minerals and so on and they make them into things and then sell them back to us – for a much higher price.'

Freddie nodded. 'They are very smart businessmen, Mma.'

'Except that if we made the things here – here in Gaborone – we would not have to spend money to buy things back.'

'That is very interesting,' said Freddie. 'But we don't, do we?'

'Not at the moment,' said Mma Ramotswe. 'But you never know what will happen in the future.'

'Nothing is certain,' said Freddie. 'Except the fact that nothing is certain. That is certain, I think.'

Mma Ramotswe laughed. 'Can you give me a leaflet about these chairs – the living-room ones?'

'Yes,' said Freddie, fishing a leaflet out of a drawer. 'Here it is, Mma. It gives all the specifications. You must check the width of your door, you see, or you may not be able to get that chair in the house. We have had one case of that already. We took the furniture back, of course, because we are a highly reputable company.'

'Of course,' said Mma Ramotswe.

She glanced at the leaflet before folding it and putting it in a pocket. 'May I try out that living-room chair, Rra? For comfort?'

'Naturally,' he said. 'It is ready for you, Mma. It would be honoured if you sat on it.'

She moved to the chair and lowered herself onto it. It was all right, she thought – just all right. There was nothing special about it in terms of comfort: it was neither too hard, nor too soft. But she had certainly sat in many more comfortable chairs than that one, she decided, as she rose to her feet once more.

'Interesting,' she said.

She prepared to leave him. There was one thing more, though, that she wanted to ask about. 'These chairs are not expensive, Rra. They are cheaper than at some other places in town.'

Freddie grinned. 'We are undercutting everybody,' he said. 'We can sell really cheaply, Mma Ramotswe. People are not fools, you know – they can compare prices.'

'Yes,' she said. 'They do that, don't they? But how is it that your chairs are so cheap and everybody else's are ... well, not so cheap? How do you explain that, Rra?'

Freddie's reply came quickly. 'Buy cheap, sell cheap,' he said. 'That is the first rule of business.'

'But how do you manage to buy so cheaply?' Mma Ramotswe pressed.

Freddie hesitated. 'I think it's done with credit,' he replied at last. 'I think you can borrow money very cheaply and then use that to get your market share. You've heard of market share, Mma?'

Mma Ramotswe assured him that she had.

'Once you get your market share,' Freddie continued, 'then you can pay back the original loan because there will not be so much competition – so you can put your prices up and pay off the debt. Simple.'

Mma Ramotswe thought about this. 'You said there will not be so much competition, Rra. Why?'

'Because they will be out of business. Then you buy up the competitors' businesses and sell off the buildings. You use that to pay off your debts.'

Mma Ramotswe struggled to conceal her irritation. He was talking about the destruction of the livelihood of others, and yet was taking it so lightly. She closed her eyes. It was not his fault: this young man was simply a small cog in a machine that did exactly this sort of thing. He did not invent the system. So she confined herself to asking, 'How do you know all this, Rra? You must know a lot about business, I think.'

The compliment was well judged. We all liked to be told that we knew a lot, even when we did not; Mma Ramotswe knew that well, and understood how inexpensive were words of praise or encouragement, and how much pleasure they could bring. 'I am doing a course,' he replied, with pride in his voice. 'It is a night-school course, and the person who teaches it works in the business. He told us all about it.'

'What sort of business?'

'Furniture,' Freddie replied. 'That is why he knows so much.'

Mma Ramotswe waited. She remembered what Clovis Andersen had written: *If you want to find something out, give the other party the wrong information and wait until they correct you – with the right information! It works every time!*

So now she said, 'I think I know who that person is. There is a man called Mr Talkmore Molome. I think that he must be the person.' She had reached for the name from nowhere. A man called Talkmore, a successful football player, had been in the news recently, and his name had stuck with her. The Molome was dredged up from memory somewhere – she was not sure where.

It worked. She watched as he shook his head. He was enjoying being in a position to correct her; so many men seemed to get pleasure from that, she thought – from showing that they knew better. But they did not, of course.

'Talkmore Molome?' Freddie said. 'No, it is Kagiso Moesi. He is our lecturer in the course.'

'Of course,' said Mma Ramotswe, committing the name to memory, *Kagiso Moesi. Kagiso Moesi.* How right Clovis Andersen had been – about everything.

Kagiso Moesi ... There was something familiar about the name, but she could not put her finger on what it was. That was the trouble with names – they often resonated within the dim recesses of your memory, but you were still left uncertain as to where you had encountered the name, and when. There were so many people who touched our lives in one way or another, who left a signature somewhere in our memory, but who had faded as the years passed. She thought of all those people whom we met on our journey through life, whom we might see briefly and then never encounter again; and we, to them, were the same thing – names, faces barely remembered, passing shadows.

Chapter Seven

A Kind Man

Charlie was muted as Mma Ramotswe drove him back to the office. He had emerged from the dental clinic looking downcast, his lips firmly closed, and had responded with a curt nod of the head to Mma Ramotswe's enquiry as to how he felt. She had said nothing, imagining that he might have had an injection and his jaw could be feeling numb. It was not easy to talk with an anaesthetised tongue, and if he had anything to say it could wait until later. But as they rounded the traffic circle near the road to the football stadium, Charlie suddenly recovered the power of speech to say, 'It is very bad, Mma. The dentist has told me I must brush my teeth every day.'

Mma Ramotswe stifled a chuckle. 'Well, there you are, Charlie,' she said. 'That is what you are going to have to do.' Then she added, as an afterthought, 'Many of us have been doing that for some time, you know.'

Charlie pouted. 'That is all right for old people, Mma. It is not fair that young people have to do it.'

The tiny white van swerved – much in the same way as it swerved when Mma Makutsi made a challenging or questionable remark.

'I beg your pardon, Charlie,' Mma Ramotswe remonstrated. 'Firstly, I am not an old person. I am just a few – well, maybe twenty years – older than you. That does not make me old.'

Charlie looked embarrassed. 'I was not saying you were old, Mma. I was talking about really old people – not people who are just a bit old, like you.'

She threw a sideways glance at the young man. She realised that he did not intend to be rude; and from his perspective, perhaps, everybody over thirty was old. Yet at some point he would have to learn to be more tactful. Perhaps he would when he himself was over thirty; perhaps the scales would fall from his eyes then.

'Everybody should brush their teeth every day,' Mma Ramotswe said, her tone even and impartial. 'That is something that even small children should do – especially if they are eating cakes and sweet things like that.' She paused. 'How often have you been brushing them, anyway, Charlie?'

Charlie gazed out of the window. 'That is private, Mma. Teeth are private.'

She looked at the road ahead. Were teeth private? It was true that there were some bodily issues that were not the business of anybody else, but did teeth fall into that category? She thought not. After all, when we opened our mouths to talk, or when we smiled at somebody, we exposed our teeth to others. There they were, open to inspection, so to speak; laid bare willingly.

She half turned to Charlie. 'That means never,' she said. 'I think you are telling me that you never brush them.'

Her comment hit home. Charlie turned to face her. 'How do you know that?' he asked, his voice heavy with reproach.

She sighed. If Charlie wished to become a private detective – and he was, effectively, apprenticed half-time to the agency for that very purpose, the other half of his time being spent as a still-unqualified mechanic at Tlokweng Road Speedy Motors – then he would have to learn some of the stratagems by which a detective elicited information. And behind each of these stratagems there lay a simple proposition about human nature. In this case the proposition was that anybody who defended the privacy of certain information almost certainly had something to hide. That was not *always* the case, of course, but it was often true. So if Charlie did not wish to reveal the frequency with which he brushed his teeth, there was a good chance that he did not brush them at all.

'It was the way you said it, Charlie,' she explained. 'If you listen to what people say about what they do not want to say, then you can work out what's what. That is something you will learn in your professional work. Read *The Principles of Private Detection*. It is all there. Clovis Andersen tells you all about it.' She paused. 'Do you have a toothbrush?'

Charlie looked out of the window again.

Mma Ramotswe sighed again. 'Charlie, if somebody looks out of the window when you ask them a question, then you know that they do not want to answer you. So that means, in this case, that you do not own a toothbrush. That is the only conclusion I can reach.'

Charlie sniffed. 'The dentist says that I have to brush my teeth all the time ... '

'Hardly all the time,' Mma Ramotswe corrected. 'I imagine he said "every day".'

'And he said that I should use something called dental fluff.'

'Dental floss,' Mma Ramotswe corrected.

'He said this dental stuff is like very thin string. He said I must pull it between my teeth.'

Mma Ramotswe nodded. 'I have sometimes used it. Mma Makutsi uses it every day, I think. She makes Phuti use it too.'

'Women are always trying to force men to do things,' said Charlie. 'All the time, Mma. They say do this or do that or you will get ill or die or something else. All the time.'

Mma Ramotswe smiled. 'You have spoken about that before, Charlie. And it is not true. Women sometimes point out to men that it would be a good idea to do something. And your dentist, he was a man, wasn't he? He is that Zambian man who helps Mma Potokwani with the children's teeth. So this is not a case of a woman telling a man to do something – it is a man who is saying to you that you should do something.'

Charlie said nothing.

'Did he say anything about gum disease?' Mma Ramotswe asked.

Charlie nodded. He looked miserable, and Mma Ramotswe's heart went out to the young man. It was not easy being a young man, she thought. You were torn by conflicting desires. You had to look strong, but might be anything but strong inside; you had to behave as if you were scared of nothing, but you might be frightened to the very core of your being; you had to refrain from crying when all you really wanted to do was to weep. It was not at all easy, and she did not blame Charlie for being what he was – a typical young man.

She tried to reassure him. 'You mustn't worry, Charlie,' she said. 'We can stop at the pharmacy at Riverview and buy you a toothbrush. It will be a present from me to you. And we shall get some toothpaste too.'

Charlie bit his lip. 'I am very ashamed, Mma,' he muttered.

She reached out to touch his shoulder. 'You must not be,' she said. 'All of us are human. You, me, Mma Makutsi – even Mma Potokwani. We are all human – every single one of us.'

'I should have been brushing my teeth.'

'It is never too late to start brushing your teeth, Charlie,' she said. And, to emphasise the point she added, 'That is well known, you know. That is very well known.'

They stopped at the pharmacy, and Mma Ramotswe accompanied Charlie inside. There was a whole row of toothbrushes on display on a single shelf, and she left it up to Charlie to choose one that appealed. Then they chose a tube of mint-flavoured toothpaste and a large roll of dental floss.

'Now you have everything,' said Mma Ramotswe.

And just as she said this, she saw Patience, Mma Makutsi's childhood friend, the young woman she had met in Mma Potokwani's office. She was standing by the pharmacy counter, waiting for a prescription to be fulfilled. Mma Ramotswe saw that she was crying.

Mma Ramotswe reached into a pocket and handed a couple of banknotes to Charlie. 'Pay for all this,' she said. 'And then wait for me in the van. I will not be very long. Just wait.'

With a sideways glance at Patience, Charlie did as he was asked. As he did so, Mma Ramotswe stepped forward and put an arm around Patience's shoulder.

'Mma,' she said, 'I see you.'

It was the oldest and simplest of African greetings: *I see you*. It implied so much more than it said, though, because it meant that Mma Ramotswe saw not only the person standing before her, but all that lay behind her – who she was, where she came from, how she felt.

Patience struggled with a sodden tissue. 'I am sorry, Mma,'

she said. 'I am standing here crying like a useless person. I am a bit upset, you see.'

'You need not be sorry, Mma,' whispered Mma Ramotswe. 'And you are not a useless person.' She paused. Patience's sobbing had stopped, and she was now dabbing at her eyes with the bedraggled tissue.

'I have a handkerchief,' said Mma Ramotswe. 'You can use it, Mma.'

She pressed into the other woman's hand the copious white handkerchief that she always carried for just such eventualities. It was, she once explained to Mr J. L. B. Matekoni, part of her professional equipment – just as a tyre-lever or a battery charger might be for him. There were occasions on which a client might be overcome with emotion, as when, at the conclusion of an investigation, a distressing fact might need to be revealed. That could easily happen in a matrimonial matter, where a suspicion of infidelity might be confirmed, or in a missing-person case when a blank has been drawn and hopes must be gently let down. Of course, there were cases when the handkerchief was not needed at all, and the client surprised her with an entirely unexpected reaction – as in one case when a woman for whom she was acting greeted the news of her husband's unfaithfulness with whoops of delight. She had been hoping, she confessed, that another woman would take him off her hands and was very pleased that this had now occurred.

Now she handed over the handkerchief, which Patience accepted gratefully, jettisoning the inadequate tissue in a nearby bin.

'There is a café round the corner,' said Mma Ramotswe. 'After you have finished here, we can have a cup of tea together, my sister.'

Once again, the words were carefully chosen. *My sister*: it was a statement of solidarity: a proclaimed, public statement, intended for the ears of others, but a private pledge of support and understanding. People who used the words *brother* and *sister* loudly, and in public, might mean it, but their words were less likely to be as heartfelt as the same things uttered quietly, to one another.

'You are very kind,' said Patience. 'I feel foolish, Mma. I do not like to display my private troubles like this.'

'I am ready to listen, Mma,' said Mma Ramotswe. 'And I need a cup of tea, anyway. I always have a cup of tea at this time of day, and I am happy to have it with you.'

'And that young man?'

'That is Charlie,' Mma Ramotswe said. 'He is a junior detective and mechanic. He is very happy to sit outside and wait for me. He has things to think about.' She wondered whether she should explain about Charlie's teeth, but decided against it. Patience, it would seem, had enough to worry about, without having the dental problems of others added to the list.

They left the pharmacy and made their way to the small café round the corner. Here there were tables and chairs placed under the shade of large umbrellas. At noon these would all be occupied by the staff of nearby shops on their lunchtime break, but at this hour of the morning only one was taken, by two women who had finished their early-morning visit to the supermarket. Both had full shopping bags tucked under their chairs and were engaged in voluble and animated discourse.

'I know those ladies,' commented Mma Ramotswe, her voice lowered, as she and Patience sat down.

'You must hear about many secrets in your job,' said Patience. 'You must know something about just about everyone.' Then she added, 'This is a big town, but it is also a small town, they say.'

Mma Ramotswe was quick to disabuse her of the idea. 'There

is a very great deal I do not know,' she said. 'In fact, every day I realise just how little any of us knows – myself included, Mma.'

It was said in a jocular way, but Patience looked abashed. 'I did not mean to be rude, Mma,' she said hurriedly.

'I know that, Mma. Of course you weren't.'

Patience looked at her in gratitude. 'Sometimes the things I say come out wrong, if you see what I mean, Mma. I think one thing, and then another thing comes out of my mouth.'

Mma Ramotswe laughed. 'That applies to all of us.' She paused. 'But you mentioned secrets, Mma, and I thought I should tell you – yes, in my job I learn secrets, but they always remain secrets. I do not speak to other people about the things that I learn in my work. It is called professional confidence.'

Patience nodded. 'I know about that. It is the same in any job. You should not go and tell everybody about the things you see and hear.'

'Although many people do,' observed Mma Ramotswe, and thought how in fact she relied on precisely that desire to talk to elicit the information that she needed in her cases. On so many occasions it had been the indiscretions of others that had provided her with the knowledge she needed to bring an assignment to a successful conclusion. So, while she would herself respect confidences, she was pleased that there were so many others who would not.

A waitress appeared, and they ordered tea: redbush for Mma Ramotswe and Five Roses Ceylon for Patience. Patience still had Mma Ramotswe's handkerchief, and she now folded it carefully. 'I shall wash this and give it back to you, Mma,' she said. 'Washed and ironed.'

'You may keep it,' said Mma Ramotswe. 'You may need it again.'

Patience smiled. 'I do not spend my time crying,' she said. 'It was just ...' She shrugged, seemingly unable to complete her explanation.

'I understand, Mma,' Mma Ramotswe reassured her. 'Who amongst us does not cry from time to time? I do. Everyone does, Mma, and nobody needs to hide it – nobody.'

'You are very kind,' said Patience. 'I wasn't crying when I went into the pharmacy and then, while I was waiting for the pills that the doctor has given me, I started to cry. It just started. You know how it is.'

Mma Ramotswe inclined her head. 'I do,' she said. 'I know, Mma.' This was familiar territory. While she had never suffered from depression, she remembered only too well how Mr J. L. B. Matekoni had been afflicted with it all those years ago. It had come upon him suddenly, and its lifting had been almost as abrupt, when suddenly the old personality had returned and with it his normal view of the world. She remembered what Dr Moffat had told her when he had first made the diagnosis – that depression was one of the commonest of all illnesses and that there was not a family in the land that would not be affected by it in one way or another at some stage. 'Almost everybody,' he had said, 'and I mean *everybody* feels low now and then, and that low feeling is just the beginning of the actual condition. Nobody is exempt, no matter how strong you are.'

'Did the doctor say you were depressed?' she asked.

Patience hesitated. 'She said—'

'You don't have to answer that,' said Mma Ramotswe quickly. 'I do not want to pry, Mma.'

'I don't mind talking about it – to you, Mma Ramotswe. Just to you. Yes, she thought I was depressed because I told her that I was having trouble sleeping. And I also told her that there was this crying and sometimes not being able to get going in the morning. That is the worst part of it, Mma Ramotswe – not being able to get going when I have always been used to getting up early for work.' Her voice faltered, and a look of concern appeared on her face. 'You won't tell Mma Potokwani now, will you? I would not like her to think that I will not be able to do the job I shall be starting soon.'

Mma Ramotswe reassured her that she would not breathe a word to Mma Potokwani – or anybody else.

'I shall not let this interfere with my work,' Patience said. 'I promise you that.'

'I am sure you will not,' said Mma Ramotswe. 'I can tell that you are a hard worker, Mma. This thing that has happened to you is not your fault.'

'And the doctor said these pills will help,' Patience continued. 'She said they may take a couple of weeks to do their work, but she said that they will make me feel better.'

'They did that for my husband,' said Mma Ramotswe. 'Suddenly one morning he woke up and smiled. That will happen to you too, Mma.'

Patience managed a smile. 'I am happy to hear that. But I would still like to talk to you about something, Mma Ramotswe. Do you mind?'

Mma Ramotswe shook her head. 'Talking about something is the first step in fixing it,' she said. 'I have always found that to be true, Mma.' And it was true, she thought, because she had proved it time and time again in her own life. Words were the very first bandage for any wound.

'Let me tell you, then,' said Patience.

Mma Ramotswe looked over Patience's shoulder, out towards the car park. She could see the tiny white van, parked next to a large red car, and she could make out Charlie standing beside it. What was he doing? It was hard to tell, but when she shielded her eyes she had a better view. And then she saw what it was: Charlie was cleaning his teeth.

'You know, of course,' Patience began, 'that I am from Bobonong. And you know that Grace Makutsi and I were friends. And then she came down here to Gaborone and I was left up there because I had a baby then, Mma Ramotswe. The baby came to me when I was only sixteen because I had been attacked by a man one night. It was not my fault, Mma Ramotswe.'

Mma Ramotswe could not help but gasp. 'Of course it was not your fault, Mma. Nobody should ever blame the woman in these dreadful cases.'

'But some do,' said Patience. 'There are always some people who say: "What were you doing out at night?" "Why were you there in that particular place?" "What did you say to the man?" They really say things like that, Mma; or, even if they don't say them, they think them. I have seen people thinking those things, Mma.'

Mma Ramotswe shook her head. 'There are always people who think the wrong things,' she said. 'That is the cause of half the trouble in this world, you know: people thinking the wrong things.'

Patience seemed reassured. 'Anyway, Mma, there were some kind French priests who helped me. I had my baby and they gave some money to my grandmother to help me look after him. He is called Modise.' She paused, and looked sideways at Mma Ramotswe. Modise meant *herd boy* in Setswana. 'I know that is not a very good name, Mma, but my father was called Modise and I wanted him to bear my father's name. My father was a good man. He became late when I was very young – about two,

112

I think – but people said to me that he was a kind man. That is the most important thing, I think, Mma Ramotswe – to be kind.'

'Oh, that is quite right,' agreed Mma Ramotswe. 'And if you have a kind father, then you have a very good start. My late daddy was a kind man too, Mma. We have both been fortunate in that.'

'I do not even have a picture of my father,' Patience mused. 'We were poor people, you see, and there are not many pictures of poor people.'

'Except in your heart,' said Mma Ramotswe. 'I think you may have a picture of him there.'

Patience said nothing. She closed her eyes for a moment, and Mma Ramotswe wondered whether she was going to burst into tears again, but she did not. Opening her eyes, she continued, 'I had a job as a cleaner, Mma. It was in a government office and it had good conditions. If you work for the government then you are sure that you will get your pay at the end of the month. And the government will look after you, as long as you do your job well. I made sure that I did that. I swept and swept and polished the floors of the government toilets so that they were shiny as any floor could be. I also washed the windows, which many people did not bother to do. The government people liked their windows being clean, and I received many commendations.

'I went to night school and got my school certificate. Then I did a course in book-keeping and passed all the examinations first time, with distinction. Just like Grace Makutsi. And I was given a promotion because you do not want to have qualified book-keepers sweeping floors. I had a good salary then and it would have been more than enough for Modise and me to live on if it had not been for a man who came to live in my house and would not move out. He said that I was his wife, but I never married him, Mma. He said that if I tried to throw him out he would make sure that I lost my job. He had some sort of hold over some of the government people up there – I don't know why – and I was worried that he would be able to do as he threatened. So I stayed with him, although he drank a lot and had a very bad temper. He would shout at me and sometimes raise his hand. I was at the hospital three times because of him.

'I know I should have left him earlier than I did, Mma, but sometimes it is hard to do the things that you know you should do. But eventually I ran away with my son, and we went to the French priests' place, and they gave us a room behind the clinic they ran. This man came after me. He came along shouting and waving his fists and he told the French priests that if they did not make me come back with him he would set fire to the school they ran up there.

'There was one of the French priests who was very tall. He was called Father Pierre, and he had a broken nose from something that had happened a long time before. He was very strong. I saw him pick up a donkey once, just like you or I would pick up a dog. He lifted the donkey in the air and put him on the other side of a fence. There were people watching and they all spoke about what they had seen for a long time afterwards.

'That man went up to Father Pierre and started shouting at him. The priest looked at him and told him to stop shouting as his voice was hurting his ears. That made the man shout even more, and then he gave the priest a push – just a small push, Mma, but it was enough. The priest hit him. Very hard on the chin, and then put his knee in his stomach. That man doubled up and when he straightened up the priest hit him on the chin again. Then he shouted at him in Setswana, because those priests spoke very good Setswana, and told him that if he came back to their place he would lift him up and carry him off to the police. He also warned him not to try to speak to me ever again or he would hit him again many times on the chin and other places too. That was enough to make him go away, and I never saw him again.'

Mma Ramotswe listened wide-eyed. When Patience stopped to draw breath she said, 'Sometimes it is necessary to be direct, Mma.'

Patience agreed. 'That priest understood that, I think. He was a very kind man, Father Pierre, and I never saw him hit anybody else.'

Mma Ramotswe was keen to hear more. 'Did you stay there?' she asked. 'Did you stay with the French priests?'

'For a short while,' answered Patience. 'Then I went back to my grandmother's house. I stayed there for a long time. Modise went to school and did very well. He was very good at mathematics, they said. But it was not easy, Mma, bringing up a boy with no father there.'

'It is best for a boy to have a father,' said Mma Ramotswe. 'I know there are people who say that it does not matter, but I think that it is important for a boy to have somebody who can stand up to him. I think that is best, although it may not have been possible for you, Mma. I understand that.'

She thought of her own experience with the two foster children, Motholeli and Puso, whom she and Mr J. L. B. Matekoni had looked after for some years now and who were now well into the difficult teenage years. Motholeli had been relatively easy, in spite of the difficulties she found in walking – her approach to life was a positive one, and she rarely complained. That, Mma Ramotswe thought, was little short of a miracle, as one might have expected a child in such a situation to express at least some resentment at what fate had dictated for her. But she had not, and had ended up doing rather the opposite, remaining cheerful about the limitations of her condition and making the most of every opportunity that was presented her, particularly those of helping Mr J. L. B. Matekoni or Fanwell in the garage. Puso, alas, had been more demanding. At heart he was a nice boy – Mma Ramotswe had never been in doubt about that – but the compliant, biddable child of eleven had suddenly become the adolescent of twelve, whose moods might come upon him at any moment, making him silent at times and monosyllabically surly at others. There had been slammed doors – a sure sign of impending teenagerdom – and complaints about how she and Mr J. L. B. Matekoni were cooking up ways of ruining his life. Mma Ramotswe knew that such accusations were levelled by just about every teenager in the world against just about every parent, and their patently ridiculous nature hardly needed to be pointed out. And yet they hurt – in spite of everything, in spite of the knowledge that they were temporary, they hurt. But being a parent hurt – that was part of the arrangement. It hurt and then suddenly it did not hurt any longer, and a loving and reasonable person emerged from the teenage shell, just as the colourful emperor moth emerges from the chrysalis of the mopane worm. It was just a question of waiting, and of biting one's tongue and keeping one's temper in the face of trying behaviour. Yet there must be circumstances – and these, perhaps, were just such circumstances – where a child could wreck everything a parent longed for. Such developments were serious, and could not simply be wished away.

Patience continued with her story. 'I was always hoping that I might find a good man,' she said. 'I looked and looked but there were very few good men about. Then a man came up from Water Affairs in Gaborone. He had to be up in Bobonong for four months to deal with some problems they we were having with the water supply. I met him in the office, and I liked him straight away. I thought to myself: this is my best chance ever of finding a man who will be a good husband. I hoped he would take notice of me, Mma – and he did. He said that I was just the sort of woman he had been looking for and that he wanted me to come and live with him in Gaborone when he went home. I said that this was very good, because I had been hoping to meet a man like him, and now it had happened.

'He said that he was very happy to have Modise live with us. He said that he would make sure that he got a place at Gaborone Secondary School and that there were very good teachers there. I was very pleased, Mma, because fourteen-year-old boys are not always easy, and I was worried that my new friend – he's called Simon – would not want to have a teenage boy in the house. So we came down with him about three months ago, Mma Ramotswe, and here we are. Simon has a house in Gaborone West, and it is the best house I have ever lived in. It has three bedrooms, Mma, and a living room that can also be used as a dining room. There is a fence all round it and a gate with the plot number on it. Anybody passing by would say, "That is a good house, that one."

'But I should tell you about Simon, Mma, because that is important in this story. He is from up north, Mma. He is a foreigner in this country. His people are from Malawi. But there is no work up there and many people are poor. Simon came to Botswana when he was twenty-two because he had heard there might be work. He came over the border at night, as he had no papers. It is not easy, Mma, to have no papers. If you are a person without papers, then you are nothing. Even cattle have papers these days, Mma – I'm joking, of course, but that is what it can feel like to have no papers.

'He was very lucky, Mma. He was given a job and managed to get permission to stay in the country. He is a hard worker, but even if you work and work, it is not easy, and the only reason that he got that job in Water Affairs is because there was nobody else with his water engineering qualifications. He is a big expert in pumps, Mma. He knows all about them.

'I was so happy when I found him, Mma. I thought that the rest of my life would be very happy. I would look after him, and he would look after me – which is the best basis for any partnership, I think, Mma Ramotswe. I was so happy. But then Modise started to behave badly. He was very bad, Mma – all the time. He turned his head away whenever Simon said anything, pretending that he could not hear him. Or he would sit at the table and frown as if he wanted Simon to go away. He would turn his back on him, or pretend that he was not in the room.

'I spoke to him, Mma. I told him that I had seen what he was doing, but he would just get up and walk out whenever I tackled him about it. He said that he did not know what I was talking about and that he did not want to listen, anyway. He called Simon "the Foreigner". That is what he actually said, Mma – sometimes to his face. He would say things like, "Foreigners don't know anything about anything." Once he said, "Foreigners should all be sent home. This country is for Batswana – not for foreigners."'

Mma Ramotswe winced. It shamed her to hear of people being berated for who they were. That, in her view, was one of the worst and most wicked things you could do: to belittle or insult another person for what they happened to be. You might disagree with others for what they said or for what they did – that was one thing – but to take against them simply for what they *were* was to blame them for something over which they had no control, and was cruel, and profoundly wrong. And yet it was done all the time, and all over the world. There were plenty of instances of it in Africa, where one group of people might dislike another group for reasons that were lost in time, or that never existed in the first place; there were plenty of instances of the same thing in other parts of the world, too, where animosities and hatreds of that nature survived; and in every case there was distress and suffering because of the failure of charity that such views entailed. We should love one another, she thought, not only because it was the right thing to do, but also because it was far easier than hating one another. People who hated often had to work quite hard at keeping their hatred warm.

She told Patience that she was sorry to hear about this. 'Of course, he is only fourteen, Mma, and young people of that age often behave in a very silly way. Your Modise is probably just the same as other teenage boys. Much of the time they do not think, you know.'

'I know that, Mma Ramotswe. But this is getting very serious now. Only this morning, before I came to the pharmacy, I had to call in at the school. He has been in trouble at school and they wanted to speak to me about him. They say that he is getting out of control. I was very ashamed to have to sit there and be told these things.'

Mma Ramotswe reflected on this. What our children did could be painful, although we almost always forgave them. And as far as fourteen-year-old boys were concerned, she had yet to meet one who was not, at least in some respects, embarrassing or difficult. That, simply, was what fourteen-year-old boys were like.

'You must not blame yourself for any of this, Mma,' she said. 'Teenage boys are ... teenage boys, I'm afraid. Then suddenly they become something different and all the surliness and awkwardness stops. It is the same with teenage girls, though a bit different. They are difficult in other ways.' She paused. 'I am very glad that I am not a teenager, Mma, but I am particularly glad that I am not a teenage boy. I am very glad of that.'

Patience listened to this. 'Yes, Mma. You are right. But this is a big problem for me because Simon is getting very angry. He says that he does not like to be treated like that in his own house – and who can blame him? I can tell, Mma, that although he is a very good man, he is getting to the end of his tether. I know that because he told one of his friends that he was thinking of breaking off our relationship altogether. That friend has a girlfriend who then passed the news on to me. You can imagine how I felt, Mma Ramotswe. My one chance of happiness after all these years of things going badly – my one chance – is being threatened.'

Mma Ramotswe shook her head. 'This is very bad,' she said. 'Perhaps you should try to speak to him again. Sometimes it takes teenagers a long time to hear what is being said to them.'

'I have spoken to him, and then spoken again. He refuses to listen. And you know what I think now, Mma? I think that this is exactly what he wants. He wants Simon to ask us to leave.'

Patience said this at the moment that Mma Ramotswe was coming to that exact conclusion. She had seen something very similar to this before when a divorced friend of Mr J. L. B. Matekoni had seen his budding romance destroyed by a jealous daughter. That man's daughter had made it her business to see off the woman who had entered her father's life because she did not want to share him. Children were often unwilling to share their parents with a prospective step-parent – that was nothing new.

'This is all very upsetting,' said Mma Ramotswe.

Patience looked at her watch. 'I am keeping you, Mma. I wanted to share my story, and I am grateful to you for listening. I feel a bit better now.'

'We can talk some other time,' said Mma Ramotswe. 'I understand how you feel, Mma. Let us talk about it later. May I talk to

Mma Makutsi about this? She has many ideas and may be able to suggest something.'

Patience nodded and began to rise up from the table. 'Yes, of course, Mma. She is my old friend. I was going to talk to her anyway.' She paused. There was resolution in her voice now. 'I am starting my new job next week. I am looking forward to working with Mma Potokwani.'

'She is one of the best women in the country,' said Mma Ramotswe. 'You will be very happy there.'

She reached out to touch Patience's hand gently. It was a small gesture, but it brought a smile to the younger woman's face. 'Be brave, Mma,' said Mma Ramotswe. As she said this, she thought: we tell other people to be brave; we tell them that all the time. Perhaps it was reasonable to tell them that, she was not sure, but it was harmless enough advice when there was very little else one could think of to say.

Mma Ramotswe paid for the tea and they said goodbye. Then, as she was making her way back to the van, Mma Ramotswe stopped. An idea had come to her – an idea that was as unexpected as it was outrageous. Would something like that actually work? Would anybody agree to it, particularly Patience, who would have to be in on it from the word go? And what if it went wrong: what damage could it do to the very thing that it was seeking to protect?

No, this was impossible. This was not the sort of plan that anybody actually put into effect. This was the sort of thing that people made up when they were telling stories or thinking of plots for films. This was not something that you actually *did*.

And yet, and yet . . .

She turned round to call out to Patience, but the other woman was now out of earshot, heading off for the minibus stop on the far side of the car park. Mma Ramotswe made up her mind: she would run the plan past Mma Makutsi before she approached Patience herself. If Mma Makutsi laughed, or rejected the idea out of hand, then nothing would have been lost. Of course, she might react in the opposite manner and say, 'Mma Ramotswe, this is a *very* good idea! This is just what we need to do to save my poor friend Patience from having all her hopes of happiness dashed to the ground – dashed to the ground, Mma!' Something like that.

She reached the van, where Charlie was waiting for her, looking pointedly at his watch.

'I'm sorry to have kept you, Charlie,' she said. 'That lady was telling me a very important story.'

Charlie said nothing, but went round to the other side of the van to get into the passenger seat. Then, when she was at the wheel and starting the engine, Mma Ramotswe noticed that Charlie's mouth had a very obvious line of white round the lips.

'I see that you have been cleaning your teeth,' said Mma Ramotswe. 'You may need to wash your face when we get to the office.'

Charlie used his tongue to lick at the toothpaste on his face. 'It is very good toothpaste, Mma. I shall use it every day.'

'That is very wise, Charlie,' she said.

They travelled in silence. Charlie looked at Mma Ramotswe and frowned. 'Something is worrying you, Mma,' he said.

'I am just thinking,' she replied. 'I am thinking of a rather peculiar plan.'

Charlie did not seem to be particularly interested. He was examining his toothbrush now, feeling the paste-encrusted bristles. 'How peculiar?' he asked.

'The most peculiar plan I have ever made,' said Mma Ramotswe. 'And possibly the most dangerous.'

Charlie's interest was aroused. 'How is it dangerous?' he asked.

'Because it involves deception,' answered Mma Ramotswe. 'And I should tell you one thing, Charlie, that you should remember if you have a career as a private detective—'

'I am going to have that career,' interjected Charlie. 'I am already doing that.'

'Yes, of course,' she said. 'But you still have lessons to learn. And one of these is that you should always pay attention to what Clovis Andersen has to say in *The Principles of Private Detection*.'

'Oh, him,' said Charlie. He had heard about Clovis Andersen on so many occasions, and Mma Makutsi and Mma Ramotswe were always going on about how he should read the book. If you listened to them, he thought, you might think that *The Principles of Private Detection* was one of the books of the Bible, or one of the statutes in *The Laws of Botswana*, or a declaration enacted by the United Nations for the whole world, instead of being just a book with a by now rather tattered cover by a man who lived in a place called Muncie, Indiana, wherever that was.

Now Charlie asked in a casual tone, 'And what does Mr Almighty Andersen say about deception, Mma?'

Mma Ramotswe ignored the insult. Charlie could insult Clovis Andersen if he wished, but he would be the loser. You ignored wisdom, succinctly put, at your peril, and he should know that by now. He would learn ...

She answered his question: 'Mr Andersen says that you should not use deception,' and then added, 'except in those cases where you need to.'

'Hah!' said Charlie.

Chapter Eight

We Appreciate Water

Mma Makutsi listened attentively. She did not move, but sat behind her desk, her hands folded in front of her, her large round spectacles pushed up on her forehead. Above her, on the faded white board of the ceiling, a small gecko, so pale as to be almost translucent, stalked a fly. She let her gaze fall on that tiny hunting scene for a few moments before it returned to Mma Ramotswe, similarly seated at her desk, who was in the process of telling her of the conversation she had just had with ~~Precious~~ *Patience* in the café at the Riverview Shopping Mall.

'I am not surprised to hear that she is depressed,' said Mma Makutsi. 'When I saw her the other day out at the Orphan Farm, she told me that there was something. She said that she would talk to me about it on another day. Now I know what it is, Mma, and I am not surprised – not at all.'

'Well, there you are, Mma. She was very upset.'

Mma Makutsi unfolded her hands and gave her fingernails a thoughtful inspection. 'Patience has had a very hard time,' she mused. 'She is one of those people who have bad things happen to them one after the other – time after time. And then suddenly something good happens to them and we all think, At last, that person has something good happening in her life. But of course, with their luck, you see this good thing being suddenly threatened and we think, This is very unfair, but it is exactly the sort of thing that happens to that unlucky person.'

Mma Ramotswe agreed with this. She nodded gravely. 'Oh, you are so right, Mma. And sometimes it makes us wonder whether there is such a thing as justice.' She shook her head. 'There is, of course, but sometimes it is hard to see it.'

'But you said you had an idea,' Mma Makutsi pressed.

Mma Ramotswe hesitated. She had almost abandoned her idea, but then she remembered the look of sheer desolation on Patience's face as she told her story and she decided that she could not stand by. She would have to do something even if it meant explaining to Mr J. L. B. Matekoni that she was taking on yet another unpaid case. He never sought to prevent her doing that, as he was a generous and sympathetic man, but every so often, when she discussed with him the finances of the No. 1 Ladies' Detective Agency, he would sigh and say, 'Of course, if you perhaps did a little more *paid* work, Mma Ramotswe, and perhaps just a *tiny bit* less unpaid work, then your accounts might look a bit healthier – just a suggestion, not a criticism.' And she would listen and then point out that from the point of view of a person who needed help, ability to pay was the last thing that should be taken into account. A need was a need, no matter whether or not there was money to back it up. And if further defence were needed, she would certainly be in a position to cite numerous instances where Mr J. L. B. Matekoni himself did work on the cars of people who did not have the money to pay his bills. He never turned anybody away, with the result that his own accounts, although usually more robust than those of the No. 1 Ladies' Detective Agency, could sometimes be perilously close to going into the red.

But now her mind was made up, and she explained to Mma Makutsi the outline of the plot that had occurred to her in the car park earlier that morning.

'All right, Mma Makutsi,' she began. 'Let us consider what we have here. We have a boy who has always lived with his mother. He has been the apple of her eye – let us assume that, because every son is the apple of their mother's eye, human nature being what it is. They live together up in Bobonong, along with a man who comes into his mother's life. This man is not very pleasant. The boy sees his mother being taken away from him by this man. Yes, she is there for her son, but then much of her time is taken up by this man.

'His mother runs away, and takes him with her. He is very happy again, and even happier after he sees a French priest knocking the bullying man to the ground. Happiness arrives once more, and he returns to being the centre of his mother's world – until another man turns up and wants some of the time that she had for her son. The old problem of being jealous of his mother's friend returns, although this time the boy decides that he will fight back. He does everything he can to annoy this new man. It is easy to be unpleasant if you are a teenage boy, and that is what this boy does. He is rude; he is surly, so that the new man will think, I cannot live with this woman and her ill-mannered son. He hopes the man will then say to the woman, "I am sorry, but I must give you up." That would be a very good result for the boy, who would then be back with his mother once more. I think many boys want their mother back, Mma ... '

This seemed to resonate with Mma Makutsi, who immediately became animated, clapping her hands together in agreement, her glasses falling off her forehead back onto their accustomed position on her nose.

'You are so right, Mma Ramotswe,' she exclaimed. 'You know that; I know that. We all know that men are looking for their mothers. All their lives, Mma, they are looking for their mothers. And that is how they choose the women they ask to marry them. They think, Oh, this person is just like my mother and I will ask her to marry me and look after me for the rest of my life. That is how men think, Mma. They don't know that is how they think, but that is how it works.'

'Possibly ...' began Mma Ramotswe, only to be cut short again by Mma Makutsi, to whom a further dimension of this insight had evidently occurred.

'There was a very famous doctor back a long time ago,' Mma Makutsi continued. 'He was called Dr Fraud. You've heard of him, Mma? You've heard of this Dr Fraud?'

Mma Ramotswe knew exactly who Mma Makutsi was speaking of, as she had read an article in one of her magazines that explained all about the theories advanced by this great man.

'Not Dr Fraud,' she corrected Mma Makutsi. 'He was called something else, I believe. He spelled his name oddly, but that is what they called him, I think. He was a psychologist.'

'Yes,' said Mma Makutsi. 'Fraud, or whatever – same man. He invented psychology. He said that all men love their mothers. He said that, Mma! That's not me saying that. He said it.'

Mma Ramotswe had been aware of that. She had always

thought that it would be strange if men did not love their mothers, bearing in mind what their mothers did for them. Who fed them when they were small? Who wiped their noses and mended their trousers? Who did all the tasks that young boys required to be done for them? It would be surprising if men did not end up loving their mothers after all that.

'I think we should get back to this boy, Modise,' said Mma Ramotswe. 'I think we can understand why he started to behave badly to this man his mother had met. He must have thought, Here we go again – another man coming to take my mother away from me. And it looks as if he might be succeeding. His mother, of course – your friend Patience – has spoken to him, but it is no use. He is determined to be so unpleasant that the new man will ask them to leave. And who could blame him?'

Mma Makutsi said that she would never tolerate that sort of atmosphere in her house. 'If I had a youngster like that under my roof, being rude and unpleasant to people, I would soon sort him out,' she said. 'I would get Phuti to give him a good hiding. Wallop, wallop – that is the way to stop that sort of thing.'

Mma Ramotswe started at her. 'My goodness, Mma Makutsi,' she protested. 'There are not many people who speak like that these days. People say you should not spank your children, because that does not help. There are better ways of dealing with bad behaviour.'

Mma Makutsi sucked in her cheeks. 'They may say that, Mma Ramotswe, but have they seen how lions behave? Have they seen that? You go out into the Kalahari or up north to Chobe or somewhere like that and you watch the lion families. I have seen it, Mma, with my own eyes, I'm telling you. The young male lions are not very well behaved. They try to push their way into things. They try to get more than their fair share of the food. That is only natural, because they do not know any better. But then what does the male lion do, Mma? He goes up to them and he gives them a smack with his paw. Smack, smack. And the young male lions run off and stop causing trouble because they know what will happen if they carry on causing trouble. That is how things work in nature, Mma Ramotswe.'

'We are different,' Mma Ramotswe ventured. 'I'm not saying that lions do not do as you say they do, Mma – all that I am saying is that you cannot apply lion rules to people. We do not hide in the grass and jump out at people. We do not eat zebras out in the bush. Most of us do not even roar all that much . . .'

Mma Makutsi looked pained. 'You are making fun of the serious point I was making, Mma.'

Mma Ramotswe apologised. 'I'm sorry, Mma Makutsi. I think now I should tell you what I have in mind.'

Mma Makutsi was placated. 'I am very interested in that, Mma. Anything to help Patience would be a good thing.'

'This may not work, of course,' Mma Ramotswe warned.

'Tell me, Mma. Then I will say whether I think it would work.'

Mma Ramotswe told her, setting out, in some detail, how she thought her plan might be attempted. At the end of her explanation, she sat back and awaited Mma Makutsi's verdict.

At first nothing was said. Outside, in the acacia tree behind the garage, the two Cape doves who lived there sang briefly to one another. Then there was silence once again.

Mma Makutsi laughed. 'I have never heard of such a thing,' she said at last. 'Only you could come up with something like that, Mma Ramotswe.'

'Does that mean you think it might work?'

Mma Makutsi did not hesitate. 'It will definitely work,' she said. 'What could possibly go wrong?'

Everything, thought Mma Ramotswe, but did not say that. Instead, she said, 'I shall need to talk to Phuti first. Should we do that together?'

Mma Makutsi thought for a moment. Then she shook her head as she gave her answer. 'I don't think so, Mma. I think that you might do that by yourself. Phuti is not himself at the moment with all this business pressure. It might be easier for you to convince him.'

'I shall try,' said Mma Ramotswe.

There was a note of sadness in her voice. She was very fond of Mma Makutsi and of Phuti. She did not like the thought that they might be experiencing difficulties. But then she thought: life has its ups and downs. If you did not have some downs, then your appreciation of the ups might be all the less for that. Hills always looked better when you looked at them from down below. Was that true? Yes, she thought it was, but she was not sure what bearing this had on what she was thinking at the time. None, she felt; and then she thought again and decided that it did have some relevance. Sometimes, she told herself, the first thing you think is the thing that you *should* think. If that was not well known, then perhaps it should be.

She lost no time in driving herself to Phuti's shop, the Double Comfort Furniture Store, at its large premises on the edge of town. Since Phuti's father had first established the business, it had grown from being a small, rather poky establishment selling cheap household furniture to being a large, air-conditioned showroom attached to a voluminous warehouse. Various other retail businesses had set themselves up on adjacent plots – including a fashion house, Smart Man, Smart Woman, and a shoe shop, Your Shoes – but these were very much dwarfed by the Double

Comfort Furniture Store and its extensive car park. As Mma Ramotswe tucked her van into a shady berth labelled 'Business visitors only' – which I am, she said to herself, because she was not here as a member of the public, she was here in her role as a sort of fixer of the problems in people's lives, and that was a business, albeit an unusual one – she rehearsed what she was proposing to say to Phuti. The agenda of their meeting had expanded since she'd first decided to seek his co-operation in helping Patience. There was other business to be discussed with Phuti, and that concerned the commercial difficulties he was facing. He had not asked for her help in that matter, but she felt that she should tell him about her conversation with Freddie, the young man selling chairs near the dental clinic. Phuti was in the sights of those who would destroy his business – there could be no doubt about that – and that, she felt, was not a battle in respect of which she could be a mere bystander: sides had to be taken. She looked once more at the 'Business visitors only' sign. Mma Ramotswe was the last person to ignore a sign, and for a moment she felt a pang of doubt. Did the sign mean that the parking place in question was for those who were there to buy furniture? If that were the case, then she could not qualify, and she should park elsewhere. But that reading of it, she felt, was too restrictive. You could not go through life like that, being too timid, too faint-hearted in the face of other people's instructions as to what you should do or not do. It was not that the sign said 'Please do not park here'; it was not as if it said, 'We would really prefer you not to park here'; it simply said 'Business visitors only', and that amounted to an invitation, even if it was a restricted one. And besides, she had Phuti's permission – in a sense – because this was, after all, his car park, and she was here to see him.

Phuti's sanctum in the Double Comfort Furniture Store was

reached through an outer office staffed by a receptionist, a small woman with braided hair and wearing a high-collared blouse. She was, Mma Ramotswe thought, typical of a certain sort of receptionist – one trained, and encouraged, to block any attempt to waylay, speak to, or even catch a glimpse of their employer. Not all receptionists were like that, of course: Mma Ramotswe had encountered many who were warm and welcoming, who made the visitor feel pleased to have wandered into the office, and who, according to traditional and approved custom, enquired after one's health and the health of one's immediate, and sometimes extended, family. Of course that could be taken too far – there was a security guard at the President Hotel who interpreted his role rather broadly and would willingly spend ten minutes passing the time of day with all those who crossed his path, asking them at length about their family, their friends, and their cattle. He had become a bit of an institution in town, and people spoke with amusement about his lengthy and unnecessary greetings until one day his interrogation revealed a potential thief intent on gaining access to the hotel bed-rooms. The thief had somehow acquired a master key and was only exposed when an answer he gave the guard, who greeted him as he sauntered into the hotel, revealed an inconsistency.

Phuti's receptionist looked up from an envelope she was open-ing. For a moment or two she did not speak, but gave Mma Ramotswe a look of frank appraisal. That, of course, was the first weapon in the armoury of the unhelpful sort of receptionist. That was the moment at which the decision was taken whether to block the visitor or allow her to proceed to the next stage of the process.

Then she spoke, and if it is possible to render icy the warm syl-lables of the traditional Setswana greeting – with its comfortable *du* and its rounded *mela* – then this receptionist managed to do just that.

Mma Ramotswe replied courteously before asking whether Phuti was in. The receptionist pursed her lips before replying, 'Mr Radiphuti?'

Mma Ramotswe tried not to smile. She had asked for *Phuti* without qualifying the name with *Radiphuti*. But how many other Phutis could there be, she wondered. Perhaps she could point that out to this unhelpful woman; but no, Mma Ramotswe was not one to score points unnecessarily.

'Yes,' she said brightly. 'Mr Radiphuti himself. This *is* his office, I think.'

The receptionist shook her head. 'No, Mma, this is *my* office.'

Mma Ramotswe was taken aback. 'But this is the Double Comfort Furniture Store, is it not? That's what the sign outside says, I think.' And then she thought: and the other sign said 'Business visitors only', but she would not bring that up in this company.

'It is definitely the Double Comfort Furniture Store, Mma. Yes, that is the case. But you asked whether this was Mr Radiphuti's office and the answer to that is that you are standing in *my* office, Mma.'

Mma Ramotswe laughed. 'Oh, I see what you mean. This is your office – this outer office, that is – while Mr Radiphuti's office is that office in there, beyond that door that, now I look at it, says "Mr Phuti Radiphuti, Managing Director".'

The receptionist nodded. 'That is broadly speaking true, Mma,' she said. 'And now can you tell me what I can do for you?'

Mma Ramotswe took a deep breath. This, she suspected would be the difficult part. 'I would like to speak to Mr Radiphuti.'

The receptionist waited a few moments before replying. Then she said, 'There are many people who would like to speak to Mr Radiphuti, Mma.'

Mma Ramotswe remained calm. 'I think he will be happy to see me,' she said.

The receptionist bristled. 'Mr Radiphuti is a very busy man,' she retorted. 'Every day there are people who come here and say that he would be happy to see them. But I do not think he is always happy, Mma, to be interrupted with this thing and that thing.' She paused, allowing time for her words to sink in. 'Mr Radiphuti needs time to think about all the things he has to do. How can he think about them if he is having to speak to every-body who wants to see him? I do not think he can, Mma – with the best will in the world, I do not see how he can.'

It would have been easy for Mma Ramotswe to barge past this obstructive receptionist. Viewed as two players of a contact sport – rugby, for example, or American football – there was no doubt at all about who had the advantage. The receptionist was small-boned and did not appear to carry much weight. Mma Ramotswe, by contrast, was traditionally built in all her dimensions and had the receptionist tried to bar her way, she would simply have pro-ceeded, as if running for the touchline, effortlessly pushing her insignificant opponent aside. It would have been no contest from the very beginning, and the goal, Phuti's door, would be reached in seconds. But she did not do that. She did not believe in physical violence of any sort, nor did she believe in escalating a tricky situ-ation. She was a detective, but she was also a psychologist, and, perhaps most importantly of all, she was an adherent of the old Botswana view that a gentle feeling-out of common ground was preferable to a victory that caused the other side to lose face. The *I win, you lose* philosophy had enjoyed rather too much time in the sun of late, but it was not a philosophy of which she approved.

'I see what you mean, Mma,' she said, in as emollient a tone as she could manage. 'You must have a very difficult job keeping people from disturbing Mr Radiphuti. I am sure you do it very well.'

The receptionist sat back in her chair. 'Well, Mma, it is a very hard job, yes.'

'I imagine that you need a lot of training,' Mma Ramotswe continued.

The receptionist nodded. 'Yes, Mma. It is a highly skilled profession.'

'I imagine that you trained somewhere like Johannesburg,' said Mma Ramotswe. 'Or even Cape Town. That sort of training always shows, I think.'

Now the receptionist was beaming with pleasure. 'That's kind of you, Mma. Actually, I trained locally, although I have done some extension courses from the Botswana Institute of Office Practice. I have done three or four of their courses. They are very useful.'

'It shows,' said Mma Ramotswe. And then she said, 'It is very rude of me not to tell you who I am or where I come from, Mma. My name is Precious and I was born in Mochudi.'

The receptionist looked interested. 'I have a cousin in Mochudi,' she said. 'She is a nurse. She is married to a man called Lepodise.'

Mma Ramotswe clapped her hands together. 'They are a very good family, Mma. They are well known up there.'

'Yes, they have a nice place just outside the village. They are related to many people.'

'I know that,' said Mma Ramotswe. 'They are very important. Do you go up there to see your cousin?'

'I do.'

'That must be very nice for the cousin. You can bring her all the news from Gaborone, because I imagine you meet many people here – in your job.'

'That is true, Mma,' said the receptionist. And then, suddenly becoming businesslike, she continued, 'What name shall I give to Mr Radiphuti?'

'Tell him it is Mma Ramotswe.'

'I shall do that,' said the receptionist, reaching for the telephone.

She spoke briefly to Phuti and then replaced the receiver. 'I was right, Mma,' she said. 'Mr Radiphuti will be very happy to see you.'

Mma Ramotswe stifled her laughter. 'You are very kind, Mma,' she said.

The receptionist raised a finger. 'One thing, though, Mma.' Glancing over her shoulder towards Phuti's door, she lowered her voice. 'Mr Radiphuti is not himself, I'm afraid. Please do not excite him. There is something troubling him, I think.'

Mma Ramotswe inclined her head. 'I hear you, Mma. I shall be very careful.'

'Thank you.'

Mma Ramotswe looked at the receptionist. Her unhelpful manner had been extremely irritating, but it was clear that she was a loyal employee and that she had Phuti's interests at heart. So she forgave her the rudeness she had shown, and thanked her again for her help. The encounter had proved the point again, not that it needed further proof: the best response to hostility was a compliment, an expression of affection, a simple smile. It always worked – or almost always.

There was something that she needed to find out, though, before she went into Phuti's office. Now, as casually as she could, she said, 'I see, Mma, that you are Mma Moesi. I saw your name on the board outside.'

'That is me, Mma,' said the receptionist.

Mma Ramotswe felt her heart beating hard. Would it be audible? Could one's heartbeat give a warning to other people?

'You aren't married, are you, to Mr Kagiso Moesi, are you?'

The receptionist laughed. 'My husband, Mma. Do you know him?'

Mma Ramotswe answered quickly. 'No, Mma. It's just that I have heard the name. I can't remember where, and I wondered.'

'Perhaps it was here,' said the receptionist. 'He used to work here. He was head of sales. He left this company about three years ago.'

Mma Ramotswe's heart did not slow down; if anything, its beat increased. 'And now, Mma? Where is he now?'

'He is working for a firm of business consultants,' the receptionist said. 'And he is doing some teaching too – business teaching. He is very busy.'

Mma Ramotswe watched her. This woman was proud of her husband; it showed in the tone of voice in which she spoke of him. Did she know what was going on, she wondered; or, even worse, was she part of it?

Phuti rose from his desk. He was old-fashioned in his manner, and always stood when a lady entered the room. Mma Ramotswe noticed this – with approval. There were some who said that men did not have to stand when people came into a room, but these people who criticised the custom were men, rather than women. And that, Mma Ramotswe thought, was because they were lazy, and if you were lazy it was very useful to be able to say that things requiring you to get to your feet were old-fashioned and no longer necessary. It was common courtesy to rise to your feet in this way because it marked the arrival of the other person and made her feel appreciated. And what was wrong with that?

'Mma Ramotswe . . .' His voice trailed off, and the welcoming smile quickly faded. 'Is everything all right?'

She lost no time in reassuring him. 'It is quite all right, Rra. There is nothing wrong with anything.'

He gestured to a chair, a look of relief on his face. 'It's just that I thought that perhaps Grace . . .'

'Grace is fine, Rra. She is at the office, I think. She will probably be doing some filing. There is always filing to be done.'

He nodded. 'That is what she is best at. Filing. She loves filing.'

'She certainly does,' said Mma Ramotswe, sitting down in the chair he had indicated. As she did so, she patted the arms of the chair fondly. 'This is a very comfortable chair, Rra. Some of the chairs we are required to sit in these days . . .'

Phuti shook his head. 'Oh, Mma, you are so right. They are making chairs that are completely unsuited to people like . . .' Once again, he trailed off.

'People like me?' Mma Ramotswe supplied. 'Traditionally built people, Rra?'

Phuti looked evasive. 'I was not singling you out, Mma. I was just saying that many chairs these days are the wrong shape – for everybody, really, not just those who are particularly . . .'

'Large, Rra?'

Now she remembered her promise to the receptionist. This sort of conversation was potentially unsettling, and so she quickly moved the conversation to safer ground with an enquiry as to how he was.

Phuti lowered his gaze. 'I am all right, Mma Ramotswe. Things are not going particularly well, but there are worse things happening out there and I am grateful I am not . . .' He searched for the right words, and decided upon 'out there'.

'I know you have some business troubles, Rra,' she said.

'I have heard from Grace that there are problems that are worrying you.'

He looked at her intensely, and for a moment she wondered whether she had spoken out of turn in revealing that Mma Makutsi had confided in her. It was possible, she thought, that he might resent being discussed in this way by his wife; but he did not, and he simply sighed and said, 'I am very worried, Mma. I do not mean to burden you, but I can tell you I am very concerned.'

Mma Ramotswe expressed her sympathy in the conventional way – a clucking sound. That sound was more eloquent than any number of words, and Phuti acknowledged it. 'You are very kind, Mma Ramotswe. I know that you have always been our friend.'

'And you and Grace are my friends too,' said Mma Ramotswe. 'And we must help our friends.'

'We must,' said Phuti. 'We must definitely help our friends.'

Mma Ramotswe hesitated. She had not intended to bring up her request quite so soon, but this discussion of friendship provided an obvious pretext for what she wanted now to ask.

'And that is why I am here, Rra,' she said. 'Grace and I wish to help one of her old friends. I need to ask you about that.'

Phuti nodded. 'I am always willing to help, Mma.'

'Thank you, Rra. So I will tell you about a plan that we have, and then I shall tell you something that you need to know about this matter that is bothering you.'

Phuti sat up in his chair. 'About my business problem?'

Mma Ramotswe nodded. 'Yes, but first this plan of ours.'

'I am listening, Mma Ramotswe.'

She took a deep breath. 'There is a woman from Bobonong,' she began. 'She is called Patience, and Grace knew her back in those Bobonong days.'

Phuti frowned. 'Patience? Ah yes, Grace has mentioned that

lady. She is the one who moved to Gaborone with her son not all that long ago. Grace said that she met her out at Mma Potokwani's place. She said something about her getting a job out there.'

'Exactly, Rra,' said Mma Ramotswe. 'That is the lady in question. She moved to Gaborone because she had met a man who works for Water Affairs. He is a Malawian who has been living in this country for some time. He knows all about pumps.'

'I do not know much about pumps,' observed Phuti. 'Mind you, I do not have much to do with them.'

'Nor do I,' said Mma Ramotswe. 'I like to hear them pumping away and to see water coming out of the pipe. I like that.'

Phuti managed a faint smile – the first time he had smiled at this meeting, which was unusual, as he was normally cheerful enough. 'There is no Motswana who does not like that sight,' he said. 'We appreciate water.'

'We do indeed,' agreed Mma Ramotswe. 'To think that there are places where they complain about rain. Can you imagine that, Rra? Imagine complaining about rain. It is very hard to picture such a thing. I cannot do it, in fact.'

'It all depends on what you are used to,' said Phuti. 'If you live in a very wet place, then you get fed up with rain. If you live in a dry place, like Botswana, you cannot get enough rain.'

'That is true,' said Mma Ramotswe, and added, 'We need rain at the moment, Rra. The land needs a good soaking.'

He looked out of the window. 'Over there,' he said. 'Over there is where the clouds come from. I sit at my desk and look at the sky through my window, and I hope that the clouds will come. I know that is a bad thing because the clouds never come when you sit and look for them. But I cannot stop myself from looking.'

'I do that too, Rra. The whole country does that. When it gets really hot, then the whole country, I think, will be looking at the sky in that direction. If you were a thief and you wanted to steal everything from Botswana, you would be able to sneak in from behind and get away with everything because the whole country would be gazing over in that direction. Then people would turn round and say, "Oh, where have all our things gone?" I think that there are people who would like to steal everything. Our cattle. Our diamonds. Our elephants. Everything.'

Phuti looked sad. 'Elephants too? Yes, I think you are right, Mma. The government has that big battle up north to deal with those poachers who come in up there. Those people are thieves. They come over the border from Angola and Zambia. From Zimbabwe. And they take the ivory from our elephants. It is theft, that. It is a very serious type of theft.'

It was Mma Ramotswe's turn to sigh – which she did. 'There is a lot that is wrong with the world, Rra, but I must tell you about that lady from Bobonong. She has moved down here, as I said, and she is very happy with her new boyfriend. But her problem is that she has a bad-news son. He is very bad news, I think.'

Phuti made a tutting sound. 'He should be given a spanking, I think.'

Mma Ramotswe bit her lip. So, Phuti and Mma Makutsi were of one view on that subject; that was unexpected. She had thought that he might be a bit less outspoken on matters of discipline, as he had always seemed to her to be gentle in his disposition, but perhaps it was only when the subject of delinquent boys arose that these views emerged.

'I think it is sometimes not quite that simple,' she said mildly. 'I think that it might be better – these days – to reason with boys like that.'

Her suggestion was put mildly, but Phuti's response was robust. 'No, Mma Ramotswe, that's exactly the wrong thing to do.

Modern people have been saying that sort of thing since 1961. They have been saying that. They have been saying, "Talk, talk, talk – that is the solution to bad behaviour." Well, I can tell you, Mma, that this has not led to there being less bad behaviour from teenage boys. The opposite, I think, is true. If we say, "Oh, we must talk about your behaviour," these boys say, "Oh yes, please talk – we are listening very carefully," and while we are talking, they go off and do the things they should not be doing. And because we are all busy talking about how they might behave in a better way, we do not see that they are not even there to listen to our lectures, but have gone off to do various bad things.'

'1961, Rra? Are you sure about that?'

He was. 'I read about it, Mma. I read an article that said that 1961 was the year when all this nonsense started. Before that, bad behaviour was not tolerated. If a young person behaved badly then he knew that he would get a spanking. And boys are not fools, Mma. If they knew they would get a good spanking, then they would think, It's not worth doing these bad things, no matter how much I like bad things. That is how they would think, Mma. There is a lot of scientific proof of all that, Mma. Lots.'

Mma Ramotswe raised an eyebrow. 'People say all sorts of things are proved by science, Rra. You have to be careful.' She paused. 'But let's not argue about that, Rra. The fact of the matter is that Patience has this difficult son, and he is being rude to this new boyfriend. He is making it very hard for her. And it is her only chance of happiness, Rra. This new man is the man she has been hoping to meet all her life, and now it is all being put in peril by this selfish boy.'

She saw Phuti's eyes narrow. He was not pleased with this story.

'I would deal with that young man,' he said through tight lips. 'I would teach him not to be unkind to his poor mother.'

'Well, Rra, she has tried to talk to him, but he is not listening. And she is very upset by this.'

'So she should be,' said Phuti. 'That is because she must have allowed him to get his own way too much. You should never let children get their own way all the time. Some of the time, yes, but not all the time. There is a very delicate balance there.'

Mma Ramotswe agreed that there was. Then she continued, 'Grace and I are very keen to help Patience, Rra, and so we have made this plan. It is a very good plan, I think, but it involves Patience and the boy leaving the house of this Water Affairs man and moving into your house for a while. Not for too long, I think – maybe a month or so, maybe less.'

Phuti stared at her. 'Moving into our house?'

'Yes, Rra. Grace says that you have the room. She says that you have two bedrooms that are not used and that Patience can have one of these and the boy – he is called Modise – can have the other one.'

'And then?' asked Phuti.

'Then we shall put our plan into effect.'

'And what is that plan?'

Mma Ramotswe hesitated. 'There are still some details to be sorted out, Rra. We shall tell you as soon as it is ready.' She paused. 'But in the meantime, are you happy for this poor woman and her son to come and stay at your place?'

Phuti shrugged. 'It looks as if I don't have much choice.'

'Nobody is forcing you, Rra.'

'Well, if Grace wants it. Yes.' He looked pensive, and Mma Ramotswe saw what she thought was an inner struggle. And she was right, as he now went on, 'No, Mma, I would be happy for this lady and her son to stay at our place. She is a friend of Grace, as you say, and you cannot say to friends that they cannot stay at your place. You cannot do that, Mma Ramotswe.'

She thanked him. Within each of us, she thought, there are two people: the person who thinks first of himself or herself, who is not all that much concerned with others, and then there is the person who worries more about what is expected by others – about what, for instance, the old Botswana morality would suggest be done. And in that respect, there could be little doubt: the old Botswana morality, followed as of second nature by her late father, Obed Ramotswe, would be clear: you did not turn friends away from your house if they needed a roof over their heads; you simply did not.

'I do not think they will bother you much, Rra,' she reassured him. 'I do not think the boy will behave badly in your house.'

She hoped that was true, but even as she said it, she wondered what would happen if the boy were to prove troublesome. Phuti would not tolerate it, she imagined, and might be tempted to confront the young man. That was understandable, of course, but could easily derail the plan that had occurred to her in the supermarket car park and that Mma Makutsi had so enthusiastically supported.

She looked at Phuti. 'It will be important for you to bite your tongue, Rra,' she said. 'I know it is a lot to ask, but it might be best if you did not try to discipline this young person when he is staying with you.'

Phuti shrugged. 'He is another person's son,' he said. 'I will not interfere.'

'Good,' said Mma Ramotswe. 'And now this other matter – this business problem. Let me tell you what I think about that.'

Chapter Nine

Never Point Out the Obvious

'Now, Rra, these chairs,' Mma Ramotswe began. 'Not your chairs, of course, but these other chairs that people are buying. What can be done about them?'

Phuti frowned. He looked up at the ceiling, and then looked down again. He sighed – a heartfelt sigh that seemed to go on for rather a long time; so long, in fact, that Mma Ramotswe felt that he was in danger of deflating before her eyes.

'Are you sure you are all right, Rra?' she asked.

Phuti nodded. 'I am just breathing,' he said. 'I am always breathing, Mma.'

'Good,' said Mma Ramotswe. 'But there is still a question: what can be done about these people who are taking all your business?'

Phuti began another sigh, but then stopped himself. 'I don't think there is anything I can do, Mma Ramotswe. I think it is the end.' He fixed her with a gaze, and it was a sad one. 'There comes a time in the life of every business when you have to ...' His voice trailed away.

She did not like the sound of this. 'You have to what, Rra?'

'When you have to say that the time has come,' he said. 'When you have to accept that the world has moved on without you.'

She drew in her breath. 'But, Rra,' she protested, 'things cannot be that bad. Surely not.'

Phuti shook his head. Reaching for a folder, he extracted a sheet of paper and pushed it across his desk to Mma Ramotswe. 'There are many figures on that piece of paper,' he said. 'You don't have to look at all of them. Just look at the figure in the right-hand column – at the bottom. Look at that one, Mma. And you will see two things about it: it is a big number, and it has a minus sign in front of it.'

Mma Ramotswe glanced at the piece of paper. She was no expert in accounts, but she was still a businesswoman and knew how to read a simple balance sheet. And there was no doubt in her mind that this was not what anybody would describe as a 'healthy' balance sheet.

'I see,' she said, her voice lowered in the sympathy that comes with reading bad news.

'Yes,' said Phuti. 'That is the position. We have those outstanding liabilities to suppliers, some of whom are beginning to get anxious about payment. Suppliers who get anxious may suddenly say, "Payment in advance, please." And when they say that, there is usually no way out. It is the end. You cannot sell furniture that you do not have because your suppliers will not give it to you. You cannot make a profit out of non-existent sales, Mma.'

Mma Ramotswe handed back the sheet of paper. She wanted to know how this situation had arisen. How could it be that customers could so quickly be lost to a rival, especially to one who had only just started trading?

'They undercut me,' said Phuti. 'And every time I start a special promotion, the day before we begin it, they come up with something cheaper. It's as if they know what we are planning and then make sure that they beat anything we offer.' He sighed again, a shorter sigh this time, but still one that seemed to come from some deep well of despair within him.

She gave a start. She knew immediately what was happening here. But before she could say anything, Phuti went on, 'And then there are their advertising campaigns. They have been very effective, Mma Ramotswe, and they are planning another one soon.'

Mma Ramotswe shook her head sadly. 'I have heard of that. Grace told me.'

'Yes,' said Phuti. 'They run these campaigns for their new chairs. They turn people's heads with all their claims. They make people think that they must have one of these new chairs if they are to be anybody at all. It is a status thing, I think. *Get one of our new chairs and you will be up-to-the-minute fashionable.* It is ridiculous, Mma. They make people feel dissatisfied with the life they are leading – they make them unhappy with the chairs they've been sitting in all their lives.'

He was right, thought Mma Ramotswe. Phuti had put his finger on what advertising was all about. 'That is true, Rra,' she said. 'But . . .'

He waited for her, and she looked out of the window, towards the horizon, a green line of acacias. There was a slight greyness in the lower part of the sky, that grey that could suddenly become purple and then, before one knew it, billow up into great rain clouds. She hardly dared hope. A sky that was stared at would never rain; you had to wait; you had to wait in hope.

'But, Mma Ramotswe?'

She brought herself back to where she was – in Phuti Radiphuti's office, discussing chairs.

'There is an expression, Rra. I have heard people say it. It is: *You must fight fire with fire.*' She gave Phuti an enquiring look. 'Have you heard that saying, Rra?'

He had. 'But I'm not sure that it can be true, Mma. I think you fight fire with water, do you not?'

Mma Ramotswe smiled. 'That is true, Rra, but I think that people are thinking about something a bit different. I think they are saying that you must use the same tactics as other people are using if you want to get anywhere. So, in this case, you must fight advertisements with advertisements.'

For a while Phuti stared at her without responding. Then he said, 'But advertisements are very expensive, Mma Ramotswe.'

'They are,' she countered. 'But going out of business is even more expensive in the long run.'

'But what can I advertise? If I advertise a sale, then they will splash some sort of offer all over the place and people will go to them. It has happened every time, Mma.'

His air of defeat seemed to have deepened, and for a moment or two Mma Ramotswe herself felt discouraged. But then she thought of what she might unwittingly have discovered, and her sense of justice pricked her into action. 'I think I may be able to say something about that, Rra,' she began. 'I think I may have an idea about how that happens.'

Phuti did not seem to have heard her. 'It's hopeless, Mma Ramotswe,' he said. 'These people are too clever for me.'

She repeated what she had said, and this time he looked up, puzzled but interested. 'What do you know, Mma?'

'I think that there is somebody in your company – here in

148

the Double Comfort Furniture Store – who may be passing on information about your pricing.'

He stared at her in disbelief. 'That is not possible, Mma. I am the one who makes those decisions. My staff do not hear about them until the last moment.' He paused. 'That was because I was worried about the exact possibility you mention, Mma Ramotswe. I know all about how important it is to keep trade secrets.' He shook his head. 'No, I do not think that can be happening.'

Mma Ramotswe glanced over her shoulder towards the door that led into the receptionist's room. Phuti followed her gaze.

'We cannot be heard outside,' he said. 'And anyway, that is only Mma Moesi. She is a very trusted employee.'

'And her husband, Rra? He was an employee too?'

Phuti hesitated. 'He used to be, yes. But now he is working for somebody else.'

There was something in his manner that alerted her to the possibility that he had reservations about Kagiso Moesi. Mma Makutsi had an expression she used to describe such speech: *speaking with only half your tongue.* Well, that was what Phuti was doing, she thought.

'Was he a trusted employee too?' she asked. 'Would you call him that?'

The question seemed to make Phuti uncomfortable. 'We did not part on the best of terms, I'm afraid. That was unfortunate, because of his wife. She had worked here for a long time, and I did not think it right that she should be judged by her husband.'

Mma Ramotswe's mind was racing ahead. She had encountered situations like this before, where a husband and wife were involved, and they always gave rise to particular difficulties. It was simple enough if both spouses were in the wrong, but it was never easy if you had a guilty husband and an innocent wife, or vice versa. She thought about what Phuti had said so far. Kagiso Moesi had left on bad terms: what did that mean? Had there simply been a disagreement between him and Phuti, a difference of opinion on how some business matter should be handled, or had there been something much more serious – such as an accusation of dishonesty or, perhaps, disloyalty?

She did not get the impression that Phuti was keen to talk about it, but she pressed him nonetheless. It was important, she felt, to find out a bit more about Kagiso Moesi before drawing any conclusions as to what role he might be playing in this matter.

'I don't like to pry, Rra,' she began. Of course, that was precisely what anybody said before they engaged in prying, but at least it gave some impression of proper reticence. 'No, I don't like to pry, but I was wondering what this Moesi did that led to . . .' She hesitated before deciding that 'bad feeling' was the right expression. 'That led to bad feeling between the two of you, Rra.'

Phuti looked out of the window. That, Mma Ramotswe knew, was always a sign that somebody found a subject awkward and would be unwilling to speak about it.

'He was a bit too fond of certain things,' he said.

He directed his gaze back to Mma Ramotswe. His expression gave nothing away.

'Uh,' said Mma Ramotswe. 'I see.' But she thought: what on earth does this mean? Clovis Andersen would have described it as 'an answer that is not really an answer'. He was good on that topic, and had many examples of how people might try to avoid answering a question. One technique was to respond to a question of one's own devising. Another was to change the subject entirely and to talk about some quite different matter – usually one that put one in a positive light. That was a favourite device of politicians, she had noticed: a question put to a politician about some grave misdeed on his or her part might be answered with a set of positive statistics about the progress of the economy, the success of school-building projects, or a recital of future construction schemes that were on the point of beginning. Phuti's answer was in a different category: he had replied to her, but had done so in terms so vague that nobody was any the wiser.

She thought of the possibilities. All of us might be said to be too fond of certain things, in that we all, surely without exception, had at least one or two failings. She herself might admit to being too fond of fat cakes, while Mma Potokwani might be said to be excessively fond of fruit cake. In his younger days, Charlie might have been described – with some justification – as being far too fond of sitting on an empty oil drum in his lunch hour and watching young women walk past. Now, of course, Charlie was a married man, and those oil-drum days should be firmly in the past. That was not to say that young men should not take pleasure in looking at young women – a world in which that sort of thing was entirely discouraged would be a very dull one – but they should do so with courtesy and respect. They should not leer or whistle, but should behave in such a way, in short, that the young women, if they noticed the glance, would feel complimented and appreciated, rather than uneasy. And women, of course, could appreciate men, although not always in the way in which men might like to be appreciated or admired. Mma Ramotswe might say of a man that he was good-looking, but she would probably not be referring to bulging muscles or broad shoulders, but to a certain cast in his features, and in particular to kindness. A man with a kind face was her ideal, which may have been one of the reasons why she was drawn to Mr J. L. B. Matekoni in the first place. His features might not be all that regular, but his face was unmistakably kind.

And while she was contemplating human failings, she thought of Mma Makutsi's particular weakness, which was shoes. Mma Makutsi took care with her appearance and always dressed neatly, but her taste in dresses was relatively muted when compared with her choice of shoes. When it came to footwear, it seemed as if all restraint was thrown to the wind, and she chose shoes that were as fashionable and elaborate as possible, often making no apparent attempt to co-ordinate their colour with the colour of the garments she wore. She would have no hesitation, if pushed, to say of Mma Makutsi that she was too fond of shoes, but would not say that because there was nothing wrong in taking pleasure in one's shoes, and nobody was harmed by this enthusiasm. And Mma Makutsi's shoes, of course, were unique, in that they appeared to speak, although Mma Ramotswe was satisfied that this was simply a trick of the hearing, of much the same sort that will make us think we have heard our name being called, or a snatch of a song, when in reality there has been nothing. The voice of Mma Makutsi's shoes may be no more than the creaking of a house – for all houses creak in one way or another – or the sound of the wind in the branches of a tree. There is rarely complete silence – there is always noise of some sort if we listen hard enough, and those faint noises, those seemingly distant noises, may easily seem to us to be something that they are not.

Thoughts of Charlie raised a particular possibility in her mind. Was Kagiso Moesi too fond of women? Was that what Phuti was alluding to in his typically quiet way? She decided to find out.

'So he was rather fond of the ladies, Rra?' she asked.

Phuti had not imagined that the meaning of his comment was so obvious, and his eyes registered his surprise. 'Ladies, Mma?'

'Yes. There are two things of which men are typically too fond, Rra: beer and ladies. It is possible that Moesi liked beer too much, but I think it is more likely that he suffered from the second failing. Both can create big problems for men – and indeed for other people.' She paused. 'Not that I am one of those people who want to stop men from being fond of anything at all – and there are such ladies, Rra. All I would say is that men should like beer and ladies in moderation. "All things in moderation" is what I say.'

Phuti shook his head, but not in disagreement. This was more a shake of the head in response to the human condition – or rather, to the male condition. 'There are many men who like beer too much, Mma Ramotswe – you are right about that. They are happiest when they are drinking beer, I think.'

'But Moesi is not like that? He was not one of those happy beer men?'

Phuti thought for a few moments. 'I believe he sometimes liked beer. But not very much. No, Mma, it was the other thing.'

'Ladies?'

Phuti lowered his voice, and Mma Ramotswe understood why. Mma Moesi was sitting directly outside.

'He was not a bad man in that department,' Phuti said. 'He was never impolite to ladies, and he never tried to become too close to them. But he used to pay them too many compliments, Mma.'

Mma Ramotswe said that she knew the type. 'He was a flirt, Rra? Was that it? Did he flirt with the ladies?'

Phuti nodded. 'Exactly, Mma. That is exactly what he did. He would say to a lady customer "You are looking very pretty today in that nice dress" or "I think your eyes are very bright today, Mma" or, as I once heard him say to a young woman who was wearing white, "You look just like the icing on the cake, Mma". That sort of thing.'

Mma Ramotswe smiled at that. 'A very peculiar compliment,

Phuti. Icing on the cake? That is a very strange thing to say to anybody.'

'I agree,' said Phuti. 'I spoke to him about it. I told him that it was unprofessional to say things like that to lady customers. They did not come to a furniture shop to have a man make remarks about their appearance, even if they were looking pretty. I said that was not the point. And I also told him that many of these ladies had husbands or boyfriends and these men would not like the thought that such things were being said.'

'And did he listen to you, Rra?'

Phuti sighed. 'Does anybody listen to anybody, Mma? Most people do not want to take advice from other people. Most people think that they are right about most things and other people are wrong.'

Mma Ramotswe felt she had to disagree. 'Oh, I don't know, Rra. I think there are times when people will take advice. I think there are times when people will change the way they behave when somebody points out to them that they have been doing something wrong.'

Phuti did not seem convinced. 'Well, he certainly was not like that, Mma Ramotswe. He seemed to pay no attention. And then one day, I heard him saying to a lady who had come in to buy a lounge suite that she reminded him of a delicious ripe pumpkin. I could tell that she did not like this, as she hit him with her handbag. It was not a serious blow, Mma, but I saw it, and I saw him sneak off like a guilty schoolboy.'

Mma Ramotswe said that Moesi had probably richly deserved the rebuff. 'You'd think he'd learn,' she said.

'I had to fire him then,' said Phuti. 'Getting rid of somebody is something that I do not like doing, but he would not listen to me and I could not have that sort of thing going on in the

Double Comfort Furniture Store. We have our reputation to consider.'

Mma Ramotswe said that she assumed he took it badly.

'He was very cross, Mma. He said that I was somebody who wanted to stop people behaving naturally. He said that any lady would love to be compared to a pumpkin. I said I did not think that was true.'

Phuti stopped, and looked enquiringly at Mma Ramotswe. 'Would you not be upset if somebody said you looked like a pumpkin, Mma?'

Mma Ramotswe thought about this. Perhaps the answer would depend on the source of the remark. She would be happy for Mr J. L. B. Matekoni to make the comparison, but she was not sure that she would like it to come from anybody else – and certainly not from a furniture salesman whom she had just met. 'I think you did the right thing, Phuti,' she said. 'You cannot have that sort of thing going on, even if he never went any further.' She paused. 'Did Mma Moesi know about any of this?' she asked.

Phuti looked uncomfortable. 'I never told her about it. And I said to Moesi that he could give his wife some other reason for leaving the job.'

Mma Ramotswe understood. 'You wanted to protect her?'

He lowered his head. 'I suppose so. I know that you are not meant to give people false reasons for doing things, but I did not want to put their marriage at risk. I think that she does not know that her husband goes around making these pumpkin-type remarks to ladies.'

'Perhaps it is best for a wife not to know that sort of thing,' said Mma Ramotswe. But then she thought about it for a few moments longer, and added, 'Although there is a strong case for telling people about things they do not know about. Husbands should not be able to think they can get away with doing things that their wives would not tolerate.'

Now they lapsed into silence. Mma Ramotswe watched Phuti. She felt that he looked somehow defeated – perhaps the memory of the disagreement with Moesi, coupled with the contemplation of the dip in his business fortunes, was just too much for him. She hesitated for a few moments, and then made up her mind. What was required here was decisiveness and action. She had a plan – in fact, she had more than one plan, and the time had now come to take the first steps in rescuing Phuti from his plight.

'There is something that I must tell you, Phuti,' she began. 'It is not an easy thing to say.'

He looked up, his face full of weariness.

'It makes no difference,' he said. 'Everything is . . . ' He waved a hand. 'Everything is all over the place. I am finished, Mma Ramotswe. It makes no difference. The bank can come in and start taking the stock away.'

Mma Ramotswe gasped. 'That is not the way to talk, Rra,' she said. 'Nothing is finished until . . . ' She was not sure how to complete the call to action. 'Nothing is finished until it is finished.'

Phuti stared at her. 'I do not disagree with that, Mma. But as far as I can see, it *is* finished.'

Now was the time for firmness, and for the plan to be revealed.

'It is very clear to me,' Mma Ramotswe began, 'that sensitive information is being passed from the Double Comfort Furniture Store to its competitors – these, these . . . ' She poked a finger in the air. 'These other chair people. They are hearing about your promotions and then undercutting you to put you out of business. They are deliberately taking a loss in order to do that. So, we must ask ourselves who is passing that information.'

Phuti sighed. 'I cannot see who would do that. All my staff are loyal.'

Mma Ramotswe shook her head. 'Loyal people can cause great damage unwittingly.'

He looked puzzled. 'You say somebody is making a mistake?'

'More or less,' said Mma Ramotswe. 'But first you have to ask yourself: who has a reason to harm you? Who would like to see the Double Comfort Furniture Store end up bankrupt?'

Phuti looked blank. 'I do not make enemies very often,' he said. 'I cannot think of anybody.'

She waited a few moments for effect. Then she said, almost whispering, 'Moesi?'

Phuti frowned. 'Him? Maybe he is a bit cross still—'

'Maybe he is *very* cross,' interjected Mma Ramotswe. 'There is something you must remember about anger, Rra. It grows. People go away and brood on things that have been done to them, and their anger grows. Then it becomes a great cloud, hanging over them. Always there. Always rumbling away. That is how anger works, Phuti.'

'But Moesi has nothing to do with the business any longer,' Phuti protested.

Mma Ramotswe raised an eyebrow. Then, half turning in her chair, she pointed silently at the closed door behind which lay the reception area and Mma Moesi's desk.

Phuti's jaw dropped. 'Oh, Mma.' He struggled to speak, but again all he could say was, 'Oh.' Then he managed a weak, almost despairing 'No', followed by another 'Oh'.

Never point out the obvious, Clovis Andersen had written – just let it sink in.

Chapter Ten

Meeting an Actor

'Mr Tutume?' asked Mma Makutsi as she sipped at her first cup of office tea the following morning. 'Mr Tutume, the drama teacher?'

Charlie was working in the garage that morning and he had joined Mma Ramotswe and Mma Makutsi for the tea break, leaving Mr J. L. B. Matekoni and Fanwell to cope with a recalcitrant gearbox next door. Now, coming into a conversation that had already started, he joined in with confidence. 'Oh yes, I remember him,' he said. 'The one who is always shouting. *Shout, shout, shout.* "All right, I can hear you, Rra! No need to turn the volume up quite so high!"'

Mma Ramotswe sighed. 'He teaches acting, Charlie. He is not shouting, as you put it. He speaks clearly – that is all.'

Mma Makutsi agreed. She shook a finger at Charlie. 'That's the trouble with your generation, Charlie. You people do not open your mouths when you speak. *Mumble, mumble, mumble.* Half the time nobody can understand what you people are saying.'

The criticism washed over Charlie. 'That's because you don't know the latest words, Mma Makutsi,' he retorted. 'The words you use – no offence, of course – are very old ones. They are not modern.'

Mma Makutsi looked up from her tea. 'I speak correctly, Charlie. I use words that you will find in the dictionary, whether it's a Setswana dictionary or an English dictionary – they are all there. I do not make up words just because I like the sound of them.'

Charlie shook his head. 'No, Mma. Nobody is making up words. These modern words, the words we use, are all out there.' He pointed to the world beyond the window; to the world beyond the Tlokweng Road, the houses, the offices, the traffic. 'Go out and listen to what people are saying. Nobody is making them up.'

Mma Makutsi had the bit between her teeth. 'Charlie, these new words that people like you use are not proper words. Why call beer *spinza* when you can call it beer? What is wrong with *beer*?'

Charlie smirked. 'People laugh at you if you just say beer. That is what old people call it, Mma – no offence.'

The light from the window caught the lenses of Mma Makutsi's glasses: a warning glint. 'And *zaka*,' she snapped. 'What is wrong with the word *money*? Is *zaka* more valuable, perhaps? And why call a one-hundred-pula note a *clipper*? Doesn't that mean hair-dresser, Charlie?'

Charlie laughed. 'Oh, that is very funny, Mma. *Chilla, chilla,* Mma!'

It was hard for Mma Ramotswe to remain uninvolved. This was a vintage exchange. 'I think Charlie is telling you to relax, Mma Makutsi,' she said.

'There!' crowed Charlie. 'At least Mma Ramotswe understands. She's a modern lady, Mma Makutsi – she knows these words.'

Mma Makutsi sat back in her chair, glaring at Charlie.

'Don't be angry with me, Mma Makutsi,' said Charlie. 'I am just having some fun. You don't need to call the *bo-4*.'

Mma Makutsi frowned. 'What is this *bo-4*?'

'Police,' said Charlie. 'That is what some guys – some *majita* – call them. A *majita* is a guy, Mma. A *brazene* is a brother. A *frying pan* is a liar.'

Mma Makutsi clapped her hands together. 'See!' she exclaimed. 'You see – that is what I am talking about. It is all nonsense. Why call a liar a *frying pan*? Where is the sense in that?'

Mma Ramotswe felt it was time to intervene. Tea breaks could very easily degenerate into protracted discussions, and when Charlie was involved they could decline even further.

'I am going to see Mr Tutume,' she said. 'And I thought you might come with me, Mma Makutsi.'

'And me?' Charlie interjected. 'Could I come too, Mma? This is meant to be one of my days for the agency. I do not want to spend it under a car.'

Mma Ramotswe glanced at Mma Makutsi, who shrugged.

'Very well, Charlie. You can come with Mma Makutsi and me, but you must behave yourself.'

'And don't use any of your slang in front of Mr Tutume,' said Mma Makutsi. 'Remember that he is a teacher, and you must treat him with respect.'

'I know how to behave,' Charlie said, a note of resentment in his voice.

'Of course you do, Charlie,' said Mma Ramotswe.

She looked at Mma Makutsi. 'I shall tell you why we need to visit Mr Tutume. It is because he is the man for amateur dramatics in this town, Mma.'

Charlie looked puzzled. 'And so?' he asked.

Mma Ramotswe addressed Mma Makutsi. 'Our plan,' she said.

It took Mma Makutsi a few moments to work out what Mma Ramotswe meant, but then she nodded. 'Of course.' She glanced at Charlie and added, 'I suppose he will need to know.'

'Yes,' said Mma Ramotswe. She turned to Charlie. 'This is a very confidential matter, Charlie. You understand that, don't you?'

'I have always understood about keeping my mouth closed, Mma,' said Charlie, making a zipping movement across his lips. 'Believe me, I have always respected confidence. I know that as a detective.'

'Trainee detective,' Mma Makutsi interjected. 'Junior trainee detective.'

'Be that as it may,' continued Mma Ramotswe, 'this matter which I am about to explain to you, Charlie, is a delicate one. It is a private matter – not one of our paying cases, but it is still very important. It involves the happiness of an old friend of Mma Makutsi.'

'And the happiness of a young boy,' added Mma Makutsi. 'In the long run it involves his happiness too. And also the happiness of a civil servant. All of these people.'

'Yes,' agreed Mma Ramotswe. 'That is why we should handle it very carefully.'

Even as she said this, she reflected on what they were about to do, and on the risk that the whole thing not only might not work, but could conceivably make matters worse. That was the trouble with plans that seemed relatively simple and straightforward on first examination: if they went wrong, the outcome might be far from what was desired.

Now she revealed to Charlie the story of Patience and her new boyfriend.

'Poor guy,' said Charlie after she had finished. 'This man has to put up with that boy? Bad news, Mma. He should give him a clip on the ear, Mma. Or get a big stick.'

Mma Ramotswe sighed. This was not the first such solution that had been proposed to her. And it was interesting that this sort of approach was suggested by men. Was it only women who saw the subtler aspects of this sad story? But then she thought: if men made a suggestion as to how to deal with male behaviour, should one ignore it? Was it possible that men understood how boys and men thought?

For a moment she wavered, but then she remembered something. Obed Ramotswe had never raised his hand to anybody, and he was as fine an example of a man as one would find anywhere. Not all men thought the same way. Not all men went through the world pushing and boasting and breaking things. That was not the only way open to men, even if there were plenty of men like that; those people belonged to the past, in her view. And she would stick to her view. 'You cannot solve problems of bad behaviour just by hitting people, Charlie,' she said.

He looked at her defiantly. 'But, Mma, when I was young, we knew that if you were rude to somebody like a teacher or an elder, you were beaten. Whack. Like that. Result? Nobody gave any cheek to teachers or elders. Or policemen. Nobody.'

Mma Ramotswe was patient. 'If you are violent with people, Charlie, then they are violent in return. All violence leads to more violence. Surely that is well known.'

Charlie shook his head. 'No, Mma. If somebody – a bad person, say – thinks you are going to be violent towards him, what does he do? He makes sure that he isn't violent in the first place. And so that is one example, Mma, of how violence stops violence, rather than leading to more violence.'

He was pleased with this statement, and Mma Ramotswe could see that he was silently repeating it to himself, satisfied at the force of his argument. She decided that she would not pursue

the matter, as Charlie tended to dig in if one contradicted him.
And Mma Makutsi was inclined to do that too, although not as
frequently, and not as stubbornly.

'Let's not argue about these things,' Mma Ramotswe said
firmly. 'Nobody is going to threaten that boy with physical pun-
ishment. We are not going to do it that way.'

Charlie looked sullen. 'Then he will continue to behave badly
to that poor Water Affairs man. And they will be thrown out.
Then it will be back to Bobonong for your friend, Mma Makutsi.
Back to the sticks.'

Mma Makutsi bristled. 'Bobonong is not the sticks, Charlie.
Bobonong is an important centre now.'

'Centre of what?' muttered Charlie under his breath. 'Centre
of yawn-yawn?'

He had not intended Mma Makutsi to hear him, but she
did. She was about to respond when Mma Ramotswe raised her
voice. 'I think we should tell Charlie what we are planning,' she
said. And then, without waiting, she went on, 'Patience – Mma
Makutsi's friend – is going to say she is leaving her new boyfriend.
She has spoken to him about this already, hasn't she, Mma?'

Mma Makutsi confirmed that Patience had laid the ground-
work. 'She has taken him into her confidence. He wants to save
the relationship but he cannot bear the bad behaviour of Modise –
he is the son, you see. So he is in on this plan. He has agreed.'

Mma Ramotswe resumed the explanation. 'Patience and
Modise will go to stay with Mma Makutsi. Then, while they are
there, she will start inviting another man to the house.'

Charlie frowned. 'But what about the Water Affairs man? What
will he think?'

It was Mma Makutsi who answered. 'Charlie, you did not hear
what we said. He will know that this other man is part of the plan.

He will be a very different sort of man. He will make sure that Modise does not like him at all.'

It dawned on Charlie. 'Ah,' he said. 'I see it. The boy will think that the new man is not a good thing at all. He will want his mother to go back to the previous man.'

'That is right, Charlie,' said Mma Ramotswe. 'It will teach the boy a lesson. Appreciate what you have, or you may end up with something much worse.'

Charlie chuckled as he thought about the plan. 'It is a very good idea,' he said. Then, after a pause, he said, 'Is Mr Tutume going to be the new man? Is that the idea?'

Mma Ramotswe explained that they would ask for his help. 'We helped him in the past,' she said. 'Remember that, Mma Makutsi?'

'Yes, I remember, Mma. We helped him sort out that argument over his inheritance – that argument over cattle. He was very grateful.'

'He said that he hoped one day he would be able to repay our help,' said Mma Ramotswe.

'It was what we call a pro bono case,' Mma Makutsi explained to Charlie. 'When we do not charge a fee, we say that we are doing it pro bono. That is the technical term, Charlie, that you should remember if you ever become a proper detective.'

Charlie resented the tone of this remark. 'I am on that career path, Mma Makutsi,' he snapped. 'Mma Ramotswe has told me that my training will only take another few months.'

Mma Makutsi looked doubtful. 'We'll see,' she said.

'You're doing well, Charlie,' Mma Ramotswe assured him. 'Carry on observing things. Carry on studying *The Principles of Private Detection*. Everything is there.'

'I have read that book twice,' said Charlie.

'Then you must read it again,' Mma Makutsi advised. 'Read it two more times. Three more times, maybe. Then it will be lodged in your mind. You will see something and you will think: yes, Clovis Andersen has something to say about that.'

Mma Ramotswe agreed. It was extraordinary, she felt, how Clovis Andersen had something to say that could guide one's response to almost any situation. There was no other book remotely like that, she thought, although there were some who spoke in those terms of the Bible. She was not so sure. The Bible had its place, of course, but it had very little to say about how to follow people, how to get information out of those who did not want to give it to you, or how to distinguish between relevant and irrelevant facts. For that, there was no doubt but that *The Principles of Private Detection* was the superior text.

They finished their tea and Mma Ramotswe looked at her watch. 'Mr Tutume said that he could see me during the school break,' she said. 'That is in half an hour.'

'Then we should go,' said Mma Makutsi.

'You may drive, Charlie,' said Mma Ramotswe. 'Do not go fast. Take your time.'

'Yes,' said Mma Makutsi. 'Where does Clovis Andersen say that, Charlie? Where does he say, *Take your time?*'

Charlie scratched his head. 'Somewhere,' he said at last. 'You're right, Mma. He says it somewhere, but I am not sure exactly where.'

'Not good enough,' said Mma Makutsi reprovingly. 'More study required, I think.'

Mma Ramotswe said nothing. She could not have answered that question. Where did Clovis Andersen talk about taking your time? She was not at all sure, but then, as she glanced across the room, it occurred to her that Mma Makutsi did not know either.

*

Mr Olivier Tutume came to greet them in the reception room at Maru-a-Pula School, having been told by the receptionist of their arrival. He was a large man but had that delicacy of gait that some large men have, a suppleness and grace of movement that often goes with an ability to dance. He was bearded and was wearing an open-necked white shirt and neatly pressed khaki trousers. He would not have been picked out in the street as a drama teacher, but then, Mma Ramotswe reflected, it would not have been easy to guess his profession on his appearance alone.

He shook hands with each of them in turn, starting with Mma Ramotswe and ending with Charlie.

'This is quite a visit,' he said. 'Three detectives – all at the same time. That is a rare honour, I think.'

'You are not under suspicion of anything,' said Mma Ramotswe, with a smile. 'You need not worry.'

Mma Makutsi, though, felt that she had to correct him. 'Our colleague, Charlie, is a trainee detective, Rra.'

Charlie gave her a reproachful look. Why did she have to spoil things for him every time – every single time?

Mma Ramotswe noticed this. She now said, 'He is an almost qualified detective, Rra. Very close.'

Mr Tutume gave Charlie an encouraging smile. 'I am sure that you will be very good at it, young man. We all have to start somewhere.' He turned to Mma Ramotswe. 'We could take a walk round the school grounds. The staff room is always crowded at break time and it will be easier to talk outside, I think – especially if you have anything confidential to ask.'

'It is definitely confidential,' said Mma Ramotswe. 'It is a confidential favour we have come to ask, Rra.'

'I am very glad that I might have the chance to help you,' said Mr Tutume. 'I have not forgotten how you helped me a few years ago, Mma Ramotswe. I have not forgotten that I promised I would help you if you ever needed my help.'

'How are your cattle?' asked Mma Ramotswe.

'They are doing very well. Once you had worked out what was going on, I got my proper share of good, healthy cattle, and they have prospered. I had a very good bull. The cows were very happy with him.'

'That is good, Rra,' observed Mma Makutsi. 'Sometimes it is not like that at all.'

'And your brother,' asked Mma Ramotswe, 'the one who was taking all your late father's good cattle and leaving you with the bad ones – what about him, Rra?'

'He is doing well, Mma. He was very ashamed to have been caught and it changed him. He has tried to make it up to me, and I have forgiven him.'

Mma Ramotswe approved of that. 'That is the best thing to do,' she said. 'If we do not forgive, then we end up carrying a big burden on our shoulders.'

Mr Tutume said that he had always thought that too. 'You know, Mma, when I am teaching the children here – the older ones – I get them to act as if they were thinking of wrongs done to them. I get them to walk in the way in which an unforgiving person might walk. And you know what they do? They all stoop as if there was a weight on their shoulders.'

'There you are,' said Mma Ramotswe. 'That proves it, Rra. Forgiveness takes a weight off our shoulders.'

They made their way out into the school gardens. Here and there, under trees or under verandas, the pupils clustered in small, talkative knots.

'The children look happy,' said Mma Ramotswe.

'They are,' said Mr Tutume. 'For the most part, these children know how lucky they are. They are getting the best education that is available anywhere in this half of Africa, I believe.' He paused. 'But, Mma, you must tell me how I can help you.'

'It is a very strange request,' Mma Ramotswe began. 'We need an actor.'

'I see,' said Mr Tutume. 'What sort? And for what?'

'We need a man,' said Mma Makutsi. 'We need a man who can come to my place for visits and who can pretend to be ... '

' ... to be somebody he is not,' supplied Mma Ramotswe. 'That is why this man should be an actor.'

Mr Tutume looked bemused. 'I suppose that's what acting is all about – pretending to be what you are not.'

'This man,' Mma Ramotswe went on to explain, 'should pretend to be the boyfriend of a lady living at Mma Makutsi's place. He should bring her gifts ... '

'Chocolates and so on,' suggested Mma Makutsi.

'Yes, chocolates would do. He should pretend to be courting this lady but he should also pretend to be a very unpleasant man. He should shout a bit. He should be boastful and demanding.'

'That is all very easy to do,' said Mr Tutume. 'Most actors can do that sort of thing very easily.'

'And, in particular,' Mma Ramotswe continued, 'he should make sure that this lady's teenage son should not like him at all. He should make sure that the boy thinks, This is the last man I would like my mother to marry – something like that.'

Mr Tutume stopped where he stood, and they all stopped with him. 'This is a wonderful role,' he said. 'It gives a lot of scope to an actor.' He paused. 'I assume, Mma, that the objective here is to get the boy to think that another man – perhaps a previous suitor – is a far better choice for his mother? Am I right in that assumption?'

'You are exactly right,' said Mma Ramotswe. And she wondered whether her plan was quite that obvious. But there was no point in such speculation; what she wanted to know was whether Mr Tutume, who knew everybody in amateur dramatic circles in Gaborone, would have an actor whom he could recommend. It would have to be an amateur, and it would have to be somebody who was prepared to help a young woman and do so with no expectation of reward.

'Do you know anybody who might act that part for us, Rra?' she asked.

Somewhere in the distance an electric bell rang shrilly, and small groups of children started to make their way back to the classroom blocks.

'Oh,' said Mr Tutume. 'I am the one to do that.'

It was what Mma Ramotswe hoped he would say.

'Are you sure, Rra?' she asked.

'Of course I am sure, Mma Ramotswe. Not only is it a challenging role, but it is also an opportunity to help this poor lady. If we can get this young son of hers to see reason, then that will be a good thing for everybody.' He paused. 'Of course, some teenage boys do not think like the rest of us. You have to bear that in mind.'

'I think I know that, Rra,' said Mma Ramotswe.

'As a teacher I can speak to that,' he continued. 'The years between fourteen and seventeen are a very bad time for a boy. They think they know everything. They think the world does not recognise how much they know. They want to be big men, but they are really small boys. They want girls to like them, but the girls won't notice them. They would like their muscles to be bigger. They would like to be able to drive cars, but the law doesn't allow them to. They would like to drink beer, but that is also not allowed. They are not much use to anybody, really. It is very sad.' He smiled. 'And then, suddenly, at seventeen – sometimes at age sixteen – they grow out of all of that and they become nice once more, just as they were before this terrible thing called adolescence happened to them.'

Mma Makutsi had been nodding her agreement. 'I have heard many people say the same thing,' she said.

'That is because it is true,' said Mr Tutume. 'I think that what I said is true.' He turned to Charlie. 'And what do you think, Rra? You are twenty-something, I think. You must remember what it was like to be fourteen or fifteen.'

Charlie looked embarrassed. He struggled for words.

Mma Ramotswe came to his rescue. 'Charlie was an exception, I think, Rra. He has always been a very nice young man.'

'That is very good,' said Mr Tutume. 'You are very lucky.'

Charlie managed to say the right thing. 'I am lucky to be working with these ladies, Rra. They are very good teachers.'

Mma Makutsi beamed with pleasure. Charlie had his moments, she thought – and this was one of them. 'We do our best, Oliver.'

Mr Tutume hesitated. He glanced at Mma Makutsi, and then smiled. It was a wonderful smile, thought Mma Ramotswe – the sort of smile of which even those members of an audience seated in the very back row would feel the benefit.

'This is all very good,' said Mr Tutume. 'I hope that I have passed my audition. If so, you can tell me when I can assume my role.'

'We shall be in touch,' said Mma Ramotswe. 'It will be very soon. Now we have everything in place, we can begin.' She paused. 'You should never start before you can begin.'

Mr Tutume looked thoughtful. 'I expect I shall agree with you, Mma Ramotswe – once I have worked out what you mean.'

Then he turned and explained, to nobody in particular, but in obvious response to Mma Makutsi's earlier use of his first name, 'And by the way, the name is *Olivier*, not Oliver. A stage name, you see, but everybody uses it now when they talk to me. Not a big thing, but there it is.'

170

Chapter Eleven

Where Are Your Tonsils?

There were two telephone calls to be made. The first was to Mma Potokwani, and the second was to a woman called Bontle Boshelo, owner of a small printing business in the light industrial sites off the Lobatse Road.

Mma Potokwani was not in her office when Mma Ramotswe called, but her assistant agreed to go and find her. 'You can stay on the line, Mma Ramotswe,' she said. 'Mma Potokwani will always want to speak to you.'

Mma Ramotswe said that the willingness was mutual. She was always prepared to speak to Mma Potokwani – about anything, really, but particularly when, as now, she was in the course of implementing a carefully thought-out scheme. The scheme involved Phuti, and she had discussed it with him and obtained his agreement to participate, even if he seemed doubtful as to the prospects of success. 'I really don't see anything working,' he sighed. 'But I suppose there's no harm in your trying, Mma Ramotswe.' He sighed again. 'If you really want to . . . '

She bit her tongue. She would have loved to give him a pep talk, to tell him that he owed it to Mma Makutsi, to their son, and to his employees at the Double Comfort Furniture Store, to do something to prevent his business from folding up in the face of this relentless competition from their rivals. But she knew that pep talks rarely worked once the person to whom they were addressed had passed the point of caring. Phuti, for some reason, seemed to have gone well past that point.

It took Mma Potokwani's assistant a few minutes to find the matron. During that time, Mma Ramotswe heard, coming down the telephone line, the sound of birdsong. At first, she thought it was some form of interference – an electrical whistling generated by a faulty junction box somewhere – but then she recognised it for what it was: there was a bird on Mma Potokwani's veranda, or on her windowsill, perhaps, and it was singing to her. She smiled as she listened to the unexpected musical performance, and asked herself why the manufacturers of telephone equipment did not use birdsong rather than the frequently strident music they inflicted upon callers when they were asked to wait. If music was intended to calm people while they were being connected, then surely birdsong would do that more effectively.

Mma Potokwani was breathless when she picked up the receiver. 'Oh, Mma Ramotswe,' she said. 'I have been running around like a mad thing this morning. I wish you were here to help me.'

Mma Ramotswe allowed her to recover her breath before enquiring as to the cause of the crisis.

'Cauliflowers,' said Mma Potokwani.

Mma Ramotswe waited for further explanation.

'Actually, worms,' Mma Potokwani continued. 'Cauliflowers *and* worms.'

'That sounds like two problems,' said Mma Ramotswe. 'Perhaps you should tell me, Mma.'

Mma Potokwani explained that the Orphan Farm had been given a big load of cauliflowers. She was grateful to the donor, a large hotel company, who regularly passed on any surfeit of vegetables and other food that was surplus to the requirements of their kitchens. These cauliflowers had been welcome, of course, but on being prepared for cooking by the various housemothers, had been found to be infested with worms.

'They are very strange-looking worms,' said Mma Potokwani. 'Not the sort that one would want to find on your plate.'

Mma Ramotswe asked if they could be removed before the cauliflowers were cooked, and Mma Potokwani replied that this is what they had been trying to do. Some cauliflowers, though, had been cooked the previous evening and served to the children in one of the houses. The housemother in that house, although one of the best cooks on the Orphan Farm, was also one of the most short-sighted, and had simply not seen the worms. As a result, the children had eaten them and one of them had been up all night being sick.

'It is just one of those things that happens,' said Mma Potokwani. 'And I should not burden you with it, Mma.'

'I am sorry to hear about it, though,' said Mma Ramotswe. 'But Mma, there is something I would like to ask you: would you be prepared to appear in an advertisement – as a sort of model?'

There was silence. The bird had stopped singing when Mma Potokwani had come on the line; it did not resume.

'Mma Potokwani?' asked Mma Ramotswe. 'Are you still there, Mma?'

'I am here, Mma Ramotswe. But I am wondering whether I heard correctly. Did you just ask me if I would be a . . . a model? Is that what you said, Mma?'

Mma Ramotswe assured her friend that that was exactly what she had said. She almost added, by way of explanation, that models came in all shapes and sizes, but decided that such a comment might be misinterpreted.

'I have not been asked to be a model before,' Mma Potokwani said. 'But you are my old friend, Mma Ramotswe, and you know that I like to do what you ask of me, if possible . . . if at all possible.'

'I am very pleased,' said Mma Ramotswe. 'Now let me tell you what is involved. There will be only one photo shoot.'

'Photo shoot?' asked Mma Potokwani.

'That is a session when they take some photographs,' explained Mma Ramotswe.

'I see.' There was a pause before Mma Potokwani went on, 'May I ask, Mma, what these photographs are for? Are they for a . . . a fashion magazine, or something like that?'

Mma Ramotswe laughed. 'Oh no, Mma Potokwani. Of course, I am not saying that you would not be very suitable for such a thing. Very suitable. But this will be for a leaflet – an advertising leaflet and also for an advertisement in the newspapers. The *Botswana Daily News. Mmegi.* And maybe one or two others.'

'Goodness, Mma Ramotswe: you mean that my name will be all over the papers?'

'We shall not need to use your name,' said Mma Ramotswe. 'We shall simply call you "a lady" maybe, or something like that.'

Mma Potokwani sounded a bit disappointed. 'I would not mind if you used my name, Mma.'

Mma Ramotswe agreed quickly. 'We can put it somewhere on the leaflet,' she said.

'With a reference to the Orphan Farm,' went on Mma Potokwani. 'In case anybody wants to make a donation.'

Mma Ramotswe agreed to that too. 'We must not put too much on it, though,' she said. 'We do not want to confuse people. The main point of this advertisement will be to get people to buy chairs.'

Mma Potokwani asked for more details. Whose chairs were these? And what sort of chairs were they?

Mma Ramotswe told her about the difficulties the Double Comfort Furniture Store had been experiencing. Mma Potokwani was fond of Phuti Radiphuti, who had been more than generous to the Orphan Farm in the past, and she expressed strong support for the idea. 'Anything I can do to help Phuti Radiphuti I shall do,' she told Mma Ramotswe. 'Tell me where to go, and when, and you will find me there, Mma.'

'You are very kind,' said Mma Ramotswe. 'I shall get back to you, Mma Potokwani, and give you all that information.'

'I'll get back to the children, then,' mused Mma Potokwani. 'A model? Me? My goodness. What will people think?'

'They will say, "There is a good example of somebody having a career change a bit further along in life," said Mma Ramotswe. 'They will be most impressed.'

'I hope so. Mind you,' Mma Potokwani added, 'you never know what people are going to say, do you, Mma Ramotswe.'

'You do not,' said Mma Ramotswe. 'Sometimes they say nothing. Then at other times they say things you think they might say. Then at still other times they say things that are completely surprising. You never know, Mma.'

They said goodbye. For a few moments, Mma Ramotswe sat at her desk, reflecting with pleasure, and some amusement, on her conversation with Mma Potokwani. It was not every day that you asked your old friend, a matronly figure – in every sense – to be a model in a photo shoot, and it is not every day that your old friend, when so asked, responds in such a positive way. But when such things happened, you felt a certain warmth of satisfaction in the result. And that set you up for stage two, if there was a stage two to your plan, which, in this case, there was. And the call involved in stage two, once again, was entirely positive in its outcome. Mma Bontle Boshelo, who ran Print Express just off the Lobatse Road, was as pleased to hear from Mma Ramotswe as Mma Potokwani had been. They too went back a long time together – to school days in Mochudi – and although life had taken them in different directions, the bonds of childhood were still there. Mma Boshelo listened to what Mma Ramotswe proposed and agreed that she was just the person to provide the services required. 'They will be at half price,' she said. 'Not only for old times' sake, but because I am happy to help Mr Radiphuti. He is a good man, that one, and if he is in trouble, then we are all in trouble. There are too many aggressive businesses around that seem very happy to crush all their competitors. Since when has business been just fighting, fighting, fighting, Mma?'

Mma Boshelo confirmed that her diary was free for the following day. She could provide the photographer and a graphic designer – 'a young man who is very good and who does not charge the earth, Mma'. All that Mma Ramotswe would need to provide would be the props and the talent. 'The talent, in this case, is the model, Mma. That is the word that creative people use: the talent.'

'I have the talent,' said Mma Ramotswe. 'It is Mma Potokwani. Perhaps you know her, Mma?'

There was silence at the other end of the line. Then, 'Mma

Potokwani, Mma? The matron of that orphan place out at Tlokweng? The one who makes those—'

'Fruit cakes? Yes, that Mma Potokwani, Mma.'

There was a further silence. 'Are you sure, Mma? Is this for an advertisement, you say?'

'Yes, I am sure, Mma. It is for a leaflet and for the newspapers.'

Mma Ramotswe heard Mma Boshelo's breathing. She decided to bring the conversation to an end. If Mma Boshelo had her doubts – as she obviously did have – then those could be dispelled the following day when, in the Double Comfort Furniture Store, all would be revealed.

Mma Ramotswe had not intended that everybody should be present at the Double Comfort Furniture Store the next morning. She had envisaged that she and Mma Potokwani would attend, along with Mma Boshelo and her cameraman, but she did not think it was necessary for anybody else to be there. She had miscalculated the appeal of the term *photo shoot*, which, to many people, and particularly to people like Charlie and Fanwell, was suggestive of a glamour they did not encounter in their day-to-day lives and was, to all intents and purposes, irresistible. Mr J. L. B. Matekoni was alone in saying that he did not think his presence was necessary, although, with characteristic kindness, he was prepared to give Fanwell and Charlie – it was one of his garage days – the time off.

'This is your chance, Charlie,' Fanwell said. 'This Mma Boshelo will be keeping an eye out for possible models. They are always needing people like you for catalogues and so on.'

Charlie was secretly thrilled, but tried to seem nonchalant. 'I have enough to do, Fanwell,' he said, 'without starting a modelling career.'

'And films?' Fanwell pressed. 'What about movies, Charlie? What if this Mma Boshelo has been asked to find somebody for a big new series over in Johannesburg? What if she is just waiting to phone a big-time producer to tell him that she has found just the man? What then, Charlie?'

'Hah!' snorted Charlie. 'I don't want women crawling all over me, Fanwell. Those big actors get no peace. There are always women running after them. Not for me, Fanwell.'

Fanwell knew, of course, that Charlie would like nothing more than that, but he did not pursue the matter. Charlie, though, had more to say on the subject. 'Of course she might spot you, Fanwell. Have you thought of that?'

Fanwell looked doubtful.

'Yes,' Charlie continued. 'Sometimes they need people to act as bodies in police series. You just have to lie on the ground and pretend to be dead. You could manage that, Fanwell, I think.'

Overhearing this, Mma Ramotswe intervened. 'You are very unkind, Charlie. Fanwell is your friend and he is always good to you. You must not be unkind to him in return.'

'I am only joking, Mma,' protested Charlie. 'Fanwell knows that I am his good friend. He is my brother, you see. We are not real brothers, but we are brothers here.' And with that, Charlie touched his stomach.

'That is your liver, Charlie,' observed Mma Makutsi. 'It is your stomach, or possibly your liver. Your liver has nothing to do with friendship. It is your heart that you should be touching.'

'I know where my heart is,' Charlie countered. 'Everybody knows that, Mma.'

'If you are so good at anatomy, Charlie,' said Mma Makutsi, 'tell me where your spleen is. Go on, show me.'

Charlie looked away. 'It is in the middle,' he said.

'Of what?' Mma Makutsi challenged. 'And your tonsils, Charlie? Do you know where those are?'

'Perhaps he has lost them,' said Fanwell, coming to his friend's rescue. 'It is easy to leave them behind and only remember once you've got to work and you think, Where did I leave my tonsils?'

Mma Ramotswe laughed. 'Enough of all this. We must go to the Double Comfort Furniture Store. There is no time to lose.'

Mma Makutsi looked at her. She admired Mma Ramotswe's decisiveness, but she was not sure whether it was true to say that there was no time to lose. In her view, there was any amount of time. There were all those tea breaks, for instance; there were all those hours spent sitting at their desks waiting for clients who were sometimes so thin on the ground that two or three days could go by before anybody knocked hesitantly at the door of the agency and entered with their problem. And often that problem was far from urgent, being about something that had happened months, or even years before, had not been solved in all the intervening time, and only now was being unwrapped and examined afresh.

They set off, with Mma Ramotswe at the wheel, Mma Makutsi beside her, and Charlie and Fanwell in the back of the van. Mma Potokwani had arranged to meet them at the Double Comfort Furniture Store. When they arrived and found her already there, they discovered that she, too, was accompanied, having decided to bring her assistant, who had, in turn, brought her brother and his fiancée, Mma Bopa, the housemother, who was accompanied by her sister-in-law, her sister-in-law's brother, and her sister-in-law's brother's daughter. Mma Potokwani also had with her her hairdresser, known for her braiding skills, and the woman who made the staff tunics at the Orphan Farm, who was attending, she said, in her role as dresser.

Phuti had watched the growing band of people from the window of his office.

'Why are there so many people down there?' he asked Mma Moesi. 'Do they need all those people to take one or two photographs?'

Mma Moesi had been angling for an invitation to join the throng herself. 'I had better go down with you and see what is happening,' she said. 'And perhaps we should take Gloria, from the accounts department. Just in case.'

Phuti did not argue. It seemed to him that far too much fuss was being made about something that he thought was hardly worth doing anyway. But he had had his instructions from both Mma Makutsi and Mma Ramotswe and he did not have the will to gainsay them. Now he made his way to the shop floor where he was introduced by Mma Ramotswe to Mma Boshelo, and her photographer, Baruti.

The introductions made, Mma Boshelo asked Phuti to identify the chairs that were to be featured in the promotion. This choice had been the subject of much discussion between Mma Ramotswe, Mma Makutsi and Phuti, and several possible chairs had been identified. These were all generously padded armchairs, replete with cushions and with stout, load-bearing legs. They were not fashionable chairs, by any stretch of the imagination, but they were inviting nonetheless. There were few who, seeing such chairs, would not be tempted to sit down.

Mma Ramotswe now took control. Pointing to one of the chairs – the largest – she asked Phuti's men, who had been standing at the back of the crowd, to separate it from the other chairs and place it against a backdrop of potted plants that had been set against a wall. Then, drawing Mma Potokwani aside, she explained to her what she had to do.

'There will be five photographs,' she said. 'We shall see you looking at the chair. That will be the first one. Then we shall see you testing the cushions for softness. Then there will be a photograph of you lowering yourself onto the chair.'

'I think I can do all of that,' said Mma Potokwani.

'Then we shall have a photograph of you smiling and looking very comfortable, followed by a photograph of you with your eyes closed, as if you have just gone to sleep because the chair is so comfortable.' She paused. 'Is that all clear enough, Mma Potokwani?'

Mma Potokwani looked slightly disappointed. 'I don't have to do anything else, Mma?' she asked.

Mma Boshelo answered. 'We can take a short video too,' she replied. 'We can do that at the same time that we are taking the photographs. Then Phuti can use it for promotional purposes. You can say something on that, Mma. We shall record you.'

Mma Potokwani looked thoughtful. 'I shall say something about how comfortable the chairs are,' she suggested. 'Just a few words.'

'That would be perfect,' said Mma Boshelo.

Charlie tugged at Mma Boshelo's arm. 'Yes, Rra?' she asked, turning to face him.

'My name is Charlie,' he said, flashing his best smile in her direction.

'I hope you are well, Charlie,' replied Mma Boshelo politely, but with a note of impatience in her voice.

'I am very well, Mma,' Charlie replied.

She looked at him, waiting to hear what he wanted. But Charlie simply smiled. And when Baruti, the photographer, set up his tripod, Charlie tried to help him, unfortunately collapsing one of the legs and trapping the photographer's finger in the mechanism.

'I am very sorry, Rra,' he said hurriedly. 'These tripods can be very tricky, can't they?'

'Not if you handle them correctly,' Baruti responded. 'Please do not touch that bit, Rra.'

Mma Ramotswe clapped her hands together. 'Silence, please, everybody. We are about to start.'

'We can do the video first,' said Baruti. 'Then we can take the photographs.'

A hush fell over the onlookers as Mma Potokwani approached the armchairs. 'Are you ready?' she asked the cameraman.

'Rolling,' he replied.

Mma Potokwani faced the camera. 'When you are somebody like me,' she said, 'who works very hard, then when you come home at night all you want to do is sit on your husband ... '

There was a gasp from Mma Ramotswe, followed by a cheer from everybody else.

Mma Potokwani put her hands to her mouth. 'Oh, I am very sorry,' she said to Mma Boshelo. 'I meant to say "sit with your husband". I did not mean to say "sit *on* your husband".'

'Don't worry, Mma,' said Mma Boshelo. 'There are many big stars who make mistake after mistake. I have heard all about that sort of thing. Start again, I think.'

This time it went without incident, and her words were delivered without any embarrassing mistakes. 'You want a chair that is made for people like yourself – not for some unfortunate person somewhere who is all skin and bone, but for people who are not afraid to look as if they are enjoying life. I am such a lady, and these chairs from the Double Comfort Furniture Store are made for people like me – and you.' She sat down, and an expression of unforced contentment overtook her. It was genuine. The chair was truly comfortable, and she sank into it with a relief that was not in the slightest bit contrived.

Mma Boshelo clapped her hands together. 'Well done, Mma!' she exclaimed. 'That is perfect.'

From behind his camera, Baruti made a thumbs-up sign. 'Very perfect,' he said. 'Top class. Cool. Super. Yes!'

There then followed the still photographs, charting Mma Potokwani's progress from an approach to the chair to the moment of blissful contentment in its upholstered embrace. These photographs were repeated several times before Baruti was satisfied, and he was able to give a thumbs-up sign to Mma Boshelo and Mma Ramotswe to indicate that the shoot could now be brought to an end.

Some of the onlookers were disappointed that it had all happened so quickly. Phuti, who had observed proceedings silently, merely shook his head and returned to his office, accompanied by Mma Moesi. Mma Ramotswe watched them go.

'There are certain things still to be done,' she whispered to Mma Makutsi. 'And they will not be at all easy.'

Chapter Twelve

You Have Been Like an Angel

It was late the next afternoon, the day after the successful photo shoot at the Double Comfort Furniture Store, that Patience and her son, Modise, arrived by informal taxi at the Radiphuti house on the east side of town. As they stepped out of the car, the boy began to complain.

'Is this the place? This one? You said it would be a nice place. This is miles from all the action. How am I going to get to school? I'm not walking through all that bush. What about snakes? Don't you care if I get bitten? And who are these people? Why have they got that water tank over there? What if there isn't enough water and we can't have a proper bath? What then?'

This reply came from his mother.

'You are always moaning, Modise. You are always saying that things are not right. What is wrong with this house? It's a big place. Expensive. Look at it. Five bedrooms, maybe six, easily. And they will get the ground under control one of these days. You can't just snap your fingers and make a garden. That's not the way it works. And they are kind people, these friends of mine. You'll get used to being here, you'll see. Two weeks from now, you'll be saying, "Did I ever live anywhere else? I can't remember." No, don't laugh, because that is what you'll be saying. I know about these things. I am your mother – I am much older than you. I know.'

The driver, caught up in this exchange, looked uneasy. 'I'm sorry, Mma,' he said at last. 'But you will need to pay.'

'You're right, Rra.' She handed him the fare and received the change. Then, as he drove off, the ancient Volkswagen rattling on the corrugations in the road's surface, she turned and began to walk up to the front door.

Mma Makutsi had been waiting inside. Now she opened the front door and hailed her old friend.

'I see you, Patience,' she called. 'We are expecting you. You are very welcome.'

Mma Makutsi had not met Modise before. 'You are just like your mother,' she said, as they shook hands. 'I can tell that that is who you are.'

This may have been well intentioned, but it was not well received. Modise scowled, and then looked pointedly away. Patience was clearly embarrassed.

'Or perhaps not,' said Mma Makutsi quickly. 'No, I think you are not like your mother. I was wrong. You are a big strong young man now. You are not like anybody else.'

Modise's scowl disappeared, or at least was suspended. 'I am fourteen, Mma. Fifteen next birthday.'

'That is very good,' said Mma Makutsi. 'And now let me show

185

you where you will be staying. I have a very nice room for you, Modise. It has a radio and also some of Phuti's weights. He used to do his weight training in that room. After he hurt his back they said he should do weights. They are gathering dust in that room, but you may like to use them. They are very good for building up muscles.'

'My muscles are already very big,' muttered Modise.

'Of course they are,' said Mma Makutsi. 'I was about to say something about them. I was on the point of doing that.'

She glanced at Patience, who shrugged, and made a complimentary remark about the house. 'This is a very fine place, Grace. And the furniture is wonderful.'

'That is because of Phuti's business,' said Mma Makutsi. 'He is a furniture man, as I think you know.'

'It is very beautiful,' said Patience.

Modise gave a quick look around the room they were in. He said nothing. Mma Makutsi watched him. She said to Patience, guardedly, 'I'm sorry, Mma, that you have had to move.'

Patience inclined her head. 'You have been so kind to us, Mma. After we were asked to leave, I didn't know where to turn. You have been like an angel watching over me, Mma Makutsi.'

Mma Makutsi tried to judge Modise's reaction to this, but he was facing the other way now, and she could not see his expression.

'Modise is very grateful too,' said Patience, loudly. She gave him a small dig with her elbow. The boy turned and looked at her, anger written across his face. She stared back at him. 'I am very grateful, Mma,' he said, although each word sounded as if it had been prised out of him by his mother.

'Come with me to your room, Modise,' said Mma Makutsi. 'You will like it, I think.'

Her tone was breezy. That, she thought, was the best way to talk to teenagers – about anything. You talked to them in that way, as if you were not expecting them to be listening to you – which, of course, they were not.

While this trying meeting was taking place, Mma Ramotswe was settling Phuti Radiphuti in the client's chair at the No. 1 Ladies' Detective Agency. She had boiled a kettle, and was now handing Phuti a cup of tea, using the best tea service – 'the client's china', as she and Mma Makutsi called it.

'Thank you for meeting me here,' she said to Phuti. 'There is a very important reason why we should meet here and not in your office – otherwise I would have come to you.'

Phuti seemed to be more his normal self than when she had last seen him, and now she commented on that fact.

'You look a bit better, Rra,' she said. 'Last time, I thought you looked a bit . . . defeated, I think.'

Phuti took a sip of his tea. 'I have seen an advance copy of the leaflet that Mma Boshelo sent over,' he said. 'I read what you had written on it. It was you who wrote all that, was it, Mma?'

'I did it together with Mma Boshelo,' said Mma Ramotswe. 'She is very good at choosing the right words for an advertisement.'

Phuti nodded. 'You were very kind to me. What you said about the store being the best furniture store in southern Africa. And then you described me as a pioneer of the furniture trade. Nobody has ever said that before, Mma. Did you mean it?'

'Of course I meant it, Phuti. And it is true. Your store was the first one to offer such a wide choice to people. You were the one, Rra. That was you.'

Phuti lowered his gaze in modesty. 'I was just doing my best,' he said.

'Well, your best was very good, Rra. Think what you have built up. Think of all those houses where there is now a dining-room table and chairs because of you. Think of all those houses where people are sitting comfortably in their chairs because you brought them those chairs. Yes, you, Rra. You have made all of that possible for so many people.'

Phuti kept his gaze fixed to the ground. 'But you have done great things, too, Mma. Before you started this agency, there were no private detectives in the whole country. It was you, Mma – you started it all.'

Mma Ramotswe smiled at the recollection of the decision – almost an accidental one – to start a private investigation business when there was no precedent for one in all of Botswana's history. It could have been an ignominious failure – and it almost was, in those early days – but then word had got round and the clients had begun to turn up at their door, hesitant in some cases, embarrassed and furtive in others, but all of them people who needed some help with their lives – help which Mma Ramotswe had given them, often without charging a fee, because she felt that this was her calling, this was what she had been singled out to do in this life.

Phuti had the proof of the leaflet with him. 'And then there are these wonderful pictures of Mma Potokwani making herself so comfortable in that chair,' he said. 'They show the chair to the very best advantage, Mma – and Mma Potokwani too, of course. She looks good too.'

They both examined the leaflet. 'Do you remember how chairs used to be?' ran the text in bold lettering. 'Do you remember the days when chairs had deep cushions and lots of room for even the most traditionally built person? If you think those days are gone, then here is news for you: they are coming back! Come to the Double Comfort Furniture Store and see the prices – the LOWEST IN TOWN!'

Phuti read this out and then looked up at Mma Ramotswe. 'I love all that, Mma,' he said. 'But there is a bit of a problem. My prices will not be the lowest in town. Those people ... ' He paused, allowing the distaste with which he uttered the words *those people* to have full effect. 'Those people will undercut us, Mma Ramotswe – whatever we do. I could charge minus ten pula for a chair, Mma – *minus* ten – and they would sell their chairs for minus fifteen. They are very cunning. And then—'

Drawing this hard commercial fact to the attention of Mma Ramotswe seemed to make him dispirited, and Mma Ramotswe was concerned lest he should revert to his defeated frame of mind. She raised a hand to stop him.

'Rra, you will remember that I warned you about Moesi.'

Phuti nodded. 'I remember, Mma.'

'Well, I think that information is getting to him through his wife. I think that she is telling him what your price plans are. That's how that company is undercutting you.'

Phuti winced. 'I do not like the thought that this is happening,' he said. 'Mma Moesi has been a very good member of staff.'

'I'm sorry,' said Mma Ramotswe. 'But we need to do something to see if I am right. We need to make sure that she knows there will be a sale to go with our advertising campaign. And she needs to know the prices you will be charging.'

Phuti sighed. 'Is there no other way, Mma?'

Mma Ramotswe shook her head. 'I do not think so, Rra.' She looked at him sympathetically. She knew that he was a generous-spirited man and did not like to assume the worst of anybody. She could see that this was difficult for him.

'Does she type your letters?' she asked.

'Yes.'

'And your memos? If you are sending a memo to the sales director, then will she type that?'

'Sometimes,' answered Phuti. 'Sometimes I write it.'

Mma Ramotswe took this in. 'This time,' she said, 'I think that she will type the memo that you are going to send to the marketing person. Make sure that it gives the exact prices that you say you will be charging for the chairs on promotion.' She paused. 'Not that it will be the real price. The price on the memo will be much higher than the one you are going to announce in the advertisement and in the leaflet.'

'But they might still undercut us,' objected Phuti.

'No, Rra. If they hear this in advance, they will plan their own campaign. They will have Violet Sephotho splashed all over the papers saying that their prices will be such-and-such. But once they have done that, you will then publish your prices, which will be lower than theirs. It will be too late for them to start all over again.'

Phuti reflected on this. Then, for the first time at this meeting, his face broke into a grin. 'That is a very cunning plan, Mma.' Then he added, 'If it works.'

'The thing about any plan,' said Mma Ramotswe, 'is that you have to believe in it. If you believe in a plan, then there is a much better chance that it will work.'

'And you believe in this one, Mma?'

She swallowed hard. She had no idea whether she really believed in her plan. She certainly had her hopes for it, although that was different from believing in it. It was a fine distinction, she thought, but this was not an occasion for fine distinctions. This was an occasion for embarking on a course of action for which there did not seem to be a ready alternative. The Double Comfort

Furniture Store could not be allowed to fail, and currently she could see no other way of averting that disaster.

'Of course I believe in this plan,' she said, holding Phuti's gaze. 'Why should I not believe in it, Rra?'

This seemed to give him the encouragement he needed. 'Then I will do as you say, Mma Ramotswe, and we shall see.'

'That is the right decision, Phuti,' she said. And then she added, 'Do not be too harsh on Mma Moesi. I think she may not know what use he makes of the information she gives him. She may be thinking that she is passing on information that he uses for his business courses. She may not realise that he is working with competitors.'

Phuti looked at Mma Ramotswe. It was a look of discomfort, a look of regret. She felt that he wanted to believe in Mma Moesi's innocence because he did not like the thought of having to get rid of her. But now she wondered whether she herself believed what she had just said. It was a possibility, yes, but she was not sure that she thought it all that likely.

They finished their tea together. There was not much more to discuss, although they talked a little about the chairs that Phuti had chosen for the promotion. As he spoke, she saw his eyes light up. It was a curious thing, she thought – that a person's eyes should tell you so much about what was going on inside them. There were so many ways in which people might reveal their thoughts and emotions – gestures of the hands, smiles, shrugs – the repertoire of human body language was an extensive one, and one that we all learned to read without ever being specifically taught to do so. How many parents sat their children down and told them what these things meant? Very few, or none, she thought. We learned how to read a face right from the very start, when we were looking up at our mother and saw her looking down upon us. And we knew, when we were still only a few months old, that a smile meant one thing and the absence of a smile meant another. And for the rest of our lives that understanding grew, until, with any luck, we could pick up all the signs that we needed. Not that everybody was equally adept at that; some struggled to understand what they saw around them, and found life difficult as a result. That was a pity, because people for whom this was a battle had their contribution to make and, anyway, were brothers and sisters to us, just as we were to them.

Now she saw in Phuti the enthusiasm for furniture that she knew had always been there, and she was pleased.

'Your chairs are going to be very popular,' she said. 'How could anybody resist?'

Phuti became animated. 'Oh yes, Mma Ramotswe. That is certainly true. I knew when I was first offered those chairs, that they were just right for . . . ' He struggled to express himself. 'Just right for our times,' he finished.

She thought about this. Were there chairs that were right for particular times? Were there periods when people needed to be sitting up straight, for example, or when they needed to be able to relax a bit more? Did we have to earn those comfortable chairs, rather than expect them, as our right?

'That is most interesting, Rra,' she said at last. 'I had not thought of it in that way.'

'Neither had I,' he admitted. 'But now that I think of it, I think I must have been thinking about it without knowing that I was thinking about it.'

She looked at him and smiled. He smiled back. Two old friends discussing chairs, and what chairs meant. The chairs were comfortable, but so, too, was simply talking about them. That was true of so much, thought Mma Ramotswe. Thinking about something, even if it was something that you did not have, could give much the same pleasure as the thing itself. That was definitely the case with love. Thinking about love imparted a warm glow to the world. It made things right. Now she thought about those she loved, about Mr J. L. B. Matekoni, about Puso and Motholeli, about her friend Mma Potokwani, and Mma Makutsi too, for all her little ways. And she thought about Botswana, too, which she loved so much even if she felt she would never be able to find words capable of expressing the full extent of the feeling she had for her country. Not that she needed to. People understood; others felt it too. You only had to look around to see that.

Chapter Thirteen

A Big Man Calls

It was on the second evening of Patience's stay at Mma Makutsi's house that Mr Olivier Tutume, drama teacher, amateur actor, and now, for a time at least, Patience's ostensible suitor, knocked at the front door of the Radiphuti house. He was expected, and when the knock sounded on the door, followed by the familiar call of *Ko ko*, Mma Makutsi, Patience and Phuti all exchanged glances. They were about to have their evening meal in the kitchen with Modise, who, being absorbed in contemplation of the ceiling and in the thoughts that fourteen-year-old boys will have, was indifferent to the prospect of a visitor.

'I am expecting a friend,' announced Patience. 'He is early.'

'He is welcome to join us for our meal,' Mma Makutsi said quickly. 'There is more than enough.'

This response was perhaps slightly too readily delivered – as if it were a line prepared in advance, which it was.

'He will be very welcome,' said Phuti, adding, out of nervousness, 'Very good. Yes, this is very good.'

Had Modise been paying more attention, he might have noticed these cues, but he was immersed in his own world and he did not.

Patience left to admit her guest.

'I am looking forward to meeting your mother's friend,' said Mma Makutsi. 'Do you know who it is, Modise?'

The boy's eyes focused as he returned from wherever he was. He shrugged. 'She knows many people, Mma.'

'And you?' asked Phuti. 'Have you made many friends here in Gaborone, Modise? Perhaps you miss your Bobonong friends.'

Modise shrugged again. 'There are a lot of people here,' he replied. 'I have plenty of friends.'

Phuti asked politely who they were. This brought a third shrug of the shoulders. 'I forget,' said Modise.

Mma Makutsi noticed Phuti's irritation. She did her best to pacify him. 'It is hard to remember everybody,' she said. 'Sometimes I find myself thinking of somebody whose name has just gone from my mind. Completely gone – as if the wind has blown it away.'

'But not friends' names,' muttered Phuti. 'It is difficult to forget those. You have to make a real effort to do that, I think.'

Mma Makutsi shot him a glance. There had been difficult moments since Patience and Modise had moved in, but the exercise of tact and self-restraint on the part of the adults had meant that conflict had been avoided. Modise did not have good manners, Mma Makutsi had concluded, but he seemed to avoid directly contradicting others. His technique of subversion – if that was what it was – seemed more subtle than that. A lot of it was in the eyes, she decided, and in the curl of the lips. There was a great deal a teenager could say with the set of his or her lips: words were hardly necessary.

'Well, who can tell?' said Mma Makutsi cheerfully. It was a meaningless question – in this context at least – but it was one that she found could defuse an awkward situation.

Phuti took a deep breath. 'That is true,' he said. This was an equally meaningless comment, but it was one that he found helped in almost any discussion. Saying 'That is true' to someone who had just said something to you cost very little; it might be flattery, perhaps, particularly when what they had said was manifestly not true, but it kept the social peace. If more people said 'That is true' to each other, so much needless conflict in human affairs might simply be avoided.

Modise continued to stare up at the ceiling, and was still thus occupied when his mother returned with their visitor. Phuti and Mma Makutsi instinctively rose to their feet in welcome; Modise hesitated, and then remained seated.

'This is Bobby,' said Patience.

Mr Tutume waved his hands, as if greeting a crowd. 'Hi, folks,' he said.

It was a modern greeting – and Modise looked up sharply, his eyes running critically over their visitor.

'You must join us for our meal, Rra,' said Mma Makutsi. 'There is plenty for everybody.'

'Are you sure?' asked Mr Tutume, his voice unnaturally loud. 'I don't want to barge in.'

'It will be our pleasure, Rra,' said Phuti, gesturing for Mr Tutume to take a seat.

Mr Tutume sat down next to Patience. As he did so, he put

an arm around her shoulder to give her a brief hug. Patience wriggled, and smiled. Mr Tutume patted her thigh. 'You're eating well,' he said. 'Build up your resources, I always say. Know what I mean?'

Mma Makutsi was watching Modise, as discreetly as she could. In spite of himself, the boy was responding to Mr Tutume's familiarity with his mother. The earlier indifference had gone.

Now Mr Tutume looked across the table directly at Modise. 'So, young man,' he said, his voice echoing around the room, 'what would your name be?'

The reply was barely audible. 'Modise.'

'What?' shouted Mr Tutume. 'What did you say? Would you mind speaking up?'

Modise bristled. 'I said, Modise.'

Mr Tutume smiled. 'Modise? That means *herd boy*. You should be out at the cattle post, surely.' He turned to Patience, laying a hand on hers in a gesture of intimacy. 'Cattle post, don't you think, Patience? Cattle post for this young man?'

Before Patience could answer, Mr Tutume turned again to Modise. 'Now let me guess how old you are. No, don't tell me. Let me guess. Twelve? Yes, I'd say twelve. Am I right?'

The effect was immediate. Modise's eyes narrowed as he opened his mouth to speak. No words came.

'Hah!' said Phuti. 'Twelve. Not at all. Modise is thirteen.'

The offence was compounded. Once again Modise opened his mouth to correct the calumnies. This time, it was his mother who responded. 'Modise is fourteen, Bobby.'

'Doesn't look it,' said Mr Tutume, grinning.

It was a brilliant performance. Even Sir Laurence Olivier, at the height of his acting prowess, could hardly have done a better job than that done here by Olivier Tutume. No male under thirty, and certainly no teenage boy, likes to be thought younger than he is. And here he was being accused of being *twelve*. And if that were not insult enough, Phuti had demoted him, by a critical few months, to thirteen. His mother had set the record straight, but any balm that might provide for injured feelings was just too late. A dented teenage ego would take longer than that to recover.

'Oh well,' said Mr Tutume. 'You can't get everything right.' He paused. 'Sometimes the evidence of one's own eyes is simply not enough.'

Turning back to Modise, he asked what his favourite school subject was. This question drew no response, and so he asked it again. This time, Modise made an unintelligible grunting sound.

'What was that?' Mr Tutume snapped. 'You said something?'

The boy glared at him.

'Well, young man?' pressed Mr Tutume. 'The hyenas eaten your tongue?'

'He is good at geography,' offered Patience. And turning to Modise, she said, 'You like geography a lot, don't you, Modise? Maps – that sort of thing.'

Modise was still glaring at Mr Tutume.

'All right,' said Mr Tutume. 'Here's a question for you – if you're so good at geography.'

'I didn't say I was good at geography,' Modise muttered.

'Oh yes you did,' Mr Tutume contradicted him sharply. 'I heard you. So, if you're good at geography, here's a question for you: what is the capital city of Ghana? You heard of that place? Ghana? That place up there?'

All eyes were on Modise, whose own eyes were now fixed firmly on his mother, gazing at her with smouldering resentment. This was *her* fault; this was *her* friend. Yet this was *his* humiliation.

'Hah!' crowed Mr Tutume. 'I see you do not know. A bit more work on geography is required, if you ask my opinion. A bit more time on geography homework.' He paused. 'Accra, by the way. That is the name of the capital of that place. Accra. There are many people who know that – but I see you are not one of them. Hah! Except, now you are. Now you know it, you see, and you can thank me for teaching it to you. Free, too. Education should be free, don't you think?'

This last question was addressed to Phuti and Mma Makutsi, both of whom nodded their agreement.

'Well,' said Patience. 'There we are.'

Mr Tutume had not finished.

'What do you want to be when you grow up?' he asked Modise.

This brought the barest of resentful shrugs.

'Does that mean "nothing"?' asked Mr Tutume. 'Is that what you mean?'

'I said I don't know,' muttered Modise, avoiding Mr Tutume's penetrating stare.

'If you don't know what you want to do, you'll end up doing nothing,' Mr Tutume said, his voice raised almost to shouting pitch. 'You hear me? Nothing. Big waste of all the effort your poor mother puts into bringing you up. I'm telling you – and I'll tell you this for nothing, my young friend – that a person who has no idea of what he is going to do ends up being a nothing sort of man. You hear me? A nothing sort of man. That's what will happen to you, you know. Mr Nothing.'

Modise stared at him.

'And you know what becomes of Nothing Men? You know what happens to them? I'll tell you – nothing. That's what happens to nothing people. Big nothing.'

Phuti glanced at Mma Makutsi, and then at Patience. Was this going too far? Mr Tutume was a most convincing actor, but surely there were limits.

'I think I shall serve the dinner,' said Mma Makutsi. 'I think we are all ready to eat.'

At the end of the meal – an affair of forced jollity and smouldering silences – Mr Tutume thanked Mma Makutsi for inviting him to join them. Then, turning to Patience, he patted her thigh and said, 'How about you and I go to a movie?' He glanced around the table. Now was the time for a further verbal grenade. 'Just the two of us, of course. Back row, know what I mean? All lovey-dovey. Smooch smooch.'

He made a sucking, kissing sound.

Patience simpered. She had a part to play too. 'Oh, Bobby . . .'

'I think it is going very well at home,' Phuti said to Mma Ramotswe when she called on him in his office two days later.

'So I hear,' said Mma Ramotswe. 'Grace told me. She said that Mr Tutume is every bit as good an actor as we had hoped.'

'Better,' said Phuti, grinning at the memory. 'He has been round three times already. The first was for dinner – a very eventful meal, if I may say so – and then he came back again yesterday and there was a big shouting match. Well, he did most of the shouting, but it was certainly noisy.'

Mma Ramotswe was intrigued. 'Grace mentioned some argument about shoes. Was that it?'

Phuti nodded. 'Mr Tutume said that he thought Modise's shoes were a disgrace to Botswana. He asked if they had been polished – ever. That did not go down well. And so the shouting started.'

'Shoes,' mused Mma Ramotswe. 'What parent has not had a row over shoes?'

'Probably none,' said Phuti. 'But it went further. Mr Tutume – or Bobby, as he was calling himself – went on to force Modise to tidy one of the guest rooms. He stood there so that the boy couldn't get out of the door. He stood there and forced him to tidy up.'

Mma Ramotswe pictured the scene. Unpolished shoes, untidy rooms ... Mr Tutume obviously knew exactly what buttons to press in order to make himself unpopular. 'Of course, he's a teacher,' she said. 'He must have a very good idea of how these young people think.'

Phuti nodded. 'I hope it does not take too long,' he said. 'Our house is not very peaceful at the moment. When there is no peace ... well, we miss it, don't we, Mma Ramotswe?'

Mma Ramotswe sat back in her chair. She knew exactly what he meant. The world at times was an unsettled place, a place of rivalry and suspicion, of complaint and dispute. Yet there was no doubt as to what most people wanted, which was comity between those who looked at things differently from one another. Most people longed for the day when they might tune into a news broadcast and hear the announcer say, 'I'm sorry, everybody, but nothing has happened. There is no news today – none at all.'

That day had never come to pass, as far as she knew, but you could still hope. That was what you could always do – no matter how bad things seemed to be – you could hope. And now she was about to say something to that effect to Phuti, and had opened her mouth to do so, when he raised his hand to stop her.

'Have you seen the paper this morning, Mma?' he asked.

She knew immediately what it was. She shook her head as she glanced at the newspaper on his desk before him.

'Page six,' he said. 'The whole page. Top to bottom.'

She waited as he paged through the paper before passing it to her. And there it was, prominent and unapologetic in its sheer, brazen awfulness: a full-length photograph of Violet Sephotho with, behind her, a shiny new chair. At the top of the page a slogan screamed: NEVER BEFORE SEEN PRICES! 'ACT NOW TO SECURE YOUR CHAIR,' SAYS VIOLET SEPHOTHO, CELEBRITY OPINION FORMER!

Mma Ramotswe read the rest of the breathless advertisement. Her eye moved to the prices printed in bold type beneath the text. Yes, she thought, yes!

She looked up. 'It is exactly as we thought it would be, Rra,' she said. Her voice was even; there was no need to get excited when a plan was going so perfectly, so completely in accordance with what had been hoped for.

Phuti looked pleased. 'You were right, Mma Ramotswe. They've pitched the price at just below the price we ...' He trailed off, looking anxiously at the door behind which Mma Moesi could be heard talking on the telephone.

Mma Ramotswe's smile gave way to a graver expression. 'I'm afraid that the information must have been passed on as we expected.' She paused. 'It is a sad thing, Rra. It is never good to make this sort of discovery about somebody one has trusted.'

Phuti showed a new firmness. 'She will have to go,' he said. 'Yes, it is very sad, but we cannot have a person like that in our midst. I will speak to her later today.'

Mma Ramotswe looked over her shoulder. The conversation in the adjoining room was still in full flow. 'Could you possibly leave it a day or two, Rra?' she asked.

Phuti frowned. 'Why wait?'

She waited a few moments before replying. 'It is sometimes important not to act rashly. Then one can avoid doing things that might need to be undone.'

He considered this. 'If that is what you really want,' he said at last. 'Then, yes, I shall not dismiss Mma Moesi today.'

'That would be good,' said Mma Ramotswe.

'And is it tomorrow that our own campaign starts?' Phuti asked.

'Yes, Rra, it is. We will have page six in the paper tomorrow. It will be our turn. There will be those pictures of Mma Potokwani and of course there will be our prices. They will be below those offered by those people in that advertisement of theirs. And, of course, people will see the comfortable chairs and they will all say, "It's time we were comfortable again . . ."'

'I hope they say that,' agreed Phuti. 'But you never know, do you, Mma? You never know whether people are going to behave in the way you think they should behave.'

'You are right about that,' said Mma Ramotswe. 'But even if they only do what you think they should do half the time, then that is still a good thing, would you not say?'

Phuti was not going to respond to that immediately; he would think about it and then take a position. He suspected that he would end up being in agreement with Mma Ramotswe because she was so often right. But he would still mull things over – just in case.

Mma Ramotswe said goodbye to Phuti.

'I can show myself out, Rra,' she said, indicating to him that he need not get up from behind his desk.

'But, Mma Ramotswe . . .'

She brushed aside his objection. 'You have work to do,' she said quickly. 'I will leave you to it.'

Her tone was decisive, and before Phuti could raise any further objection, she was at the door that led, through Mma Moesi's office, to the showroom beyond. Standing there, she turned and waved to Phuti before letting herself out. Now all she had to do was navigate her way past the protective fortress of Mma Moesi's desk – but she had a conversation to get through before she did that.

The receptionist beamed up at her. The bristling protectiveness displayed during Mma Ramotswe's earlier visit to Phuti's office was no longer in evidence, having been replaced by a recognition of the fact that Mma Ramotswe was obviously family. With that, there came a rather unctuous friendliness that Mma Ramotswe found made her feel somewhat uncomfortable.

'So, Mma,' began Mma Moesi brightly. 'So, that is your meeting with Mr Radiphuti over then.'

Mma Ramotswe was unfailingly courteous, whatever the situation, and she returned Mma Moesi's smile. 'Thank you, Mma. I had some matters to discuss with Mr Radiphuti and . . .'

Mma Moesi looked at her enquiringly. 'And now, Mma?'

'And now, Mma, we have finished discussing these matters.'

Mma Moesi looked disappointed, and Mma Ramotswe realised she must have expected more revealing information than that.

'Successfully, Mma Ramotswe?'

'Yes. Nothing too important, of course. Just this and that.'

This brought more obvious disappointment. 'I see. Well, that is good, then. Very good.'

'Yes, Mma. Very good.'

Mma Ramotswe smiled again. 'It is another warm day, Mma,' she remarked.

'Yes, Mma. It is always warm.' Mma Moesi paused. 'It is a long time since it was cold.'

Mma Ramotswe gave this observation the attention it deserved. 'Yes,' she said, thoughtfully. 'Of course, we are lucky in this country – it never gets really cold, does it? I mean, really freezing cold.

Except in the Kalahari at night – in the cold weather. Then it can be very cold. That is because it is dry. They talk about desert drop – the drop in temperatures, that is. Very cold.'

'But only in the cold months,' said Mma Moesi.

'Yes, only in the cold months.'

They looked at one another in silence. Then Mma Ramotswe spoke. 'Phuti says that he is starting a big new promotion tomorrow. That will keep you busy, I imagine.'

Mma Moesi laughed. 'But we are always busy, Mma Ramotswe. This thing, that thing, the next thing, the thing after that. Our work goes on and on.'

'That's the way life is,' agreed Mma Ramotswe. 'And I suppose the furniture trade is the same as any other business in that respect.'

'Yes, it is, Mma.'

Mma Ramotswe waited a few moments. Then she continued, 'It must be an interesting business. And rewarding. All those . . . all those tables and chairs . . . and people, too. Helping people to sit down, so to speak. That is good work.'

It was just the right line of approach. Mma Moesi became animated. 'Oh, Mma, you are very right. It's a calling, my husband says. He says that he gets great pleasure from the thought that the work he does with the furniture industry means that people get a good sleep at night. That is because of the beds they sell, you see.

Mma Ramotswe was careful not to appear too interested. That was important, as Clovis Andersen was at pains to point out. *Never seem too keen to get a piece of information*, he wrote. *That will alert people to your interest. Hold back. Make it seem that you are not all that interested in the answer.*

'Your husband is still involved in furniture, Mma?'

Mma Moesi looked proud. 'He is, Mma. He is a business

consultant, you see. He has dealings with some other furniture firms.'

'Of course,' said Mma Ramotswe. 'And he must know just about everything there is to know about the business.'

'He does, Mma. He knows a great deal.'

'But I suppose you do too?'

'A little, Mma. And yes, my husband is not too proud to ask me about things. He understands that it is always possible to learn more.'

Mma Ramotswe held her breath. 'So the two of you must have some very good chats about what is going on in the furniture business.'

Mma Moesi laughed. 'Yes, we do. We talk a lot, Mma.' She looked thoughtful. 'You know, Mma, there are some married couples who don't talk to one another. Have you noticed that? They seem to have said everything there is to say, and they are silent. We are not like that, Mma.'

Mma Ramotswe held her breath through all of that. Now she exhaled. Poor woman, she thought. She is innocent. This is not her fault. She smiled at Mma Moesi. 'You're very fond of Mr Radiphuti,' she said. 'I can tell that.'

Mma Moesi was momentarily taken aback by the change of direction in the conversation, but then she said, 'Oh, Mma, yes. Mr Radiphuti is such a good man. He is so kind.'

'Yes,' said Mma Ramotswe. 'He is.' She paused. 'I think you look after him very well, Mma.'

'I do my best, Mma. Often, with these good men, it is for us women to protect them, don't you think?'

Mma Ramotswe answered immediately. 'Yes, Mma, it is.' And she thought about Mr J. L. B. Matekoni. Mma Moesi was right. It was the duty of women to protect such men from the many things that could harm them. It was like looking after children. Women did that because it was in their nature to do it. It was in the nature of women to care for the world.

'Without us,' Mma Ramotswe said to Mma Moesi, 'where would men be?'

Mma Moesi shook her head. 'Nowhere, I think, Mma.' She paused. 'Or in trouble, perhaps.'

They both laughed. In Mma Ramotswe's case, her laughter was partly caused by relief. She had reached a conclusion that she had hoped she would reach: Mma Moesi would never do anything to harm Phuti: she was innocent.

Mma Ramotswe decided it was time to leave. She had learned what she needed to learn, and she felt all the better for it. To have eliminated something negative – something like disloyalty – always left a person feeling more hopeful about the world. She felt better now. Each time you saw the good where you feared you would only see the bad, was a victory; a small victory, perhaps, and one that might appear to be dwarfed by surrounding defeats, but a victory nonetheless. And small victories counted, especially when you lined them up and thought about them warmly; they counted for a great deal. That was true, she thought; indeed, it was well known.

'Goodbye, Mma Moesi,' she said. And on impulse, she reached forward, across the receptionist's desk, and clasped her hand in a gesture of fellow feeling; it was the gesture that one person might make towards another in a moment of understanding that she, like you, is just trying to get through this life as best she can.

Chapter Fourteen

Never Sell Your Bed

Mma Potokwani learned of the start of the campaign when she looked out of her window to see Mma Bopa, one of the housemothers, running up the path towards her office, waving a newspaper in her hand, and ululating in the time-honoured way of a woman with something to be happy about. So excited was she, so jubilant, that she stumbled on the steps leading up to Mma Potokwani's veranda, and would have ended up sprawling on the floor were it not for a miraculous act of self-righting that saved her from disaster. Observing this alarming stumble from her window, Mma Potokwani put a hand to her mouth in shock, only to drop it as Mma Bopa, back on her feet, hurtled through her doorway.

'Mma!' Mma Potokwani exclaimed. 'Mma Bopa! What is all this?'

The stocky, traditionally built figure of Mma Bopa came to a halt in front of her. 'It's the newspaper,' the housemother explained, panting for breath. 'Your photograph is in today's paper, Mma Potokwani. Look, here it is. That's you, I believe. And that one too, and that one. You are everywhere, Mma – everywhere!'

Mma Potokwani had not been forewarned of the exact date of publication of the advertisement. She knew that publication was imminent, but now that it had happened she was not sure whether she was prepared for the sudden limelight. She reached for the paper that Mma Bopa had thrust in front of her. Yes, there she was, looking at Phuti's chair and then, in a series of manoeuvres, each captured in subsequent photographs, she was to be seen sinking into its comfortable embrace.

She could not think of much to say, other than to confirm that the figure in the photographs was, indeed, herself. 'I think that is me,' she said to Mma Bopa. 'And look, if you see what is printed down below, you'll see that it refers to me.'

She hoped that she did not sound immodest. Mma Potokwani was relentless in her pursuit of the interests of the children entrusted to her – and of her staff and their families – but when it came to her own interests, she was reticent to a degree. Seeing her photograph in the paper now, she began to wonder whether her head had been turned at the thought of being a model. There she was, a respectable matron of a certain age, and surely such a person was not meant to entertain thoughts of modelling – in whatever capacity. Suddenly a disturbing thought crossed her mind: what if the Secretary of the Child Welfare Board were to ask what she was doing flaunting herself in newspaper advertisements? And what if some busybody, of which there always seemed to be more than enough, were to ask how much she had been paid and whether the photo shoot had taken place in working hours, when, under her contract with the trustees of the Orphan Farm, she was meant to devote her time exclusively to the affairs of the orphanage? Then there were the trustees themselves – a group of sober citizens who might well object to her appearing as a photographic model. Even as she thought of that disquieting possibility, she recalled that her contract specifically stated that she should do nothing that would bring the Orphan Farm into disrepute. Was appearing in an advertisement something that would bring disrepute? Surely not. And yet even the mere thought of it made her feel uneasy.

Mma Bopa tugged at her sleeve. 'Mma, are you all right?'

Mma Potokwani brought herself back to reality. 'Yes, Mma. I'm sorry. I was thinking – that's all.'

'I am so proud of you, Mma,' said Mma Bopa. 'These photographs are so flattering. And it is such a good thing you are doing.'

Mma Potokwani was puzzled. Why, she wondered, would Mma Bopa consider her appearance in the advertisement to be a good thing?

The explanation was not long in coming. 'When I look at advertisements, Mma, what do I see? I see thin, fashionable people smiling at me. These people say, "Buy this, buy that." They try to make me think I will become like them if I use their toothpaste or their lipstick or whatever it is. But, Mma, let's be honest – we are never going to be like those people.'

Mma Potokwani nodded. 'No, Mma, I think you are right. We are never going to be like those people.' But did she really want to be like them? That was another question, of course, but it was one to which she was fairly sure she knew the answer.

'But this advertisement,' Mma Bopa continued, 'is ... is ...' She stopped as she searched for the words to express how she felt. And then it came: 'Is just so *happy*, Mma. Yes, it is a happy advertisement.'

Mma Potokwani smiled at Mma Bopa. The housemother had never been one for wasting her words. She was a modest woman, who sometimes seemed to fear that what she said would sound uneducated, but now she had found her voice.

'I can tell you, Mma Potokwani,' she continued, 'if I could afford it, I'd buy one of those chairs on the spot. You see, these legs of mine . . . ' She looked down apologetically at her legs.

'Those are very good legs,' Mma Potokwani assured her. 'They are strong legs, Mma.'

'It is kind of you to say that, Mma,' said Mma Bopa. 'But all legs feel the strain eventually. At the end of a long day most legs say, "Isn't it time to sit down now?" And that is just the time that you need a good, comfortable chair, I think.'

Mma Potokwani looked again at the full-page advertisement. It was very attractively laid out and it was, she felt, not something that one would pass over too readily. Some advertisements were only too easy to ignore – some, indeed, were so *shouty* that you felt that you had to avert your eyes. This was a *comfortable* advertisement, one that addressed you in a polite, helpful manner; one that did not set out to browbeat or intimidate – or, even worse, to make you feel that you had to do something that you did not want to do if you were not to be thought a failure. This advertisement let you be yourself, which is what most people really wanted, when you came to think of it. That was the problem, she reflected; that was the source of so much unhappiness – there were people who made it their business to stop other people from being themselves; who tried to make people be something they did not want to be. That led to swathes of unhappiness as wide as the Kalahari itself.

She smiled at Mma Bopa, who returned her smile and said, 'I'm so glad that you are famous at last, Mma Potokwani.'

Mma Potokwani quickly brushed this aside. 'Oh, Mma, I wouldn't say that.'

'Well, I would, Mma. That is why I have just said it.'

Mma Potokwani changed the subject. 'That is very kind, Mma, but I think we need to talk about carrots. I have ordered carrots for all the housemothers because one or two people said that supplies were running low. Plenty of potatoes, but not so many carrots.'

They were back on the familiar track of their daily lives. There were children to be looked after, and that meant thinking about practical things – like carrots. Comfortable chairs, both Mma Potokwani and Mma Bopa thought, could wait.

At the Double Comfort Furniture Store, the effect of the advertisement began to be felt at around eleven in the morning. Prior to that, Phuti and his staff had waited nervously as a handful of customers – certainly no more than was normal for that time of day – drifted into the store. These were people, Phuti decided, who had clearly not read their newspaper. Although now, as they came in, they looked with interest at the large posters erected throughout the store setting out the details of the special sale. But then, as the hours passed and Phuti began to feel the first doubts as to the efficacy of the entire plan, cars started to appear in the car park in increasing numbers. In the chair department, where several examples of the featured chair were arranged in a tasteful circle, people could soon be seen lowering themselves onto the inviting cushions, and registering, in one way or another, their positive reactions to the experience.

'This is a big success,' one of Phuti's sales staff remarked. 'They like the chair. They like the price.'

'I am very pleased,' said Phuti.

'One woman sat in the chair and immediately went to sleep,' the assistant continued. 'I had to go and wake her up. She said it was as comfortable as a bed. She said if she bought the chair, she would probably sell her bed.'

'Never sell your bed,' said Phuti. And then, for some reason, perhaps because of the sheer gravity of the advice, he repeated it. 'I say: never sell your bed.'

The assistant nodded. 'You are very right, Rra,' she said.

At the end of the day, fifteen chairs had been sold, and orders taken for a further twenty-three that would be delivered within days. By any standards, the campaign had been a success, as Phuti's demeanour made abundantly clear. When he returned home, and Mma Makutsi greeted him as he came in the door, she knew at once what the result was. Of course, she and Mma Ramotswe had discussed the matter at the office, and Mma Ramotswe had assured her that she thought the outcome would be a positive one. But now Phuti's smile was proof of what they had hoped would be the case.

Mma Makutsi drew Phuti aside, putting a finger to her lips to tell him to keep his voice down. Taking him by the arm, she led him out of a side door and into the kitchen yard. She glanced back into the house before whispering, 'I didn't want them to hear. Or, rather, I didn't want *him* to hear.'

Phuti followed her backward glance. 'Modise?'

'Yes,' said Mma Makutsi, leading Phuti off towards the outer reaches of the vegetable garden. 'Our young friend hears everything. I think there's something about that boy ... ' She stopped, and gave Phuti a meaningful look.

But if there was a discreet message to be conveyed, Phuti did not seem to pick it up. 'Something what?' he asked.

'Something ... ' Mma Makutsi floundered. She was not at

all sure what she meant – or if she meant anything. 'Something something,' she concluded lamely.

Phuti continued to look puzzled. 'I'm not sure what you mean,' he said.

Mma Makutsi sighed. Now a note of anxiety crept into her voice. 'I'm afraid it has failed,' she said.

He stared at her. 'This?' He gestured towards the house.

'Yes. Our plan has failed.'

He asked her whether it might not be too early to draw any conclusions. 'They've only been here a few days,' he pointed out. 'And Modise won't have seen all that much of Mr Tutume. How many times has he been round? Four? Five?'

Phuti could not help but smile at the recollection of these visits, all of which had taken place round about a mealtime. They had sat, the five of them, round the table, in an atmosphere that was fraught with danger. At any moment, Phuti feared, the surface politeness that prevailed could have been replaced with outright and overt hostility between Modise and his mother's putative suitor, but somehow that had been avoided. That, Phuti had decided, was owing to Mr Tutume's extreme skill as an actor – knowing just how far he could goad the boy without pushing him over the edge. It had been a performance worthy of a five-star review, and Phuti had resolved that the next time the Gaborone Amateur Dramatic Society put on one of their famed productions, he and Grace would be there in the front row, ready to give a standing ovation to the obliging and talented drama teacher.

Mma Makutsi made a gesture of helplessness. 'He has had lots of time to form an opinion, but you know what, Phuti? Patience told me that he just doesn't seem to care.'

Phuti waited for her to elaborate.

'She spoke to him about it,' Mma Makutsi continued. 'She

asked him outright: "What do you think of my new boyfriend?" Those were her exact words, Phuti. And you know what he replied? He said, "He's all right, I suppose."'

Phuti shook his head. 'He can't think that. How could anybody think a man like that is all right?'

'Well, he seems indifferent. That's the word, I think. Indifferent. He doesn't seem to care. He's still difficult with his mother, but he seems to be taking no notice of Mr Tutume – in spite of everything.'

Phuti was silent. He had been wondering how long they would be saddled with Patience and Modise – not that Patience herself was an unwelcome guest, but she did come with what could only be described as baggage.

'How much longer should we try?' he asked.

Mma Makutsi thought that a further week was about as much as she could manage. 'There comes a point when you have to decide that a plan just isn't working. I think that we are very close to that point, but not there just yet.'

'And what will Patience do?' Phuti asked.

Mma Makutsi had discussed that with her. 'Mma Potokwani says that there is staff accommodation out at the Orphan Farm. Patience is entitled to that now that she has started her new job out there.'

'And the Water Affairs man?'

'She says that she will try to keep seeing him, but she thinks it will be difficult. He will be here in Gaborone and she will be out at Tlokweng. It won't be easy. She thinks it's already fizzling out.'

'That is very sad,' said Phuti. 'She is a nice person. She deserves a bit of happiness.'

Mma Makutsi agreed. They had tried, they had done their best, but not all plans worked out, particularly rather unusual ones like this. 'I would like my friend to be happy,' she said. 'But I suppose not everybody gets the happiness they deserve.'

And then she thought: and some people get happiness they don't really deserve. Like me, she thought. I have the best husband in Botswana. I have this well-built house. I have my young son. I have a young woman to help me look after him. I have a job with a woman who is one of the finest women in Botswana, and she is my friend as well as my colleague. I have everything, and yet I cannot really think that I deserve all that. Perhaps it's just luck. Perhaps it's luck that determines how much happiness we get in life. But no, that can't be true. You reap what you sow – everybody knows that. So if luck played a part, it must be a relatively small one.

She brought herself back to the present. 'Tomorrow is Saturday,' she said.

'I knew that,' said Phuti, with a smile.

'Charlie has offered to take Modise off our hands for the day. He is going to be working at the garage on some old car or other. It belongs to a friend, apparently, and Mr J. L. B. Matekoni is letting him do the work in the garage.'

It was kind of Charlie, and Mma Makutsi had been impressed with the offer. 'Charlie is becoming much more mature,' she had whispered to Mma Ramotswe. 'He's thinking of other people more than he used to. It's very good.'

Mma Ramotswe agreed. She had always seen Charlie's goodness of heart, and knew that it would eventually eclipse all the nonsense that went with being a young man.

'Modise will enjoy that,' said Phuti.

'Possibly. He never says anything about enjoying anything, but he may, I suppose.'

'He'll come round,' said Phuti. 'He'll come round eventually. He probably just needs time.'

Mma Makutsi was not so sure. 'We shall see,' she said. *We shall see* implied that matters could still go in an unexpected direction, that there was some doubt as to outcome. But that, in this instance, was not what she meant. *We shall see* in this context meant *highly unlikely*, but there were times, and this was one of them, when one did not necessarily want to say what one meant.

That was Friday. Six days later, on a warm Thursday, Mma Ramotswe was late in arriving for work, having done an early-morning shop at the supermarket. The following day was the end of the month, and payday, and the shops would be busy as people stocked up. By going the day before, not only could she avoid the crowds but she would also get the pick of the items that would already be put out on special offer for the following day. So it was that she did not arrive in the office until Mma Makutsi was about to make the mid-morning tea.

She could see at once that something momentous had happened. And she could tell, moreover, that whatever event had taken place was a positive one. Mma Makutsi was never one to hide her feelings, and now, as she stood by the kettle waiting for it to boil, she had about her the unmistakable air of one who had received good news. Even if the kettle perversely failed to boil, as their rather antiquated appliance sometimes did, it did not seem that it would matter too much.

They greeted one another. Then Mma Ramotswe said, 'Now then, Mma Makutsi, I can tell that something has happened.'

Mma Makutsi was restrained. 'Possibly, Mma.'

'Only possibly?'

It was too much for Mma Makutsi. Clapping her hands together, she gushed, 'Oh, Mma Ramotswe, it has all worked. It has worked perfectly.'

It took Mma Ramotswe a moment or two to order her thoughts. She made her way to her desk and sat down. Then she said, 'Our plan, Mma? Modise? Patience?'

In her excitement, Mma Makutsi spoke so rapidly that Mma Ramotswe struggled to catch what she was saying. 'Yes, Mma. Yes. It came to a head last night. She was with Modise in his room for . . . oh, for a long time, Mma – I heard them talking. And then when she came back into the kitchen I could tell that something had happened.'

Mma Ramotswe raised an eyebrow. Miracles occurred. There were those who were sceptical about the seemingly impossible ever happening, but Mma Ramotswe knew that sometimes it did. In any human affairs, there was always a possibility that people would surprise you, and they did. They surprised you in ways you never expected. They changed. The meek became bold; the angry and agitated became calm and accepting; the complaining and the critical became accepting and tolerant. There were any number of ways in which things might turn out otherwise than we expected.

'What did she say, Mma?'

Once again, Mma Makutsi spoke with breathless enthusiasm. 'She said that Modise told her he hoped they would move back into the house they had left – the home of Water Affairs man. He asked her whether she could ask him to take them back.'

Mma Ramotswe gasped. 'Well, that's a change, Mma.'

'Yes. She was very pleased. Of course, she had to get a promise from him. She had to make sure that he would behave himself if they were to move back.'

'Of course,' said Mma Ramotswe. 'And did he promise, Mma?'

'He did. She said that he promised her several times that he would not be troublesome if they moved back.'

Mma Makutsi made the tea, preparing a pot of redbush for

Mma Ramotswe and a pot of ordinary Five Roses for herself. After allowing a short time for infusion, she poured them each a mug of their respective brews and then delivered one to Mma Ramotswe at her desk. Mma Ramotswe noticed now that Mma Makutsi had acquired a new mug. She saw that something was printed on it in large blue letters – a word she had to crane her neck to read and that now revealed itself, simply, as *Boss*.

Mma Ramotswe took a sip of the steaming liquid. She had read somewhere that it was bad for you to drink liquids that were too hot, and that you could damage the tissues of your throat if you did so. But now she did so almost distractedly, because of the implications of seeing that word on Mma Makutsi's mug. Did she really think of herself as *the* boss of the agency, or, less ambitiously, as *a* boss? Mma Makutsi was not *the* boss, but she could quite realistically be described as one of the bosses.

And that reminded her of the desk. She had been expecting Mma Makutsi's carpenter to turn up in the office to install the new, enlarged desk, but so far nothing had happened. Was that another change that had suddenly occurred? Had Mma Makutsi abandoned her earlier ambition to outdo her in the size of her desk, or was that still a work in progress? Mma Ramotswe wanted to know the answer to that, but it was not the time, right then, to venture into such contested and potentially awkward territory.

Mma Ramotswe decided to let her tea cool down before taking another sip. Looking across the room at Mma Makutsi, she observed, 'It seems that our plan worked after all, Mma Makutsi. Mr Tutume has succeeded in convincing Modise that if you think you don't like something, then you'd better be careful you don't end up with something far worse.'

Mma Makutsi nodded enthusiastically. 'Oh, Mma Ramotswe,

it is really quite funny, isn't it? That will teach that young man to watch his tongue.'

Mma Ramotswe thought that there was a certain justice in the outcome, but she did not want to crow. It was not easy being a fourteen-year-old boy and although Modise had to learn a lesson, she did not like the thought of his having been further discomforted. It must have been very difficult for him to be faced with Mr Tutume and his overbearing and aggressive ways, and yet it was something that had had to be done. In the end, it was very much more in Modise's best interests that his mother should be happy and that he should have a stepfather who would help him over the next few years as he matured. She decided that what they had done was, for this reason, the right thing to have done and they could congratulate themselves – modestly, of course – over the outcome.

And then Charlie came in for tea. Today was a garage day and he stood in the doorway, wiping the grease off his hands before pouring himself a mug of tea. Mma Makutsi was most particular about grease or oil on the handle of her teapot and it had taken her some time to train Charlie to wipe his hands. But now he did it automatically, and she was pleased about that.

'You ladies look very happy,' Charlie remarked as he poured his tea. 'Have you solved some big, important case? Has somebody paid their bill at last?'

Mma Makutsi exchanged an amused glance with Mma Ramotswe. 'You might say we have solved something, Charlie. Yes, we have sorted something out.'

Charlie perched himself on the top of one of the lower filing cabinets. Mma Makutsi did not like him doing this: there was no reason why he could not stand while he drank his tea – he had two perfectly good legs, after all. But now she chose to ignore his sitting on her filing cabinet – she could afford to be generous and she could also thank him for spending some time with Modise. Not that this had helped very much, she imagined, but it was a kind gesture on Charlie's part.

'Thank you for spending last Saturday with Modise,' Mma Makutsi said. 'I think that he must have enjoyed working on that car with you.'

Charlie said nothing, and Mma Ramotswe thought that he looked a bit shifty. 'Yes,' she said, adding her thanks to Mma Makutsi's, 'that was kind of you, Charlie.'

'No problem,' said Charlie, in a casual, throwaway tone. Then he asked, 'This problem you say you've solved – is it anything to do with him?'

Mma Makutsi laughed. 'Yes, he was the problem, Charlie. He himself.'

Charlie stared into his mug. 'He's behaving himself?'

'Yes,' said Mma Makutsi. 'You know about the plan we had, don't you?'

Charlie nodded. He was still looking into his mug of tea.

'Well, it worked just as we had hoped it would,' Mma Makutsi said, adding, 'Thanks to Mr Tutume.'

Charlie looked up from his mug. Mma Ramotswe caught his eye. He looked away. 'Charlie,' she said. 'Is there something you want to say?'

Charlie was all innocence. 'Me, Mma Ramotswe? Why should I have anything to say?'

'Because to me you look just like somebody who has got something to say,' said Mma Ramotswe.

She stared at him. His gaze settled back on her. But he still looked reticent.

'Maybe,' he muttered.

'Maybe what?' snapped Mma Makutsi. 'You can't just say *maybe*. What does *maybe* mean?'

Charlie hesitated. 'It means that maybe I helped. I don't know. Maybe I did.' He turned to face Mma Makutsi. 'But you in particular, Mma Makutsi, would never say, "Oh, you've been a big help, Charlie." You are always saying that everything I do is wrong.'

Mma Makutsi was having none of this. 'You're wrong, Charlie!' she exclaimed.

'See,' said Charlie. 'See what I mean. You've just said I was wrong – just as I told you.'

Mma Makutsi defended herself. 'I said that you were wrong to say I always say you're wrong. That is a very different thing.'

'You're wrong,' retorted Charlie. 'You're the one who's wrong now.'

Mma Ramotswe cleared her throat. 'I don't think it helps anybody to talk about who thought what in the past. Tell us, Charlie, what you did. Let us see what we think of it. I'm sure Mma Makutsi will be fair.'

Charlie clearly did not think so, but he began anyway. 'I spoke to him,' he said. 'I spoke to Modise on Saturday.'

They waited.

'About what, Charlie?' asked Mma Ramotswe.

Charlie shrugged. 'About everything. I spoke to him about how lucky he was to have a nice mother when there were people with no mother at all. I told him that he was lucky to live in Botswana, where there are schools and hospitals and where the government doesn't hit you with a big stick if it doesn't like you. I talked to him about how you should never make your mother cry. I told him that he wasn't the only person around and that he should think about how other people were feeling. All of that sort of thing. You know the stuff.'

Mma Ramotswe nodded approvingly. 'That was all good, Charlie. That was the sort of thing he needed to know.'

'Well, I told him,' said Charlie. 'Twenty minutes, maybe half an hour. I spent a long time telling him.'

Even Mma Makutsi had to express her admiration for what Charlie had done. 'You are a big psychologist, Charlie,' she said. 'That is very good. Mr Charlie, No. 1 Psychologist. First class diploma in psychology, maybe one day.'

Charlie acknowledged the compliments with an inclination of the head. 'He told me some things, too,' he said.

'Such as?' asked Mma Ramotswe.

'He said that his life was getting a bit better. He said that there is a girl in his class at school who says she likes him. He is very pleased with that.'

Mma Ramotswe smiled. That was positive news. Perhaps Modise was simply growing up – and the influence of a nice girl would help him to make the transition.

'But then I said some other things to him,' Charlie continued. 'I told him that he would have to behave himself. I told him he should not be cheeky to that Water Affairs man. I told him to apologise to his mother and to that other man.'

'To Mr Tutume?' asked Mma Makutsi.

Charlie shook his head. 'No, to the Water Affairs man – the first boyfriend – the one he had been so rude to.'

'But what about Mr Tutume?' Asked Mma Makutsi.

'He knows about that man,' Charlie replied.

Mma Ramotswe asked him what he meant.

'He knows that he is just acting,' Charlie explained. 'He said he knows that because his friend is at the school where Mr Tutume works. His friend told him he was one of the nicest teachers there. He's never cross and he never raises his voice.'

Mma Ramotswe shook her head. She was sure there was more to this story than Charlie was telling her. 'But Charlie, what did you say to him?'

Charlie put his mug down on the filing cabinet. He glanced at Mma Makutsi, as if he was worried that she would take exception to what he had to say. 'After I had given him the first talking-to, I spoke to him again. This time I spoke very strongly, Mma Ramotswe.'

There was complete silence. Then, from the garage outside, there came the sound of metal being struck by metal. 'That's the boss,' said Charlie. 'There is a nut that is refusing to shift. It has corroded. You have to watch corrosion because it—'

Mma Makutsi interrupted him. 'Strongly, Charlie?'

'I told him that I would ... I told him that I'd speak to my friend, Lesibo Modisane.'

Mma Makutsi gasped. 'The famous boxer? You know that man, Charlie?'

Charlie brightened. 'We are very close, Mma Makutsi,' he said proudly. 'He is the cousin of my brother-in-law's wife's cousin. We are that close.'

Mma Ramotswe and Mma Makutsi exchanged glances. Then Mma Ramotswe said, 'Did you say something more than that, Charlie?'

Charlie looked up at the ceiling. 'I may have,' he said. 'I cannot remember exactly, Mma. You know how—'

'Just give us a rough idea,' interjected Mma Makutsi.

'I told him that I would be watching him. I told him that his mother would tell you, Mma Makutsi, if he was even a little bit difficult – just that much ... ' He held his thumb and forefinger a fraction of an inch apart. 'Just that much, and I would get to hear of it, and I would come round with Lesibo and ... '

'And?' pressed Mma Makutsi.

'Talk to him again,' said Charlie. 'But with Lesibo.'

Mma Ramotswe closed her eyes. This was not how things were done.

She opened her eyes. Charlie seemed unrepentant. 'And he was scared, Charlie?' she asked.

'Very scared,' Charlie answered. 'He knew all about Lesibo. All teenage boys admire him big time – and not one of them, Mma, would like to be on the wrong side of him, I can tell you that for certain. Ow!'

Mma Makutsi lifted her mug of tea to her lips and drained it. She put the mug down on her desk with a flourish. 'So!' she exclaimed. 'That is the end of all that.' She looked across the room at Mma Ramotswe. 'Is that what you call psychology, Mma?'

Mma Ramotswe shook her head. She could not approve. Well, she could not approve entirely. And it was not at all clear to her exactly what had happened. Had Modise listened to Charlie and been convinced of the error of his ways? That was possible. Some people did actually heed advice, even if many did not. Or had he changed because he had become more secure and had found a girl-friend who might help him to be less emotionally dependent on his mother? That, too, was perfectly possible. Or had he simply decided that he should avoid incurring Charlie's displeasure because of the awkward interview with the boxing champion that might result?

Mma Ramotswe could not decide which of these was the operative cause of the change that had taken place. One could discuss it at great length, she suspected, and at the end of the discussion be no surer of what was what. That was the trouble with human affairs: sometimes it was simply impossible to tell what worked – even Clovis Andersen could be at a loss at times, difficult though that was to imagine. So the best thing to do, perhaps, was to keep an open mind and to realise that when a good result is achieved, it might not matter all that much how it came about. The important thing, when all was said and done, was that a happy outcome ensued. That was all that mattered – and that, beyond any shadow of a doubt, was well known.

A week went past, and now it was Friday again. Patience and Modise left Mma Makutsi's house and returned to the house of Simon, the Water Affairs man. He was pleased to see them, although he showed slight trepidation in his dealings with Modise. He need not have worried: not so much as a single surly glance emanated from the boy, and certainly no out-of-order remarks. All, as Patience reported to Mma Makutsi, was sweetness and light. And more than that, she said: once Modise started to be polite to Simon, they discovered that they rather liked one another. They went to a football match together, to watch the Zebras play a team from over the borders, and returned full of smiles, chatting and joking, following the Zebras' resounding victory. Patience was happy: she had almost lost a good man, but had found him again. Modise was happy too: he had come to accept that his mother was not going to abandon him just because there was another male in her life. And he had formed a friendship with Charlie, who was allowing him to help him work on the project car over which they had first met. He respected Charlie, because the young man had been firm with him, and because he knew Lesibo Modisane, which was quite something to consider. A psychologist observing the situation might say that Charlie had become a role model for the teenage boy, to which Mma Makutsi, were she to hear of such a conclusion, might have said, 'Some role model!' But she did not say anything of the sort, as she was grateful to Charlie for what he had done for her friend Patience.

That Friday, Mma Ramotswe had planned a special trip out to see Mma Potokwani. She was going with Mma Makutsi in the tiny white van, although they were to call in at the Double Comfort Furniture Store on the way out to the Orphan Farm. But before they set off there was a surprise waiting for Mma Ramotswe when she entered the office that morning.

She saw it from the door, and it stopped her where she stood. She looked at her desk, and then at Mma Makutsi, who was sitting at her own desk, nonchalantly – too nonchalantly, perhaps – filing her nails.

'Mma Makutsi!' stuttered Mma Ramotswe. 'My desk . . . '

Mma Makutsi looked up. 'Oh, that. Well, I thought, Mma, that you probably needed a large desk a bit more than I do. I am the number two round here – you are the number one. And so I arranged for the carpenter to come in early this morning and install the extension on your desk, rather than mine.'

Mma Ramotswe crossed the room silently. She sat down at her newly enlarged desk and ran her hands over its surface. 'It is very fine, Mma Makutsi. There is so much space.' She struggled to keep her voice even. She had not expected this, but perhaps, she thought, she should have. After all, Mma Makutsi, for all her little ways, was one of the best women in Botswana. When it came down to it, behind those round glasses were eyes that looked upon the world with love – tough love, sometimes, but there were times when tough love was just what was needed.

'Thank you, Mma,' she said. 'I am a very fortunate woman to have a colleague like you. I am very fortunate.'

They called at the Double Comfort Furniture Store, where Phuti arranged for his men to load into the van the exact chair into which Mma Potokwani had sunk for the photographs.

'Tell her that this is a present from the Double Comfort Furniture Store,' Phuti said. 'Tell her that we are very grateful for the effect that the advertisement has had on our trade. It has picked up more than I would ever have thought possible.'

'And no more undercutting from the opposition?' asked Mma Ramotswe.

Phuti shook his head. 'I think that has stopped,' he said. 'Mma Moesi did not know what her husband was doing with the information she let slip to him. She was very ashamed.'

'And the husband?' asked Mma Ramotswe.

Phuti smiled. 'He is not one to argue with his wife. I think she has dealt with all that.'

'And no word from Violet Sephotho?'

Phuti smiled. 'Not a squeak,' he said.

'Then everything has worked out well?' asked Mma Ramotswe.

'It could not be better,' said Phuti.

He smiled at Mma Ramotswe. 'And, Mma,' he said, 'I think I have learned something in all this.'

She waited. Phuti nodded, as if agreeing with some internal proposition. 'I think that I have realised that a bit of competition is a good thing. Those people gave me a wake-up call, I think, and I am very pleased that I have had it. It has given me all sorts of ideas.'

Mma Ramotswe said that she was pleased to hear that. 'Perhaps you can have more advertising campaigns featuring Mma Potokwani,' she said.

Phuti laughed. 'She has more than enough to do,' he said. 'She has all those children to look after.'

'Yes,' said Mma Ramotswe. 'Perhaps she has more than enough on her plate.'

Out at the Orphan Farm, Mma Potokwani was waiting for

them on the veranda of her office. She watched as the two men who worked in the garden unloaded the chair and brought it up the steps outside her office.

'This is for you,' explained Mma Ramotswe. 'It is a thank-you gift from the Double Comfort Furniture Store.'

'For me?' asked Mma Potokwani.

'All for you,' said Mma Makutsi.

Mma Potokwani looked at the chair. She touched its back. She sighed. 'It is the most comfortable chair in the country, I think,' she said.

Then she looked across the yard, past the small *kgotla*, or meeting place, they had created for the children and the staff. That was a popular spot, built by the Orphan Farm to introduce the children to the core of Botswana democracy – the place where everyone, high or low, could speak his or her mind. Mma Potokwani looked beyond that to the house presided over by the housemother, Mma Bopa; to the small building that was home to eight children for whom the world at first had found no place, but whom it now embraced in love and care.

'This chair is mine now?' asked Mma Potokwani.

Mma Makutsi nodded. 'It is entirely yours, Mma.'

Mma Potokwani looked thoughtful. 'So I am allowed to do what I like with it?' she asked.

Mma Makutsi said that the chair was hers, and she could do whatever she liked with her own property. No offence would be taken.

Mma Potokwani smiled. 'In that case, Mma Makutsi, I think I know a lady who would be very happy to have a chair like this.'

Mma Makutsi had seen the direction of Mma Potokwani's gaze. She agreed. Of course she agreed.

The two men were summoned to lift up the chair once more

and carry it to Mma Bopa's house. And behind the chair and its bearers there walked a small procession of Mma Potokwani, Mma Ramotswe and Mma Makutsi. As they walked, Mma Ramotswe found herself humming a tune, a song, that she really was not sure she actually knew, but that seemed to come from somewhere not too far off. It was a song of comfortable chairs, perhaps, or something like that. It had no particular words, but it was a song that made her feel warm inside.

The men put the chair down on the veranda of Mma Bopa's house. Then Mma Potokwani knocked on the door.

Mma Bopa came out. She saw the chair, and her eyes opened wide. She listened as Mma Potokwani explained that this chair was a gift, to thank her for all the hard work she had done, for all the love she had given to the children over all these years.

Mma Bopa looked at the chair. She sat down. She deserved to.

Read the next in the series ...

Precious Ramotswe takes on a quest to find the relatives of a man who, many years ago, left Botswana for the uncertainties and dangers of a distant conflict. She must not be distracted by the shocking news that a club calling itself the Cool Singles Evening Club is encouraging married men to pretend to be single and meet women under false pretences. Or by a local emergency that occurs when a new dress – intended to be a birthday present – is tried on and splits in a way that is thought to be irreparable. Mma Ramotswe and her friends can only hope that disaster will be averted so life in Botswana continues smoothly ...

From a Far and Lovely Country

Alexander McCall Smith is the author of over one hundred books on a wide array of subjects, including the award-winning The No.1 Ladies' Detective Agency series. He is also the author of the Isabel Dalhousie novels and the world's longest-running serial novel, *44 Scotland Street*. His books have been translated into forty-six languages. Alexander McCall Smith is Professor Emeritus of Medical Law at the University of Edinburgh and holds honorary doctorates from thirteen universities.

Help us make the next generation of readers

We – both author and publisher – hope you enjoyed this book.
We believe that you can become a reader at any time in your life,
but we'd love your help to give the next generation a head start.

Did you know that 9% of children don't have a book of their
own in their home, rising to 12% in disadvantaged families*?
We'd like to try to change that by asking you to consider the role
you could play in helping to build readers of the future.

We'd love you to think of sharing, borrowing, reading, buying or talking
about a book with a child in your life and spreading the love of reading.
We want to make sure the next generation continue to have access
to books, wherever they come from.

And if you would like to consider donating to charities that help
fund literacy projects, find out more at www.literacytrust.org.uk
and www.booktrust.org.uk.

Thank you.

 hachette
CHILDREN'S GROUP

little, brown
BOOK GROUP

*As reported by the National Literacy Trust